(Poor White Trash Part 3)

Bret McCormick

A HellBound Books Publishing LLC Book
Houston TX

Bret McCormick

**A HellBound Books LLC
Publication**

Copyright © 2019 by HellBound Books Publishing
LLC
All Rights Reserved

Cover and art design
By Carlos Villas
For HellBound Books Publishing LLC

**No part of this book may be reproduced, stored in a retrieval
system, or transmitted by any means, electronic, mechanical,
photocopying, recording or otherwise without written permission
from the author
This book is a work of fiction. Names, characters, places and
incidents are entirely fictitious or are used fictitiously and any
resemblance to actual persons, living or dead, events or locales is
purely coincidental.**

www.hellboundbookspublishing.com

2

Dedication

This book is dedicated to the memory of S.F. Brownrigg, whose Poor White Trash Part 2 opened up a whole new world for me.

Acknowledgements

Thanks to my beloved partner, Patrice Kleypas, for her unwavering support and enthusiasm.

Thanks to my partner in crime, E.R. Bills, for renewing my interest in the outré, while helping me set my sights on higher goals.

A million thanks to James H Longmore and Xtina Marie of HellBound Books, for making *Skin Dreams* a reality.

(Poor White Trash Part 3)

Chapter 1

They call me Liza McWhorter. Notice I say, "they call me?" Some folks'll say, "my name is," or, "I am." I don't go about it that way, because I realize that name was given me by ignorant people. They gave me that name for reasons of their own or because that's just the way things are done in the here and now. Those folks have no grasp of the vastness of life. Even their own lives. They call me Liza because that was the name of my mother's favorite aunt. Liza is followed by McWhorter on account of that's the last name of the man legally considered my father. But even that's a lie. Mama told me Dan McWhorter wasn't my true daddy. She just married him so we'd have a roof over our heads. The man who shot his seed between my mama's legs and called me down from the soulish realm into this vale of shadows, was the Reverend Archibald Gooch, pastor of the Zion Hill Church of Redemption. Brother Archie, most folks called him. They all said he was a very godly man, but he wasn't above the temptations of the flesh. He seduced Mama the same day he baptized her in the pond behind the church.

My mama was a pretty woman. At least by local standards. Folks said she had the prettiest smile and that she probably could've been a movie star. I suppose it's only normal that a healthy man–man of God, or not–would want to take a poke at her. Everyone thought the man was a pillar of the community, salt of the earth, even if he was susceptible to an occasional sexual temptation. Even my mama spoke well of him, carrying the burden of my illegitimate birth on her own young shoulders. No one suspected just how deeply flawed old Brother Archie really was. Not until much later.

I ain't, in my heart, Liza McWhorter. And even if Brother Archie had married Mama, like the church folk believe should be done, I wouldn't be Liza Gooch. Not in my heart. In my heart, I know myself to be a soul, nameless and eternal just like all souls and like the good Lord, himself. It's only for these short little visits on planet Earth that we have need of such things as names. And I've had a lot of visits and a lot of names. Most of them wouldn't mean a thing to you. Except for one. If you're god-fearing and Bible-reading you might know it; Amos, one of the twelve minor prophets. That was me in another time on another mission.

Now, I know beyond a shadow of a doubt that this is true. And I don't care if anyone else on God's green Earth knows it, believes it or gives a blessed damn about it. But folks are touchy about certain things and religion's one of them. Most run-of-the-mill Christians in our part of the country don't believe in what these days is called "reincarnation." Souls returning again to Earthly life is most definitely mentioned in the good book, but Christians don't read their scriptures very carefully. They usually just let their pastors do the reading and interpreting for them. And pastors generally don't endorse the idea of rebirth. It undermines their most potent tool. You know; the fear of eternal damnation. The only thing that keeps people coming back to the church week in and week out and contributing their hard-earned money is the fear of the fiery pits of hell. Hell with a capital H, if you're real serious about it.

Another thing I'm real certain about is the fact that hell is not a place, like Dallas or Cincinnati; it's just a state of consciousness. It's a resonance, a vibration. It's no more a 'place' than happiness or love are places. You get there by your own habitual thoughts and you can pull yourself up out of it the same way. This is just as true of heaven. Or Heaven, if we're being traditional in our religious grammatical requirements. Heaven is a vibration. That vibration, or at least the potential of it, exists in every last one of us. Stop and think about the evilest person you know. Now consider that person has a line to heaven just like you do. All that's needed is for that person to change their way of thinking and slowly, surely come into resonance with that higher vibration. That heaven vibration. Anyone can do it, no matter what misdeeds they've performed in the past. That line to heaven is like a string on a guitar, see? Just because you haven't plucked it for a good long while doesn't mean it won't sing when you do pluck it. It may be a little out of tune and require a bit of TLC to make it ring true, but the potential is always there. Always.

And getting back to hell for a minute; did you know there's a scripture that says, "Even if I make my bed in hell, thou art with me?" The writer of the Psalms is addressing the Lord with that statement. Even if a soul's in hell, God is still with that soul. Want to know why? Because God is us, just on a higher level. Everything you do, good or bad, it's really just God doing it. Can you wrap your head around that? It was hard for me at first. Anyway, it's like the Bible says, "What they meant for evil, God meant for good." And that's just another way of saying, in the long run, God gets his way. It all turns out the way God intends it, no matter how things look to us. All the killing, raping, cheating, lying and downright meanness the human race can spit out into the world don't mean a damn thing in the long run. Because it's God's game and in the end, God's going to win. Think of it like a child playing with dolls or a writer dreaming up the plot in a novel. All of it comes from one mind, one source. And that source is what most folks call 'God.'

Now, maybe you think I'm a nutball. From your personal perspective, I guess I am. From a divine perspective, I am just playing my part. I just trust that whatever I do, it's because the good Lord wants me to. So, I don't get all caught up in self-judgment and doubt. I leave that to the confused souls. I am just here doing my job and I've got it on good authority that I'm doing a fine job of it. I don't let the opinions of others sway me one iota to the right or to the left. I just keep on trudging through. I just play my part like any other soul in the game. One thing's sure, I'm not really what most folks would call a Christian.

All that doesn't mean I haven't faced my own personal tribulations. I damn sure have! And I've come through every time. Put it plainly, most think I am insane. Maybe not most, because *most* don't even know that I exist in this world, but a few authorities saw fit to lock me up a good long while in the Terrell State mental facility. When it first opened, back in 1883, it was called the North Texas Lunatic Asylum. Doesn't that sound like something out of an old black and white horror picture? Just a few years later they changed the name to the North Texas Hospital for the Insane.

Somewhere along the way, words like 'lunatic' and 'insane' became sort of politically incorrect. The official name now is just Terrell State Hospital. Terrell's not the name of a doctor or anything, it's a town in east Texas. When you say 'Terrell' to a Texan, they all pretty much know what you mean. They think of the mental hospital, not the town in general. People say things like, "You belong in Terrell!" It's just a way of jokingly implying your friend is crazy.

But, they weren't joking when they said I belonged in Terrell. They sent me there when I was ten and they didn't let me back out until I was eighteen.

Have you ever seen that movie, *Sling Blade*? It's an old picture from before I was born. I probably never would've heard of it if not for my friend, Jerry. He's a pretty sharp fellow who writes books and articles about movies. Well, in this picture Billy Bob Thornton plays a fellow who was locked up in a state mental hospital just like I was. He got put away when he was just a kid for killing his mama and her lover with a sling blade. Some folks call it a Kaiser blade. This character is called Carl, and he pretty much likes to eat mustard on everything. He's partial to starchy foods, like French fried taters and biscuits. He's got a funny way of talking and he sort of growls, "Mmm hmm," a lot. When people have seen the movie, they usually go around saying "Mmm hmm" just like Carl for a few days afterwards. Frankly, I think this was Billy Bob Thornton's best performance. In all his other movies he just seems to play the same skinny, ignorant redneck guy that looks like he probably uses meth, doesn't brush his teeth or bathe much and never does a damn thing worthwhile. In fact, the character he plays in *Sling Blade* ends up killing a character a whole lot like the ones Billy Bob's still playing in other films. This is what my friend Jerry calls, 'becoming the dragon you set out to slay.' I guess you could say he got pigeon-holed by Hollywood. And I'm sure it's hard to say no to the kind of money they pay him to reprise his role as a worthless redneck, but to my way of thinking, he should've just walked away after *Sling Blade*. But then, that's not my call to make, is it?

Anyhow, the only reason I brought up Mr. Billy Bob Thornton and that movie *Sling Blade* is because I borrow that Carl character every once in a while, just to mess with people. See, when folks first hear I was in Terrell for eight years, they get a little stand-offish. They take a step back and view me askance. "You were in Terrell?" they'll ask me, all wide-eyed and concerned.

"Mmm hmm," I'll answer back, doing my best to sound like Carl. "But, they done let me out of the nervous hospital." *Nervous hospital* is what Carl calls the mental facility he was locked up in. You'd be surprised how many times this turns things around. If folks have seen the movie, they usually bust out laughing. After that they'll give me a chance, because they can see I've got a sense of humor. It doesn't work with everyone. A lot of people are just flat terrified of crazy folks. But, you know what? Crazy's a lot like heaven and hell. It's a vibration, a resonance. And everybody walking around on this planet has got the potential for crazy locked up inside them. All that's needed is the right set of circumstances, the exact set of stressors to allow all that craziness to come spilling out into the world. If you've been paying attention, you've noticed this sort of craziness pollution happens a lot. Daily it happens. A lot of times the craziness spills out of the people voted least likely to do that kind of stuff.

That's what happened to me. Just the right thing happened to press my buttons, to step on my last nerve and I took matters into my own little ten-year-old hands. Plain and simple. It was the consensus among the authorities that I was insane and a danger to myself and others. They thought they were doing the right thing to lock me up. Who knows? Maybe it was the right thing, but I'm certain I would never have hurt anyone had the circumstances been different. Those eight years I spent in Terrell just seems like a sort of waste of time, you know? I could've been out in the world living life. Still, it's God's call, so I got to go along with it. Like I said, God's just the long phase of you and me. God is where we end up when we're done playing these human games and maybe a bunch of other games we don't know a damn thing about yet. Like games where we play other creatures in other parts of the galaxy. We got no way of knowing from our present position, because we're seeing it all "through a glass, darkly." You follow me?

I try not to speculate about the unknown too much. I'm pretty certain we have far greater creative powers than we realize. It could be that everything we imagine becomes a reality somewhere, sometime. I don't see much point in bringing a lot of frivolous realities into manifestation unnecessarily. I try to keep my imaginings to a minimum. I try to live in the here and now.

When they first let me out of the nervous hospital … just kidding. Terrell. When they let me out of Terrell, I spent the first several weeks at a group home. It was pretty much like what I imagine a half-way house is like for ex-cons. You get a clean place to stay and three meals a day so you don't get overwhelmed with having to provide for yourself right away. There's a sort of house mother who looks after everybody and gets you to talk about how you're feeling, if anything's bothering you and things like that.

Some of the others in the group home were kind of skittish. I don't blame them. They had a right to be. Some of them were seriously nuts, not like me. I did what I did because it needed doing. These others, some of them, really didn't have any control over what was going on in their heads. They'd hear voices telling them to do things or they'd see ghostly people none of the rest of us could see. It's no wonder they were afraid of getting out into the world. They couldn't trust their own perceptions. With the right drugs, they could keep from doing anything drastic; the sort of things that'd get them sent straight back to Terrell or some other loony bin. But, even with the drugs, their grasp on what most people call reality was tentative at best.

For me it was different. All I could think about was how much time I'd lost, cooped up in that mental facility. See, it seemed to me I had a lot of catching up to do. All sorts of experiences were waiting out there in the big, wide world and I was damn sure ready to plunge right in.

Plunging's not something they recommend for the recently released. They want you to take it slow. They want you to find a boring job at a quiet place where you won't get stressed out.

That just wasn't my style.

After a little more than a month of that nonsense, I packed a bag and hit the road. Austin seemed like a place with a little more flavor than anywhere else in Texas. There was a sort of "alternative" scene there, meaning people who weren't eaten up with conservative, right-wing, Christian fundamentalism. You know, because I've already told you, that I don't have a blessed thing against the good Lord. I've read most of the Bible and truly believe it's a good book. But, I am most definitely not the sort of tight-ass bitch who'd feel comfortable living in a gated community and wearing clothes that were sewed together by slaves in some foreign country. Not that I'm condemning those folks, mind you. It's not my job to judge. I just felt like I'd find some people I could get along with down there in Austin. If not there, I could always head on out to the west coast to Portland, maybe.

I really had no deep-set fear of heading out on my own. I trusted that things would work out. Faith, you know. Besides, I've looked in a mirror. I know I am pretty good looking. And as long as male humans have the traditional hormones in their bodies, it's easy for a pretty young woman to survive. That may sound sexist or weird or un-feministic, but I think it's just facing facts. We all do what we've got to do to get by. Sex is part of it. Most women my age, 'young millennials' they call us, would balk at my plain talk about sex. They've got a sense of themselves as inviolate little princesses or goddesses in a world full of male buffoons who need their guidance. You see a lot of this sort of thing on TV. Those millennial gals have been indoctrinated. I'd like to think most of them could reason their way out of that bull if they unplugged their brains from their smart phones long enough to give it some thought. In one sense I'm glad I was locked away for eight years and sheltered from the world. If not, I might be just another bubble-headed young girl who thinks the world owes her everything. Entitled, you know?

Now, when I start in talking about sex, a lot of people, both men and women, step back and think this doesn't sound like a Bible-reading gal talking. That's mainly because they've been sold a bill of goods. That bill of goods has a name: dualism. They've been taught to look at themselves in terms of eithers and ors. They've been brain-washed to believe if you're one thing, it automatically means you're not this other thing. That's nothing but a pile of horse shit. And I don't mind saying so. Pretty much everybody has the potential to be or do anything at all. All those things, the ones we call good and the ones we call bad, are all just laying there in the toolbox of your mind. You reach into the toolbox and pull out which ever piece is right for the situation. Violence is a tool. It's a tool I've used. Sex is a tool. I've used that one, too. Sometimes doing nothing at all is the best tool.

All that to say, sex is just a part of life. For all of us. And it's been a part of my life since I was just a little girl. See, Mr. Dan McWhorter, the man who was supposed to be my daddy, but wasn't, took a liking to me early on. He taught me all about sex. By the time I was ten, I guess you'd say I was fairly well experienced in the matter. Truth be known, I liked it. It felt good. I had no way of knowing it was inappropriate for an adult man to have sex with a female child. It was just a part of my life.

The trouble started when my mama found out about it. She threw a fit.

I was in my bedroom and I had no idea at first what all the yelling was about. They fought sometimes and I just figured it would blow over in a few minutes like it always did. Only it didn't. My mother did a certain scream and I knew it meant she'd been hurt. Hurt bad. I cracked the door and peeked out into the living room. Mama ran off to her bedroom, leaving Dan McWhorter on the sofa, holding his head in his hands. I could tell he was real drunk.

Mama came back in the room with his pistol in her hand. Then she started screaming at him and I realized it was because she'd found out he had been having sex with me. The disgust in her voice hit me like a splash of icy water. It made me feel sick. I had never thought of it as a bad thing. It was just a private thing. We didn't tell Mama about it because we wouldn't want her to feel jealous, on account of the fact that he liked doing it with me better than he liked doing it with her. That's the spin he'd put on it for me. I had no way of knowing any different.

She pointed the gun at him. He lurched forward, just as drunk as could be. And she shot him.

"No, Mama!" I screamed. I knew she was real upset. It was dawning on me that what me and Dan had been doing was wrong. But, still, I didn't want her to kill him. I wish I hadn't said a word, because I distracted her. When she looked at me, he dove on top of her and got the gun out of her hand. He didn't shoot her. He just beat her in the face with that gun until she was all bloody and not moving.

Then it was like he came to his senses a little bit and he took her up in his arms and bawled like a little baby. He was saying something like, "Why'd you make me do it?" but I can't be certain of his words because he was just too damn drunk and crying on top of that.

"Mama?" I called out, moving into the room. He looked at me through bloodshot eyes and tried to wave me back, blubbering away. He squeezed Mama tight and rocked back and forth. Then he started throwing up. He just vomited everywhere. He let loose of Mama and when he did, she fell hard on the floor like a sack of potatoes. I figured she was dead. That made me turn savage all of a sudden.

The gun was on the floor beside him and while he was vomiting, I just picked it up and put the barrel right against his head. I squeezed the trigger and that was all she wrote. He fell into his own puke and blood just poured out of his head.

I tried to rouse Mama, but she was gone. She wasn't breathing.

I don't remember anything after that, but they say I burned the house down. Did I? I got no recollection of it and since I was the only one left standing after all the killing, I don't see how anybody else could be certain I started the fire. Just another one of the many questions I was left to ponder for eight years in the nervous hospital.

So, that's how I came to spend time at Terrell. It's also how I knew I wasn't a danger to society. I killed Dan McWhorter because he killed my mother. Now that she's gone, I can't imagine much that would make me turn savage again. It's just a tool, like I said before. I used my savagery because it was called for. Dan deserved what he got. Do I feel bad about it? Sometimes I do. Would I do it again? Yes, I'm pretty sure I would.

But, as I hitched my way to Austin, I felt pretty sure my killing days were behind me.

Chapter 2

Hitch hiking is one of those things everybody warns you about. And I can understand how if you're the sort of gal who's got a family, what the staff at Terrell called a 'support network,' and you have options regarding transportation, then maybe you wouldn't want to mess with hitch hiking. You could end up riding with a psychopath. You could end up dead and dumped in a ditch alongside some country road. Those are very real concerns. For the sake of the peace of mind of nervous types and fearful women, I'd advise them against hitch hiking. Why ride with a stranger if it's going to freak you out?

I'm a different story. I'm not afraid of dying. A much higher power's got the decision-making authority on that matter. And, support network? Well, I ain't got one of those, unless you count the group home I was living in before I struck out on my own. That bunch of loonies wasn't even capable of supporting themselves, much less me. Not that I'm faulting them for that. They were very damaged people. I'm a different kind altogether. I'd set my sights on Austin, Texas and I was going to get there come hell or high water. Yeah, I could've walked the whole way. Good exercise, but a hellacious waste of time and good shoe leather.

So, I just headed over to the Interstate and parked my ass out in front of the diner at the Tri-County Truck Stop. I had my stuff: a few clothes, some snack food and some bottled water in a backpack. I wrote the word Austin on a manila file folder and stapled it to the outside of my backpack. That way I was sending a message every minute that I was headed that direction. I wouldn't have to waste a lot of time explaining it to folks. Besides, I knew if I stood alongside the road with my thumb stuck out, then a cop'd probably pick my ass up in no time at all.

As it was, I knew I only had so long to advertise my intentions, so to speak, before I'd be shooed away by the truck stop manager. I sat where everyone going in or coming out of the diner was sure to notice me. I got some stern looks and one old, gray-haired man started to step toward me, but then thought better of it. He just shook his head and muttered something or other, then went on inside the diner.

The smell of fried food got my stomach to rumbling. My mouth watered and I was tempted to dip into my snacks, but I realized it was way too soon for that. I had no idea when I'd get my next square meal. The chips, peanuts and crackers would have to last until then. I just cracked the top on a plastic bottle of purified water and sipped a little. That didn't stop the noise in my belly, but it wet my whistle nicely. I sat there for about forty-five minutes and I was thinking it was almost time to move on of my own volition, before I was forced to move on or worse, hauled off by the law. I stared at the stream of cars on the highway, wishing I was inside one of them.

"You can get in trouble hanging around like that."

I turned and saw a man with black hair, black beard, black t-shirt and a black jacket looking my way as he groomed his teeth with a wooden pick. I figured he was wearing all the black for the slenderizing effect. Like most truck drivers, he did have a gut on him. They said picking your teeth was bad manners at Terrell and at the group home, but I never found it offensive to see folks do it. He smiled. And I forced a smile right back at him, though I'm pretty sure I must've looked scared when I first glanced up and saw him there.

"What's your story, kid?" he asked.

"No story, really. I'm headed to Austin to see my brother." I added that lie about having a brother because I figured it could cause a little hesitation in the mind of a psycho if he believed I did have a support network, however meager that network might be.

"Your brother think it's all right for you to catch rides with strangers?"

"Well, I'm sure he'd prefer otherwise, but you see my friend Penny was supposed to drive me." See what I did there? I made him think I did have a real support network by creating a friend named Penny. "But she wrecked her car. Ended up in the hospital, poor thing."

He nodded, just chewing on that toothpick. I figured he was evaluating the likelihood of my story being true. In that moment I realized that anyone who gave me a ride needed to consider it as carefully as I did. I could've been part of an outlaw band or just a girl who'd scream rape and try to get something out of the accusation. Understanding he had something to lose made me a little bolder. "If I wanted to wait another week, Brad–that's my brother–he said he'd drive up and get me. Truth be told," (but not by me) "my mother is driving me crazy. She's going through the change of life and she's making my life miserable every way she can think of. I figure the sooner I'm out of her hair, the happier we'll both be."

I paused, thinking I might be overplaying my hand. He stared.

"You got a name?"

I didn't want to give him my real name, just in case our association ended up going sideways somehow. "Sadie," I answered him. "Sadie Richards." Sadie, I got from the *Beatles'* song about sexy Sadie. Richards was the last name of the woman in charge of the group home. Mrs. Richards listened to the *Beatles* a good deal and I'd gotten used to hearing the songs about sexy Sadie and polythene Pam. Sadie seemed a decent alias for the spur of the moment. Alias means false name. Learned that from watching old *Perry Mason* reruns on the TV.

"Well, Sadie Richards, are you hungry?"

I shook my head. He took me off guard with that. I wanted a ride, but I wasn't expecting him to buy me a meal. "I'm fine."

"You sure? I don't mind buying you a sandwich."

"Oh, no. I'm full as a tick. Couldn't eat a blessed thing." Right then my stomach growled pretty loud and I guess he may have heard it. He smiled. "Besides, I have food packed in my bag for later."

"Suit yourself, Sadie." He tossed his toothpick aside. "I'll give you a ride to Austin, because I don't like the idea of leaving you here on your own. You could end up with some nutcase or something. But, I got to tell you, I could lose my job for giving you a ride. And I can't afford to lose my job. I want you to look me in the eye and tell me you ain't a hot mess of trouble."

I think I squirmed a little just then. Nutcase, he'd said. Couldn't help but think he'd call me the same if he knew the truth about me. "I can't look you in the eye with you wearing those dark glasses. Could you pull them off?"

He grinned. "Fair enough." He took off the glasses and when I saw his friendly brown eyes, I felt like everything was going to be okay.

"You got a name?" I asked him.

"Joe Farrell, out of Paul's Valley, Oklahoma."

"I feel a lot better about you, now that I've seen your eyes, Mr. Farrell. And I won't be one bit of trouble to you. I just need to get to Austin as soon as I can."

"You can call me Joe. Let's get rolling, Sadie. That is if you're sure you're not hungry."

"I'm positive!" I said, jumping up onto my two feet. I was so happy about having a ride, I didn't give two flips about my empty stomach.

"I'm over here," he said, pointing to a rig parked out on the lot.

I followed him to the truck, climbed up high into that passenger seat and in just a short while we were headed for Austin.

Once we'd got to rolling pretty good, he asked me, "You like music?"

"Who doesn't?" I planned on being just as agreeable as a soul could be. In less than an hour I'd hooked up with a ride all the way to Austin. That night I would be exploring the state capitol and starting the life that had been postponed for so long. My life, not the one some bureaucrats and backwater psychologists wanted to trap me in. I felt on top of the world.

"What do you like to listen to?" he asked, turning a switch on the dashboard of his truck.

"I'm not picky."

"Good. About the only stations out this way are country and western. Classic country mostly."

"Suits me just fine."

Pretty soon ol' Glen Campbell was singing about being a lineman for the county. It was pleasant enough. Joe had pulled his jacket off when he climbed up into the captain's chair and now I was noticing all the tattoos he had on his arms. "You got a lot of nice tattoos," I said, by way of conversation.

"Thank you. You like tattoos?"

"Sure do. In fact, I hope to be a tattoo artist before long if all goes well in Austin." God so help me, I don't know where that claim came from. I didn't really plan it. It just sort of bubbled right up out of my throat. I surprised myself and I was thinking, *Liza ... or Sadie ... girl, don't let your alligator mouth overload your hummingbird ass.* But, what I'd improvised seemed to be just the right thing. Joe eyed me with appreciation.

"Aren't you full of surprises!" he said, laughing. "I guess it figures. Any girl who'd hitch a ride with strangers in this day and age probably has the balls to be a tattoo artist."

"Balls?" I couldn't help myself. I just burst out laughing.

"Sorry ... ovaries ... whatever."

"It's okay. You just made me laugh."

"So, how long have you planned on doing skin art?"

"Not too long really." Boy, was that the truth. About a minute to be exact. "But, I've always been sort of artistic. I mean I'm not a Picasso or a Rembrandt or anything, but I enjoy doodling."

"Got anything you can show me? In your bag there? Got a sketchbook or something?"

"Not really," I told him. "See, I mailed most of my artwork to my brother last week, so I wouldn't be lugging things around. Didn't want to clutter up Penny's little Toyota, you know."

"Oh." Joe frowned. "That's too bad."

Then, I remembered a doodle I'd done on a sheet of the spiral notebook I carried for journaling. Journaling is strongly encouraged by all the mental health professionals and I'd been doing it for years. "I do have one little thing I could show you."

"Great!" His eyes lit up and I could tell he was sincerely interested and wanted to be supportive of me.

"Promise not to laugh at me."

"I don't have to promise that," he said. "I'm sure you do good work. Especially if you're moving to Austin with the intention of becoming a tattoo artist. In fact, I'll bet your choice of profession has a lot to do with your mother giving you such a hard time."

His assumption pleased me. "You guessed it. It's just not a ladylike thing to do."

"Well," he said, "don't let it bother you. Times are changing. Tattoos aren't the scandal they were when I was coming up."

Unzipping my backpack, I dug around until I found my spiral notebook. In the process, I reckon Joe got a good look at my provisions.

"You should've let me buy you a hamburger, girl."

I don't know why, but that little comment of his made me blush. I felt the fever in my cheeks and knew my face was beet red. Funny how a little thing like that can embarrass a person. I flipped through the notebook until I found my drawing. I scrutinized it a second, before letting Joe have a look. It wasn't half bad. Suddenly, I had a feeling that I could actually become a tattoo artist, like it was meant to be and I was just now finding out about it. Destiny, you know?

I turned the book so he could see. It was a skull with some roses and other flowers and vines gathered around it. Joe reached over and grabbed the notebook from me. He took a minute to check it out, letting his eyes dart back and forth between the drawing and the road stretched out in front of us.

"That's actually pretty good, Sadie." He handed it back to me and gave me a real warm smile that sort of melted me a little. "I could see a lot of young women wanting something like that."

"You mean I'm not the only one that likes skulls and such?" I tucked the notebook away on top of my bag of potato chips.

"Far from it. I bet Kathleen might even like it. That's my wife, Kathleen."

Now, as much as I hate to admit it, that little four-letter word "wife" sort of threw me for a loop. You see, Joe wasn't wearing a wedding band and I'd kind of half-way begun fantasizing about what it might be like to have a roll in the hay with him. I know that's wrong and I shouldn't have harbored such lustful desires for a man I hardly knew. Truth is I'd had an itch I couldn't really scratch ever since they let me out of Terrell.

It was wrong what Dan McWhorter had done to me. I was just a child and he was a pervert for having sex with his little stepdaughter. I get that. But, biology is biology. Humans are adaptable and that exposure to sex at such an early age created a desire for more. I'd cozied up to a couple of the girls in the nervous hospital and we'd taken care of one another. Darlene was my favorite. Real pretty and hot as a pistol. And nothing against her, but I hadn't had a man since I was ten years old. Here I was eighteen years old, pretty near grown, and a girl of my age has rambunctious hormones. There's no getting around that fact. I had a hankering for a hard peter and there was no two ways about that. The spot between my legs was warm and wet now, but I knew I needed to cool my jets. I had no doubt I could find a randy young fellow when I got to Austin. I just hoped I'd find one as good looking as the one sitting next to me in the cab of that truck.

Joe noticed my wheels had spun off in a different direction. "You okay? I didn't say something wrong did I?" He seemed genuinely clueless.

I smiled and said, "No, of course not, Joe. You've been a perfect gentleman. I'm worried is all. This is the first time I've really been away from home. I believe you when you say you like my drawing, but I'm a little insecure about becoming a tattoo artist. I'm not real keen on waiting tables and all that. Not saying I'm too good for it. Just saying I don't want to do any more of that sort of work than I have to. I don't think it's my calling."

"It's not your calling. I bet you'll do fine. It's a good thing you got your brother to lean on until you get up and running."

I had to fight real hard to hold a big smile on my face. "Yeah. God bless him."

"What'd you say his name was?"

Now that made me pause. I couldn't recollect if I'd given my imaginary brother a name. I didn't want to draw attention, so I just blurted out my stepfather's name. "Dan. Daniel McWhorter." As soon as I spoke the name, I realized I'd told him earlier that my brother's name was Brad. I hoped he didn't remember, but if he did I was already thinking up another lie to tell him.

"Oh. I thought you said your last name was Richards."

"I did." I looked down at my lap, thinking I could disguise my fumble by pretending I was a little ashamed. "Same mama, different daddy."

"That's nothing to be bothered about," he said, lifting my chin with a finger. "Lots of divorces these days. I'm surprised you even give it a thought."

"Thanks for your kindness." Emotions are a funny thing. We don't always have a good tether on them. I felt a choke in my throat and tears welled up in my eyes. I don't know if it was because he touched me and I was disappointed about him being married. It could've been I was realizing just how alone I really was in this world. I still can't say for sure.

"Don't cry, Sadie," he said. "I'm sorry I asked you too many questions. I should just keep my nose in my own business."

"You didn't do anything wrong. I'm just a little worried. It's a big change for me."

"That it is. Now, I want you to promise me something."

"What's that?"

"When you get established, you let me know. The next time I'm passing through Austin, I'll look you up and hire you to put some ink on me."

"How will I let you know?"

"I'll give you my number. Get your cell phone out and I'll give it to you now."

"I don't have no cell phone." I felt about as low as a snake's belly admitting that to him. Hell, every little child on the street had a cell phone these days. But not me. They'd told us at the group home they were going to get us phones, but they wanted us to have at least part-time jobs first. Responsibility, you know? Plus, it's harder to keep tabs on a girl who's got her own phone.

He stared at me a moment like he could hardly believe what I'd told him. I thought he was about to say something, but he cleared his throat and shook his head. Joe just stared out through the windshield a minute, then he put on a happy face and said, "My business cards are right there by the ashtray. See 'em?"

I looked where he indicated and there they were. I nodded.

"You take one of those and keep track of it. When you're ready, you just call me up and I'll set an appointment with you to get a fresh tattoo. We may have to look pretty hard to find a blank space for it. I'm pretty tatted up."

"Thank you, Joe," I said, drawing a card out of the stack. I unzipped the pouch on my pack where I kept my pencils and band aids and dropped the card in. "It'll be a real honor to give you a tattoo. And it'll be on the house. I owe you for rescuing me from the truck stop."

"Don't talk nonsense, girl. I did what any decent man would do, if it wasn't for all the prying and pestering and regulations they foist on us these days. It hasn't cost me a blessed cent to give you this ride. Didn't even buy you a hamburger, which I should've done. You've made this trip a pleasure instead of a drudgery. So, when I get an original Sadie Richards tattoo, I'll be paying full price, thank you very much."

His sincerity and downright goodness just made me feel like I could pop. I knew for sure he was a good man. "Thank you, Joe. You're better than just decent. God's looking out for me."

"That he is, little sister. That he is."

Chapter 3

The trip to Austin seemed like it took no time at all.

"Okay," Joe said, when we got right in the big middle of the city, "I'm going to have to just let you off along here. I can't afford the time to make any detours. Next red light, you just hop out real quick like, okay?"

"You bet."

We'd pulled off of I-35 a few minutes before and we were moving through the heavy traffic on the street that ran along under the freeway. "6th Street okay?"

"Any where's fine, Joe," I answered. "I'm just glad to be here so quick."

"Dan going to be able to come get you?"

Took me a split second to recall that Dan was the name of my imaginary brother. "Sure. Maybe not right away, but I'll just poke around a bit until he can come get me. Do some window shopping or something."

"Here," he said and when I looked he was holding out two brand new, crisp twenty-dollar bills.

"No, sir. I ain't taking your money."

"It's not charity. It's a down payment on that tattoo you're going to give me. Now take it and use it to get food or something. Make a down payment on a cell phone. Young lady your age shouldn't be wandering the streets without one." He had a sincere look in his eyes and we were coming up on a red light, so I took the money and shoved it into my pocket.

"Thanks, Joe."

"You're more than welcome. Hop out real quick now. We don't want to be calling too much attention to ourselves here."

"Yes, sir."

"Don't lose my number and be sure to let me know when you're officially tattooing. Hell, as long as you got the proper tools and know what you're doing, call me before you're official if you like. I'll buy a bootleg tattoo from you."

"I'll call you," I said and I leaned over and give him a real quick hug. "You're a good man, Joe. I won't forget you."

"Better not. Now scoot."

I opened the door and climbed down as fast as I could. Then he was pulling away and I watched him go. A woman in an SUV looked at me with some powerful judgment in her eyes. Guess she thought I was a lot lizard. That's what they call the girls that sell sex to truckers. Lot lizards. I just smiled and gave her a little finger wave and she looked away.

There I was on 6th Street and I started walking. This was a right popular part of town. You could tell by the number of people walking on the sidewalks and the kinds of businesses that lined both sides of the street. There was all sorts of restaurants and shops everywhere you looked. Now, this was a real city! I don't mind saying so. It made the places I'd been look kind of sick by comparison.

My stomach started telling me it was empty just as soon as I got a whiff of the Mexican food and meat smells drifting out of those kitchens. I had Joe's forty dollars and was mighty tempted to go in one of those cafes and stuff myself. The older, wiser part of my mind won out, though. I had no idea how long it would be before I had a place to stay or any kind of a real routine to my life. I knew I needed to hang onto that money until spending it couldn't be avoided. I told myself I'd find a quiet place to journal and nibble on some of my snacks after I'd walked around for a while.

The street was plumb busting out with sights, sounds and smells. There was quite a few boutiquey places that sold gifts and souvenirs for tourists. Seems *'Keep Austin Weird'* was a popular saying on 6th Street. Lots of the shops sold tie-dyed t-shirts with that slogan and there were bumper stickers, too.

Keep Austin Weird. It brought a smile to my face and made me feel like I'd landed just where I belonged. I was nothing if not weird, myself. And though I'd always been pretty sure of myself, in my heart where it really counts, I think it was only then that I really identified with my own strangeness. You might say I took ownership. Weird sounded like a pretty good thing to be, no matter what anybody else thought about it. *Keep Sadie Weird.*

Music could be heard all over the place. All sorts of music and I've got to admit it put a spring in my step. In addition to the smells of good food, I caught the scent of perfumes and coffee and incense. I probably smelled a bigger variety of odors in my first hour on 6th Street than I was used to smelling in a whole week back at the group home.

But, just like at the group home, not all the smells were good ones. When the bunch of us crazies watched TV together in the group home, pretty much always, somebody'd cut loose with a fart. Only natural, I suppose. Here on 6th Street it was clear that folks did a lot of peeing in the alleys. Some little areas were downright overcome by the smell of piss. I just held my breath and kept walking. It was clear a lot of the folks around me were homeless. Not just homeless for a day, like me. Some of those poor, haggard old guys looked like they'd been on the streets for years and years. That made me a little sad, so I just focused my attention on the colorful sights and refused to make any space in my head for bad thoughts. It may sound a little cold-hearted but I figured the path ahead of me was rough enough without me taking on anybody else's burdens, too.

Late in the afternoon I ran into a group of three girls about my age. They were sitting outside a café together, each one looking at her own phone. I wondered what it would be like to walk in their shoes for a day. Did they have good homes full of people who loved them? One of them looked up at me. I guess she found me interesting, because she nudged one of her friends and soon all three of them were eyeballing me. It wasn't a friendly way, either, that they were staring at me. I felt kind of like a bug under a microscope. They didn't like my looks, but I wanted to see if I could turn that around. There was no point being stand-offish if I was going to make a go of it in the real world.

"Hey," I said, giving a little wave. "How y'all?"

One of them laughed and mimicked me. "How y'all?" The other two laughed with her.

Another one said, "Nice backpack! Where'd you get that?"

Well, my cheeks started burning. I probably did look a fool walking around the streets with that backpack. It was the only pack I had even if it was intended for a younger girl. I'd become sort of attached to it and still liked it until that moment. It was one of the few possessions I could truly say was mine. Now, I felt ashamed. I just turned and walked away. I could hear them talking and laughing at me behind my back.

I walked around all over for a good long while. After some time had passed I felt less self-conscious and I renewed my commitment to make a life for myself in this town. The way those girls made me feel was something I knew I had to get used to. Basically, I was a runaway. To my understanding most folks were going to look down at me on account of that. I couldn't let other people's ideas keep me from following my dream. That's what I told myself.

Toward sunset, I found a real fine tattoo parlor. It was called Skin Dreams. I watched it from a distance for a while, gradually making my approach like a cat hunting down a mouse. The window was filled with neon and the place sort of felt like a carnival to me. I could see hundreds of designs posted on the walls. There was everything from angels to alligators, zombies to zebras. There were simple little symbols right next to portraits of Jesus so detailed they looked fit for a museum or an art gallery.

Inside the place, a guy who looked about thirty was inking a word in fancy script on a fat woman's arm. He glanced up at me a couple times and offered a smile on the second look. I wanted to go in and talk to him, introduce myself and start my education about the tattoo business, but I didn't have to be told it would be rude to just barge in when a customer was being inked on. I hung back, intending to slip inside for a chat when the fat lady left. But that took forever and by the time she walked out, three other potential customers had gone inside and were perusing the tattoo choices. I like that word 'perusing,' don't you? Kind of smart sounding. I wanted to peruse, too, but it just didn't seem like the right time.

Looking around, I saw there was a good spot for journaling right across the way. I could sit down and watch Skin Dreams for a break in the action. Maybe I'd get a chance to slip inside and make my intentions known. My stomach was really rumbling now and I was damn sure ready to break into those potato chips. The spot I'd noticed was a concrete ledge surrounding a little planter full of flowers, in front of a hair salon. It wasn't exactly a beauty shop and it wasn't a barber shop. It was something in between. A place that cut hair for both men and women.

So, I perched on the ledge and opened my backpack. Just about then, Grannie Fry showed up. I don't guess I've told you about Grannie yet. Her full name was Rose Fay Fry. Course, I never called her any of that because she was my grannie and I was just a tiny thing when she passed away. I love that name Rose and I sometimes smell roses just before she shows up. Grannie's been showing up about as long as I can remember. The night she passed away she was right there at the foot of my bed. She has a way of showing up when I need her the most. Helped me through many a rough spot in Terrell. I'm sure she came to check on me since I was homeless and dead set on starting a new life for myself.

I was pulling the spiral notebook out and all of a sudden it was like somebody shoved a whole bouquet of roses right under my nose. My heart filled up with love and I whispered, "Hi, Grannie." Now, when Grannie communicates with me, it's not in words. It's mostly in feelings. Every once in a while, she'll push a picture into my mind real forceful like. Sometimes I just know things. That's her way of helping me along the road of life. In that instant I just felt her there with me and it felt good.

Grannie's always been the kindest, most beautifully loving soul I've ever known. She was really good to me when she was alive and she didn't let death put an end to that habit. I loved my mama dearly and I would've done anything for her, but Grannie and me just have a special bond.

She didn't whisper back to me, still I understood her. I felt her and I knew she was concerned about me, but she was proud that I was striking out on my own. She knew I'd set my heart on being a tattoo artist and she let me know she was all for it. Seemed like she had a little plan in store for helping me achieve that goal.

It'd been a couple of months since I'd felt my Grannie nearby, so I was just bubbling over with warmth and gratitude.

I understood she didn't want me starving myself. "Grannie, I'm fine. I got a bag of potato chips right here," I said, laying the notebook down and pulling my snack out where I could break into it.

"Who the hell you talking to?" It was a mean-sounding man. He growled at me kind of hateful.

Try as I might, I never have gotten full control of myself where Grannie's concerned. So many times, I've surprised people by speaking out loud to her. In Terrell it didn't bother folks much, because I was supposed to be a whackjob anyways. But, around regular folks it often raised eyebrows.

The man looked to be homeless. He was wearing a dirty t-shirt and some oversized jeans. His old shoes were about to slip into tatters around his feet. Even though he was glaring at me, I felt sorry for him and I wasn't scared because Grannie was with me. "Nobody," I said. "Sorry, just talking to myself."

His eyes narrowed and I could tell he was focused on whatever he could take from me.

"Want a potato chip?" I asked him. "Here, you can have the whole bag." That probably seems overly generous, but I knew I still had crackers and peanuts in my pack. And with the forty dollars Joe had given me, I figured I was quite a bit better off than this old fellow.

He snatched the bag away from me and tore it open. When I saw him reach his filthy fingers into the bag I knew I wouldn't be eating any of those chips no matter what. He opened his mouth real wide and shoved a few chips in. I could see a lot of his teeth were missing and the ones he did have were stained and in need of a good brushing.

"Got any money?" he asked. There was nothing friendly about the way he spoke the words. I think I understood right on the spot that he intended to take any money I had if I gave him the chance. Most times I would've cut and run. And I was pretty sure I could outrun the guy. But he was a lot taller than me and he was crowding in on me. Intimidating, that's what you'd call the way he was acting. I forced myself to stay cool.

Grannie was right there with me though. That's why I wasn't scared. When she wraps me up in her love it's like a sweet, gentle breeze in the springtime. Hard to put it into words exactly, but I can tell you there's nothing else like it. I stood my ground until the old guy made a move for my backpack. He tugged hard, but I pulled just as hard.

"No! Stop!" I shouted, before I realized what I was doing.

I heard feet slapping the pavement and I looked up to see the tattoo artist from across the street and a man who'd been inside the shop looking at the designs. They were running toward us and they grabbed the old man, one on each arm. He let go of my bag and he spilled the rest of the potato chips all over the sidewalk. No loss for me, because you couldn't have paid me to eat those chips after his nasty hand had been in the bag. Even so, I hated seeing food go to waste like that.

The tattoo artist seemed to know the old guy. Called him Gus or Bud or something and told him if he didn't want his ass kicked and the cops called, he'd better stay off that block from now on. The man walked away, looking back over his shoulder a time or two.

"You all right?" asked the man who'd been perusing the tattoo designs.

"Yeah, I'm fine," I told him, feeling just a touch embarrassed. Then, like lightning, that's the way it always happens with Grannie, I came to understand she was pulling the strings behind the scenes. She was making all this happen, including the guy trying to take my bag. This understanding put a big smile on my face. It just happened, I couldn't help it. I respond that way to my grannie.

Well, when I smiled I just happened to be looking at the tattoo guy. I'm sure he thought I was smiling at him. For all practical intents and purposes, I was, wasn't I? He smiled back at me. "Are you sure you're okay?" he asked. I have to say, he sounded as good as he looked, his words just husky and gentle.

I was finer than frog hair. Grannie was plucking the strings in my consciousness, playing a real pretty tune and letting me know what I should do next. "I'm okay," I said, "but would it be okay if I sat for a while in your shop?"

"Of course," he answered, without hesitating a lick. "Come on over. I noticed you were looking in earlier."

"Yeah. I love good tattoo art," I told him as I put my notebook back in my pack and zipped it up.

"Well, come on over and take a closer look."

Mr. Tattoo Guy and Mr. Customer walked me back across the street. And I'm sure you realize Grannie was there with us.

The two people who'd come into the shop with the man who helped me turned out to be his girlfriend, Honey and his friend Chet. Chet had something wrong with one leg and walked with a limp. Otherwise, I suppose he'd have run over to chase the dirty man away, too.

"You all right, honey?" the woman asked me. The fact she'd called me 'honey' seemed a little funny to me after I learned that was actually *her* name. She was in her thirties, I'd say, and kind of motherly toward me. We talked for a good long spell while Chet got a nice-looking panther inked on his upper arm. By keeping my ears open, I learned Honey's old man was named Ronnie. That's what she called him, her old man. The tattoo artist was named Thompson. That was not his last name, but his first. It seemed to fit him somehow. He was good-looking and smart and it didn't take any time at all before I let myself start feeling a crush toward him.

Grannie prompted me all the while I was talking to Honey. By the time Chet was paying for his tattoo, she was asking me if I needed a place to stay. I guess she'd started out sort of like I had. She knew what it was to need a roof over your head in a strange town. I have to admit, I was tempted to say yes. But, more than a place for one night, I wanted to start moving toward my new career. I told her I was fine and that I'd be spending the night with my brother. There was more than a bit of skepticism in her eyes, but she didn't fight me on it.

Ronnie, Chet and Honey walked out of the place. That left me alone with Thompson. He kind of straightened things up a bit and looked like he was getting ready to close the place up for the night. I just stood there.

"When's your brother going to come get you?"

So, he had been listening to my conversation with Honey.

I can't say Grannie prompted me. I'm not sure it's what she intended. I think she would've preferred me to go home with Honey and her old man. Anyhow, the next thing I knew I was blurting out a whole ration of truth to Thompson. "Thompson," I said, "you're going to think I'm crazy, and maybe I am, but I don't have a brother. I don't have any family at all." That wasn't exactly true. I had Grannie for sure and I could feel her right there with me. But, I meant I had no living family, which was pretty much straight up truth if you didn't count my illegitimate daddy. "I don't have a home. I just got in town today. I came to Austin because I'm dead set on being a tattoo artist. You're a tattoo artist and a damn good one from the looks of things. I want to learn from you. I'll work for you for free until I'm ready to really work. I'll do anything, sweep floors, clean your toilet, whatever. Please, just let me be here and learn from you. I won't let you down, I promise."

Thompson stared at me a long time without saying a word. He had kind of a stunned expression on his face. It reminded me of the time at Terrell when an old light fixture had fallen from a hallway ceiling and hit smack dab on top of Cindy Thornhill's head. She just stood there with that blank look in her eyes a few seconds before she tumbled to the floor like a heap of dirty laundry. I sure was wishing that Thompson wasn't going to do the same.

In retrospect, with hindsight, I'm pretty sure Thompson imagined he was thinking over what I'd told him. Weighing the pros and cons of my offer. That's what he thought he was doing, but I'm dead certain my grannie was having her way with him, nudging his own thoughts away and scooting her ideas into his head. She's good at that.

After a bit, he smiled at me. It was a good, clean smile, friendly and honest. "Okay, I'll give you a place to stay for now."

I started to jump up and down in an excited frenzy about to tell him how grateful I was, but he put up a hand to stop all that and said, "I'm not making any promises. I don't know you and you don't know me. Things might work out the way you're planning, it's possible. But, it's just as possible that things'll be different. I can tell you right now, you steal from me and I'll press charges. So, don't thank me and don't get all excited. Now, is that all you have?" He pointed at my backpack.

"Yes, sir," I answered all timid like.

That put a sad look in his eyes, but only for a moment. Guess he thought it was pretty awful that everything I owned would fit in that backpack. And it wasn't even a big backpack. It was a kid's pack, intended for a girl much younger than me. For an instant I thought I'd cry from shame, but then Grannie boosted me and I felt like things were going to be okay.

"Come on, then," Thompson said. "I'm parked out back." He locked up the front door and turned out most of the lights, then I followed him through the back room and out through a heavy metal door into the alley. He had a real nice pickup truck parked there and we both got in.

Chapter 4

Thompson lived in an old house that looked like it was built maybe in the 1920s. I say that because it resembled the place where Grannie lived before she died. I'd heard my mama say Grannie's house was built in 1928. Noticing Thompson's house had such a resemblance to my grandmother's home made me feel extra good. Things were working out just the way they were supposed to. But, I guess they always do.

When he brought the truck to a stop out on the driveway, he turned to me and said, "I don't even know your name."

Now that was a quandary. Did I tell him my real name, which would've been the honest thing to do? Or did I stick with Sadie Richards? I couldn't spend more than a second deliberating the matter. "Sadie," I said. "Sadie Richards." The reason I went with Sadie Richards is because it's just a sexier name than Liza McWhorter. And I was hoping Thompson would come to see me in a sexy way. Besides, if anybody from the group home came looking for me, they'd be asking for Liza McWhorter, not Sadie Richards.

"Okay, Sadie, come on up onto the porch, but wait outside for a minute. I have a roommate named Jerry. I need to fill him in on what's going on. Have a seat on the porch swing and I'll come back out in a minute."

"All right," I said, climbing out of the truck. I was sure hoping that roommate wasn't a romantic thing. I didn't figure Thompson for a gay man, but who was I to be making assessments? I'd been locked up in the loony bin for almost half my life. I was about as inexperienced as a body could be. Besides Jerry could be a guy's name or a girl's.

Thompson went in through the front door, closing it behind him. I settled myself down onto the swing and just rocked back and forth a little. Right then I felt Grannie real strong. It was like a big psychic hug. Then a powerful gust of wind blew across the porch, stirring the windchimes and making the dead leaves dance. Seemed to me it was Grannie's way of reassuring me and telling me not to worry. Then she was gone, back to wherever souls go when they're not reaching out to the living.

"Thanks, Grannie," I whispered.

A cat mewed in the bushes. I looked and saw a pair of golden eyes peering up at me from the shadows cast by the porch light.

"Hello," I said.

That's all the encouragement he needed. He hopped up onto the porch and then right into my lap, just purring away and rubbing up against me as friendly as you please.

"How are you, little guy?" I said, running my hands over his black fur. "You looking for a home, too? Are you a homeless soul like me?" I said these things softly, not really meaning anything by them. Just speaking in a low voice to be comforting, the way a mother does to her newborn baby. I felt comforted by the energy I'd received from Grannie and that felt so good I just wanted to share it. The cat had no collar, but he was sleek and well-fed. He had none of the tell-tale scruffiness of your usual stray. Somebody had been looking after him, feeding him regular.

As I stroked the cat, I heard voices inside the house. It was Thompson talking with his roommate. Two male voices, I noticed. They were just chatting in a regular conversational tone, so I couldn't really make out their words. I was glad to notice there was no stress in either of their voices. That meant Thompson's roomie wasn't pitching a fit because he'd brought home a stray. "Yep," I said to the cat, "you're a pretty sleek-looking fellow. I can see I'm the only stray on this porch, for sure." The cat purred and rubbed back and forth against my body and my backpack, soaking up the attention I was giving him.

The front door opened and when I looked up I saw Thompson smiling down at us. The cat made a little yerp of a sound and jumped off my lap and ran in through the open door. Thompson didn't try to stop him, so I figured he was a regular member of the household.

"I see you've met Satan," Thompson said.

"Satan? What kind of a name is that for such a sweet animal?"

"Not guilty," Thompson said. "Jerry named him, but that's just the sort of thing he does. He's got a weird sense of humor and a great appreciation for the grotesque."

"I see," I said, standing up off the porch swing. "In that case I hope I'm grotesque enough to meet his standards."

Thompson didn't have a reply for that. He just grinned, shook his head and gestured me into the house.

Now, I've got a habit of saying a little prayer whenever I go into somebody's house for the first time. My grannie taught it to me when I was a little girl and I've been doing it all my life. It's such a habit I do it automatically without even giving it a thought. The prayer goes like this, *God bless this house and all who enter into it now and forever.* I muttered these words very softly as I crossed the threshold and I guess it caught Thompson's ear.

"What was that?"

"Huh?" Like I said, it's so automatic for me now that I sometimes don't even realize I've said it.

"Was that some sort of spell or something? You're not a witch are you, Sadie?"

It truly was not until that very moment that I understood what he was talking about. "No, that's just a prayer my grannie taught me," I said. "It's such a habit now I forget I'm even saying it."

Thompson seemed a little skeptical. "A prayer? Say it again. I want to hear it."

"God bless this house and all who enter into it, now and forever." No sooner had I spoken the words than there was a huge crash, like breaking glass in the kitchen and the cat came running like a bat out of hell.

"What the fuck?" Somebody shouted. It was Jerry and he came running out of his bedroom, dressed in some pretty funny-looking, plaid pajama pants and a T-shirt with a T-Rex on it.

Thompson said nothing, but walked to the kitchen. I followed him and so did Jerry. Sure enough, there was broken glass all over the floor. The place was none too clean. There were dirty dishes stacked all around the sink and the trash can was filled to overflowing. "The cat must've knocked them off," Thompson said, a little disgust creeping into his voice. "I thought you were going to wash those dishes today."

"Sorry, bro, I didn't have time. Besides, it's not my fault if the beast scatters our dishes."

"He's probably hungry. Have you fed him?" By the way Thompson was glaring at Jerry, I was pretty certain this was an on-going discussion between the two of them.

"Not yet, man. I'll feed him now."

"Watch your step," I said. "You're barefooted. Let me clean up this mess. No sense in you bloodying your feet."

Jerry just stared at me. He looked witless, like a mentally challenged person, his mouth hanging open and his eyes sort of dull. I didn't realize it then, but his demeanor was on account of the fact he'd been smoking dope. It wasn't until a good while later that I learned Jerry was pretty much a daily pot smoker. I smelled it on him, even then, but I had no way of knowing what it was. Marijuana's not a part of the Terrell State Hospital experience. What folks take for granted out in the free world was largely not even on my radar yet.

"Jerry, this is Sadie," Thompson said.

"Hi." I stuck my hand out toward Jerry in spite of his blank stare. "Pleased to make your acquaintance, Jerry."

He slowly rose to the occasion and offered me his hand. "Yeah. Likewise."

"You go back to whatever you were doing," I said, trying to sound as cheerful as I could. "I'm sure you're busy with important things. I'll have this mess cleaned up in no time."

"Well, that doesn't seem right." Thompson just glared at Jerry.

"Listen, I apologize that the place is such a mess. I meant to have it cleaned up by…"

I wanted to diffuse any tension, so I just cut right in. "You folks are kind enough to put a roof over my head tonight, so the least I can do is help with a little cleaning." I was careful to slip that word 'tonight' in there so they wouldn't think I was taking it for granted that I had a regular place to stay. I definitely wanted this to be my regular place and I didn't mind working so they'd see it as a benefit having me around. I figured if I made myself useful they'd want me to stick around.

Jerry looked at Thompson and shrugged. Thompson frowned and said, "Just so there's no misunderstanding, this place is *always* a mess and Jerry's *always* running behind on his chores."

"Well as long as I'm staying here that won't even be a concern for either one of you." I smiled real big at both of them and Jerry smiled right back at me. Thompson tried to hang onto a stern expression, but I poked him in the belly with my index finger. "Let's not let this little mishap put a sour mood on the evening. Now, show me where the broom is and I'll have this all cleaned up in a jiffy." I never knew exactly what a jiffy was, in fact I'd never even used the word before that very moment, but I'd heard it often enough from Ms. Ina Steeple, one of the counselors at Terrell.

"Sounds reasonable to me," said Jerry. He shrugged again and headed back to his bedroom. Thompson showed me where everything was and I started sweeping up and bagging trash and washing dishes. My stomach growled real loud a couple times and that, as always, was a bit embarrassing. I expected Thompson to say something, but he just left the room. I hoped he wasn't disgusted with me, but then I heard him talking on the phone. He was ordering pizza.

"Hey, Sadie," he called out, "what kind of pizza you like?"

I poked my head out of the kitchen. "I only like two kinds of pizza," I said.

"What's that?" he asked me, holding the phone to his ear.

"Hot and cold." I said.

That put a smile on his face. He ordered what I imagined was his regular choice; pretty much a little bit of everything. Supreme or some such. I went back to my chores in the kitchen, gratified that I'd made him smile and damn pleased to know I'd be eating some pizza before long.

Grannie had really outdone herself this time. She wasn't there hovering over me in that instant, but she'd set everything in motion and it was all falling into place, like a line of dominoes that somebody's thumped just to watch them fall.

"Thanks, again, Grannie," I whispered as I pulled the drain plug and let the dirty dish water out of the sink. Now, right when I said those words, I heard a loud yowling at the back door. I opened it and found Satan, crying and moving around. It wasn't lost on me that the cat seemed in tune with my prayers and thoughts. He'd smashed the dishes right when I told Thompson my prayer of blessing and now he was yowling for my attention at the same time I was thanking Grannie.

I stooped down and picked him up. "You picking up on my thoughts, boy?" I asked, nuzzling into his fur to show him I meant to be friends. He yowled right loud. "You're just hungry. Here, I'll find you something." I set him back on the floor and started going through the cabinets in search of cat food. There was a box of dry food in the closet where the cleaning supplies were stored. I poured what was left out into a bowl and set it on the floor. Satan didn't say grace over it, he just dug right in. I filled another bowl with water and set that beside him. He finished his food and washed it down with a bit of water. He purred and rubbed up against my legs.

"You're a very friendly fellow, even if you are prone to making messes," I said. "Seems to me you deserve a better name than Satan. I'll study on that a while and see if I can come up with something that suits you a little better." I knew Jerry and Thompson might not go along with my choice of name for the cat. Whether they liked it or not, I reasoned I could call him whatever I pleased. It'd be like a nickname. Satan could be his proper name, but I'd call him something else that reflected our relationship to one another, the way friends do.

Chapter 5

That pizza was about the best thing I'd ever laid lip to. There was plenty of it and Thompson encouraged me to stuff myself. Once my belly was full, I got real sleepy all of a sudden. I yawned, even though I was trying hard not to. I imagined they'd give me a blanket and have me sleep on the sofa, but Thompson noticed my yawning and showed me to a room that was mostly windows.

"This is the solarium," he said, "but it doubles as a guest bedroom. Make yourself comfortable. If you need anything during the night, just help yourself. Restroom's over there." He pointed to the first door on the right down the hallway.

"I sure appreciate your hospitality, Thompson." I was considering whether or not I should step forward and give him a hug. He didn't give me time to make up my mind, though.

"Goodnight," he said, turning and walking away. "Sweet dreams."

"Sweet dreams to you, too," I said, pushing the door closed. When I turned and looked at the little bed, I thought to myself that I'd never seen one so low to the floor. I found out later it was what you call a futon, sort of a Japanese-style bed. Though I hadn't noticed earlier, ol' Satan had crept in and was curled up on top of the blanket. I dropped my backpack and plopped down on the bed next to him. "You rooming with me tonight, fellow?"

I pet him for a while and silently gave thanks for all the good that had befallen me that day. This time the night before I was in my bed at the group home. I never could've imagined how things played out in the course of my first day of freedom. I'd been real fortunate to catch that ride with Joe. Then I'd stumbled onto Skin Dreams, a totally cool tattoo shop. Grannie had stepped in on my behalf and sort of moved things along in my favor. I wasn't forgetting her influence, but I really couldn't say just exactly how much power a spirit like my grannie has to shape the experiences of the living. It was definitely good fortune that Thompson was such an easy-going man. Plenty of folks would've told me to hit the road when I asked for help.

Now, I was sitting on a warm bed, in a reasonably clean room. I was about as pleased as I could be with the way things had played out. Satan seemed pretty happy about it, too. I got up and opened the door a few inches, just in case he needed to go out during the night. I felt like I could sleep forever, but I knew cats only slept for an hour or two at a time.

I must've been out like a light, because I don't remember a thing after cracking the door open for the cat. Somewhere during the night, I dreamed of hitchhiking. It wasn't at all the way things had played out in real life. In my dream, I was standing alongside a freeway with my thumb out. Trucks and cars were just whizzing past me. Clouds rolled in and the sun set. It was kind of beautiful, all red and gold, with the billowing purple clouds, but at the same time it felt a little threatening. Rain started falling and I got soaked, but nobody was stopping to give me a ride.

I walked along the roadside until I noticed a big storm drain the water was flowing into. I figured maybe I could hide out inside there for a while until the rain slacked off. Once I stepped into the big concrete tunnel, it was like everything sort of shifted. The best way I know to describe it was like I'd entered another world. You know, like another dimension maybe? Instead of darkness, there was light flickering way off in the distance ahead of me. There was lots of graffiti spray-painted onto the walls of the storm drain. Someone had painted the word Satan in big black capital letters. I remember a five-pointed star, too.

As I moved toward the light, I could hear voices. There was like a group of voices chanting some words I couldn't make out. I don't know if the words they were saying were in another language or if they were just muffled and distorted by the distance and the echo effect of the hard concrete surfaces. It occurred to me that I might be in danger, though I couldn't say why. I didn't know who those voices belonged to and I was just compelled to see whatever it was I would find at the end of the tunnel. Even though I felt the hair standing up on my neck, I just edged along in that storm drain toward the light.

Finally, I came out into a big space that didn't look at all like anything you'd expect to find in a storm drain. It was more like an old church. Not like any church I've ever seen in real life, but maybe along the lines of a really old Catholic church. Like something you might call gothic. There were ornaments, statues and alcoves all over the place and the ceiling was so high up I couldn't really make it out. Candles were flickering by the hundreds. There was a large circle of folks in black robes all hunkered down close to the floor. Their faces were hidden from me, but they were the ones doing the chanting. I still couldn't make out their words. I guess you'd say they had an ominous tone. I didn't know if their intentions were evil or good, but I felt pretty confident that either way I was all right.

In the center of this big chamber was a man standing and shouting with a shiny knife held in one hand, high over his head. His back was to me. I was just downright overcome with the desire to see this man's face. I felt somehow that if I saw him, if I knew his identity, then everything would be okay. Not just for me, but for others, too. I crept along the curve of the circle of bodies on the floor, taking care not to step on anybody or disturb any of the statues or other decorations that were crowded into the place.

All of a sudden, the man turned to face me. I let out a little gasp when I saw he had no face. Just two eyes. His head was topped with some bright red hair. You know the kind I mean. That real brassy looking hair some people have. The kind folks'll refer to as a 'carrot top.' Next a funny thing happened the way they sometimes do in dreams. The man was a woman with long black hair, but I still couldn't see a face. Then I was fighting for air.

The chamber gave way to a vast expanse of flickering light. I was pushing up toward the light. I realized I was under water. The water was very clear and that bright light I was moving toward was the sun. I was swimming for all I was worth, trying to reach the surface. My heart was pounding and my lungs seemed ready to burst. Then I broke through and sucked in all the air I could hold.

When I came to being fully awake I was sitting up on the futon in Thompson's solarium. The room looked much nicer by the early light of day. In that instant I just knew that Thompson was in the habit of meditating in that room in the morning sunlight. Though I'd heard of meditation and seen pictures of people sitting in meditation, I didn't really know what it was, but I had the definite insight it was something Thompson did on a regular basis in this sunlit room. I eased myself down onto the mattress and stared up at the ceiling. I felt good. Safe. Grateful. I heard Thompson and Jerry talking.

"We need to get some groceries," Thompson said. "Let's stock up the refrigerator."

"How long you planning on letting poor little white trash camp out?"

"Don't call her that." Thompson's tone was low, but full of authority. I imagine he was worried about me hearing what Jerry said. It did sting a bit. So that's how I came off to folks? Poor white trash? I decided right then and there to start working on my ways to shape them up into something a little more presentable. The bright side was that Thompson was taking up for me against his friend. That gave me a little courage.

"I didn't mean anything by it," Jerry said.

"You need to watch what you say, Jerry. You're way too careless with your words. Words have power. They create effects in the world. Be responsible, man."

"What? Don't tell me you're thinking about hooking up with her. How old is she?"

Thompson's voice dropped real low now. So low, I had to turn toward the door to make him out. "Let's be perfectly clear," he said. "You have a roof over your head because I'm willing to put up with your late rent payments and lazy ways. My problem may be that I take in strays, but you need to remember, you *are* one of those strays. You need to be a little more impeccable with your words, bro."

Jerry must have gone to his room, because I didn't hear them say anything else. In a minute or so I heard the front door, then Thompson's truck started and pulled away.

I lay there on the mattress taking inventory of the situation. Good news was that Thompson was sticking up for me. He seemed to be a pretty decent person. My feelings may have been a little hurt by what Jerry said, but I was pretty sure he was an okay person, too. He was probably just a little insecure. I made up my mind that I'd work on making a friend out of Jerry right away. If I could bring him around to my side, then I'd have no opposition. With no opposition, I could plan on staying. At least for a while, anyway.

After mulling things over for a good while, I decided it was time to get up and about. I went to the bathroom and took a quick shower. If I was going to be staying here, the first thing I was going to do would be to give that bathroom a good cleaning. There was soap scum and hair everywhere. Still, it felt good to get washed and to brush my teeth. I got into some clean clothes and went back to the solarium and made the little bed. When that was done, I went to the kitchen in search of coffee.

There was a shallow bit of stale coffee in the pot, so I rinsed it out and dumped the old grounds into the trash can. It occurred to me that maybe I should make enough coffee for Jerry, too, just in case he was a heavy coffee drinker like Mrs. Richards back at the group home. I'd already made up my mind to turn Jerry into an ally. They say there's no time like the present, so I plucked up my courage and went to his bedroom door. I gave a soft little rap.

"Yeah?" It was a loud and not a very friendly-sounding greeting.

I forced a smile onto my face and tried to squeeze that smile right into my words, so maybe Jerry'd pick up on my positive intent. "Jerry, I'm about to make some fresh coffee. Should I make enough for you, too?"

There was a long silence, then, "Yeah, sure, I could drink some more coffee."

"Okay then. I'll make a full pot."

"Sounds good." I may have imagined it, but it seemed to me the edge was off his voice by a little.

I went to the kitchen and brewed a fresh pot. I can honestly say; few things smell as good as fresh-brewed coffee in the morning. I don't drink it all day long, like some folks, but I have to admit, I do love that first cup. It just seems to lift the clouds a bit, if you know what I mean. Mrs. Richards explained to all of us once that caffeine is a mood enhancer. Though there are pros and cons about how much coffee is just the right amount for a body to have, Mrs. Richards was fond of pointing out that coffee drinkers lived a long time. It wasn't the sort of killer that alcohol and cigarettes were.

I sat at the little table in the kitchen and sipped that first delicious cup. I heard Jerry's bedroom door followed by the shuffling sound of his socks on the floor. He entered the kitchen wearing the same plaid PJ pants and the dinosaur t-shirt he'd had on the night before. He glanced at me a little standoffish, like he didn't really want to make eye contact.

"Morning, Jerry," I said, pretty cheerful, but not overdoing it.

"Morning," he muttered.

I watched him pour himself a cup of coffee. "Nothing better than a cup of coffee in the morning." I commented.

Jerry didn't take his coffee black the way I do. He dumped a nice little pile of sugar into his cup, then he pulled a quart of milk out of the fridge. He sniffed it before deciding it was safe enough to add to his coffee. I guessed spoiled milk was another of the regular hazards of this household. That never happened at the group home. The milk was always gone before it had a chance to sour in that place.

"Did I make the coffee too strong or too weak for your liking?" I asked. I was trying to engage him in a conversation, so I could begin showing him I was a friend, not a foe.

He took a sip. "It seems fine," he said. He glanced at me as he stepped toward the door. "Thanks for making the coffee."

I could see he was on the way out of the room and probably wanted nothing more than to hole up again in his bedroom. There was nothing to lose really by going out on a limb. Either I'd make an ally of Jerry or I'd piss him off. I trusted that Grannie had helped to bring me to the right spot. So, I just blurted out, "Us strays got to stick together."

He stopped in his tracks and looked over at me a good, long moment. "So, you heard that?" He sighed and looked at me with an expression I couldn't rightly read. It might've been disgust, muted anger or even defeat.

"Jerry, I really want you to know something. I may be down on my luck, just starting out in the world with nothing, but I'm not a user. I won't be taking advantage of Thompson or you either. I just need a starting point and I have no idea how to go about getting one. I promise this, though; whatever good is given me I repay in at least equal measure."

Again, he was real slow to reply. Finally, he said, "What am I supposed to say to that?"

"Only the truth," I answered. "What I'd like to hear you say is that you'll give me a chance to be your friend. That you'll see what kind of person I am before you judge me."

"I don't…" I could tell he was not at all comfortable with anything emotional. He felt he was being put on the spot.

"I know you're probably real busy, but if you could take just a minute or two to drink coffee with me, maybe you'd begin to see that I'm okay."

He took a deep breath. Clearly, he was not keen on the idea, but Jerry didn't return to his room. Instead, he pulled out the other chair at the little table and sat down. "Okay," he said, cradling his coffee mug in both hands and staring over with his glasses about to slip off the end of his nose. "So, how'd you end up here?"

Though I felt certain I'd eventually share the whole truth of my life with both Jerry and Thompson, I felt it was too soon to lay all that mess out on the table. Instead, I told him a story pretty much in line with what I'd told Joe, minus the imaginary brother. In short, I said I wanted to be a tattoo artist and my mother didn't approve. I had no money and no idea of how to get started, so I just hitchhiked to town in hopes of figuring out the answers to my questions. As I finished up my story, I had no idea what kind of response I'd get from Jerry and I was more than a little surprised when I looked up and saw admiration in his eyes.

"Wow," he said, "that took some guts, just striking out on your own that way."

"I didn't feel like I had a choice," I said.

He whistled in admiration and stood up. He went to the coffeemaker and refilled his cup. After he doctored his beverage up with milk and sugar, he came back over to the table with the pot in his hand. "You ready for a warm up?" he asked.

I truly appreciated his gesture. Maybe we were going to be friends. "Thank you, sir." I said.

"My pleasure," he answered. He poured coffee in my cup, then went to replace the pot on the coffee maker. I didn't want him to disappear back into his room just yet.

"So, you know a little bit about me," I said. "What about you? What is it you do, Jerry?"

"I have a website and a blog. I review movies and sell some limited-edition DVDs. I write for a few magazines."

"Now, I'm impressed!" I was truly surprised by this revelation.

He frowned, but returned to his seat across from me. "Don't be. If you heard me and Thompson talking this morning, then you know my income is sporadic at best."

"Is there a chance it'll get better?"

"Well, there's always hope. I'm writing a book about super-low-budget-indie films shot in Texas in the 1950s and 60s."

"I'm sorry, I guess I'm not the sharpest tool in the shed, but I don't even really know what that means … super low what …?"

Jerry laughed. "Yeah, I forget sometimes, it's a pretty niche area of interest. Back in the 50s and 60s, some adventurous guys began making movies in Texas. Mostly, these were monster shows or exploitation films with some sort of sexy angle. They made these movies for very little money. The films would usually play regionally in a few theaters, then sort of vanish after a little while. After home video became a thing, then people started rediscovering these forgotten films. They're generally pretty trashy fare. Definitely an acquired taste. I always liked these cheesy flicks. I especially liked the posters and the trailers. It was almost like they'd do or say absolutely anything to get people to buy tickets. Kind of like a carnival, I guess."

"Well, you've got me interested. I never really knew such things existed. Can I see one of these movies sometime?"

With a big grin on his face, Jerry stood up. "Any time you like."

"Really?"

"Follow me. Right this way, ma'am."

He took me into the living room and pointed at the wall. There on rows and rows of shelves were thousands of DVDs. I'd only halfway noticed these things the night before. In the back of my mind they probably registered as books. Truthfully, I don't know if I would've recalled seeing books or anything else on that wall, if you just asked me out of the blue. I went over to the nearest shelf and started looking at the titles on the spines of the plastic cases. They said things like *Free, White and 21* and *Forbidden Planet.*

"All of these movies were made in Texas?" My eyes must've been wide as saucers.

Jerry laughed good and hard at that. "No. Only a small percentage. My book is about Texas films, but I collect films from all over the world."

"How many movies do you have?"

"About five thousand all together. Some are duplicates. I've got quite a few in storage. They're in alphabetical order for easy access. The letter 'a' starts over there and ends up with 'z' over here." He swept his hand in an arc indicating the shelves that wrapped halfway around the living room.

"My god, it must've taken forever to watch all of these."

"Yeah, the results of a misspent youth. It's about the only thing I know much about."

I walked along the shelves glancing at titles. Two really just jumped right out at me; *Poor White Trash* and right next to it, *Poor White Trash Part 2.* "Poor White Trash," I said, "that's one I need to watch for sure!" Jerry didn't respond and when I turned around he had a mournful look on his face. "It's okay, Jerry," I said, trying to sound as sincere as I could.

"I'm sorry about that." I could tell he was genuinely sorry. It showed in his eyes.

"Don't be. You hit the nail right on the head. You have no idea how accurate your assessment is … or was. But, I want to change all that and I'm going to need the help of people like you to put me on the right track. Will you help?"

Jerry clearly took my request seriously. "Sure." He nodded. "I'll help any way I can."

Chapter 6

When Thompson came back home, me and Jerry were on the sofa in the living room watching *Poor White Trash Part 2*. Now, Jerry knew more than you'd ever guess about the movie; where it was made, details about the man who directed it and the woman who wrote the script. The director's name was S.F. Brownrigg, but Jerry mostly just called him Brownie. This man was a filmmaker in Dallas, Texas back in the 1970s and he directed four movies that Jerry was real fond of. These movies were: *Don't Look in the Basement*, *Poor White Trash Part 2*, *Don't Hang Up* and *Keep My Grave Open*.

Watching movies with Jerry was a whole new kind of experience for me. You might say it was sort of layered. The first layer was the movie itself. The second layer was the background information on all the people who made and distributed the movie. The third layer was all the stuff that Jerry and other writers had done with their knowledge of the movie. And you might even say there was a fourth layer; that was what I thought about the movie. Jerry was real keen on getting my reactions. He said some of my observations were astute. Astute was not something I'd ever been accused of being before. Watching a movie with Jerry was kind of wonderful in a completely unexpected way.

We'd started out watching *Poor White Trash*. That was a movie made in the late 1950s by a fellow named M.A. Ripps. It was a pretty typical movie for that time, nothing special. The original name of the thing was *Bayou*. It was distributed by a big company in Hollywood, but it didn't do so well. Old Mike Ripps wasn't the sort of man to give up easily, so he bought the film back from the distributor. I think it was United Artists or some such. Then he shot a scene of a woman running naked down a trail. That was considered pretty nasty for the time. He changed the name of the thing to *Poor White Trash* and started making the rounds to all the drive-in theaters all over the southern United States. That new title drew people in. It's what Jerry called 'lurid.' And after folks saw there was a naked woman in the movie, word spread like wild fire and Mr. M.A. Ripps made a bundle of money.

When this Brownie Brownrigg character made his movie sometime in the early 1970s, it was called *Death is a Family Affair*. A woman ends up stranded in a swamp and she's being chased by a mysterious killer. She's taken in by this hillbilly family and things just go from bad to worse. There's a bunch of gruesome murders and a lot of sleazy talk. This movie didn't really have a blessed thing to do with the first one. Just like the first one didn't really have anything to do with poor white trash. But, when Brownrigg asked Mr. Ripps to help him sell the movie, they came up with the idea of calling it *Poor White Trash Part 2*. Enough people in small towns remembered seeing a naked woman in the first movie and they came to see the second one for more of the same. I don't recall any nudity to speak of, but there sure was a lot of killing. I guess that word of mouth thing works just as good for violence as it does for sex.

Anyway, me and Jerry were having a fine time watching the movie and sort of poking fun at it when Thompson came in through the front door with his arms full of groceries.

"What are you two doing?" he asked. I imagine he was a little surprised to see the two of us getting along so well. Jerry paused the movie with the remote-control gadget.

"We're watching *Poor White Trash Part 2*," I told him.

Thompson shot Jerry a frown. I guess he thought Jerry might've picked that movie to poke fun at me.

"She picked the movie, dude, not me," Jerry said, holding his hands up like a teller at a bank robbery.

"Have you ever seen this movie?" I asked. "It's really a lot of fun. Especially with Jerry here to tell me all the behind-the-scenes tidbits of information."

"Yeah, he's good at that," Thompson said. He didn't seem too impressed. He continued on into the kitchen and set the groceries down on the countertop. "You two want to carry the rest of the bags in? I'll start putting this stuff away."

Jerry frowned, but I slapped his knee and called out, "We'll be glad to do that. Won't we, Jerry?"

"Sure. Nothing I'd rather do," he said real loud and sort of phony. Sarcastic, you might say.

I hopped up and went out the front door to the pick-up truck. Jerry followed along right behind me. It didn't seem to bother him one bit to be out in the front yard in his pajama bottoms, T-Rex t-shirt and bare feet. We each grabbed a couple of bags and carried them into the kitchen.

"You really bought a lot of food," Jerry noted, looking down into one of the bags to see what was in there.

"Yeah. I figured we might as well stock up. We've got an extra mouth to feed and the money'll go farther if we cook at home instead of buying so much pizza and Mexican food. I imagine Sadie here's a fair hand in the kitchen."

Now that threw me for a loop. Other than heating up Pop-tarts in the group home, I didn't have much experience in any kitchen. It was easy to see how he thought I would know how to cook, though. He was thinking of my disapproving mother back home and imagining a woman like that would've taught her daughter how to cook. My mama would've taught me, if she'd lived long enough. Anyway, I hesitated but chimed right in with, "I can boil water. I know that much. Don't expect any gourmet meals from me just yet, but I'll do my best." I was thinking I could get on Jerry's computer and look up some recipes. I did know how to use a computer to access the internet. Mrs. Richards made sure all us girls could do that. She taught us at the public library and she was always saying any information you wanted was at your fingertips, thanks to the internet.

"I'm sure you're just being modest," Thompson said.

"I'll give it my best shot," I assured him.

After a few minutes we had everything put away.

"Man, we're going to be eating good around here," Jerry said, rubbing his hands together. "What's for dinner?"

"Well, for lunch I think we should finish off the leftover pizza," I said. "It's taking up space in the fridge and we should eat that first. You boys okay with that?"

"Sure," Jerry said.

"I like the way you think. First in, first out." Thompson put his hand on my shoulder in a friendly way. I liked the way his touch felt. I wanted to do what I could to meet his expectations of me.

"Waste not, want not," I said, taking the pizza out of the fridge. I put the box of leftover pizza on the table and offered to warm up slices in the microwave. That was something I knew how to do for sure.

The three of us sat around the little kitchen table and ate lunch together.

"You know," I said, "I think pizza's even better the second day."

"You're right," Jerry mumbled through a mouthful. He swallowed and washed it down with a swig from his soda, then added, "That's equally true of all Italian food in my opinion. And soups. Soups are all better after a day or so. I don't know, I guess the flavors have a chance to mix together."

"Looking ahead toward dinner," I said, "What do you think you'd like me to cook?"

"Well," Thompson wiped his mouth with a napkin, "I do most of my business in the evenings, as I'm sure you can imagine. And since you're wanting to learn the tattoo business, I figured you'd want to come along and start checking things out. I close the shop at nine and we usually eat dinner after that. Why don't you throw something in the crock pot and that way it'll be ready when we get back?"

"Sounds like a plan," I answered him, wondering to myself how to use a crock pot.

Fortunately for me, right after he finished eating, Thompson said he was going to grab a shower. When he'd left the room, I confided in Jerry.

"Jerry," I whispered.

He was still eating and when he heard me whispering he got a surprised look on his face, like he wondered what was up. "Yeah?" he asked, sort of apprehensive.

"I've never used a crock pot in my entire life. I don't know how to do it."

He started laughing and a bit of food flew out of his mouth. He grabbed it with a napkin, coughed a bit, then took a large gulp of his drink. His face was red. "Is that all?" he asked me. "No problem, Sadie. It's the easiest thing in the world. Come on, I'll show you how."

We went to the fridge and he looked at the meats Thompson had brought home.

"You like pork chops?"

"Sure." I shrugged. Pork chops were about as good as anything.

Jerry pulled the pork chops out and put them in the sink. "Crock pot's down here." He reached under the countertop into one of the lower cabinets and took out an oval-shaped thing trailing an electrical cord. It had a lid to it and the thing looked vaguely familiar, but I honestly couldn't tell where or even if I'd seen one before.

He took a spray can out of the spice cabinet. "You spray it with a little of this olive oil," he said, demonstrating for me. "That keeps the meat from sticking." Next, he opened the package of pork chops, rinsed them and set them carefully into the crock pot. "You can put a little water in there to make them cook more tender and to disperse the seasoning."

"Seasoning? What kind of seasoning?" I asked, paying close attention to everything he was showing me.

"Well," he looked through the spice cabinet, "garlic, first and foremost. You can never go wrong with garlic.

I suppose there is such a thing as too much garlic, but I have yet to discover that threshold." He sprayed the top of the chops with the olive oil. "A little oil on top of the meat helps the spices adhere." He sprinkled garlic on pork chops. "You like garlic, don't you?"

"Sure. Well enough."

"Okay, so once the garlic's in position, I sprinkle on some salt and pepper. Not too much. Just enough so you know it's there. Now let's add some water. Anywhere from a half cup to a cup. If you wanted to make a soup, you could add a few cups of water and throw in some vegetables."

"Mmm hmm." I nodded, making a mental note. He was telling me how to make not just one dish, but two.

"With pork chops I really like to add this." He held up a pouch of something called French Onion soup mix. He tore the pouch open, dumped it into the crock pot and swirled it around in the water a little with a spoon. The pouch had flecks of dried onion and some dark brown powder. "This stuff adds a lot of flavor. And it's cheap. Lots of bang for the buck, you know?"

"Yeah. Good tip, Jerry. You're a good cook. I can tell I'm going to learn a lot from you."

"I'm no chef, but I know a trick or two. When you like to eat as much as I do, you learn a little bit about cooking as a matter of self-defense." He put the lid on the crock pot and pushed a button that lit up with the message 6 hours. "You can choose four hours, six hours or eight hours. I've found six works best for most stuff. You want the meat cooked tender, but not absolutely falling apart. Unless you're making soup. Then it doesn't matter if the meat's falling apart."

"Thanks for the lesson, Jerry," I said. "The meat's taken care of. What do y'all usually like to go along with it?"

"We can just heat up a can of corn and a can of green beans if you like. Those are simple and they go good with pork chops."

"You've sure made it easy on me. The whole menu's taken care of now. Thanks."

"My pleasure, young lady. Now, as much as I'd like to spend the rest of the day watching movies and sharing my brilliant insights with you, I'd better get some writing done. Otherwise our benefactor might become a little disgruntled."

I stepped forward before he could disappear into his room and put my arms around him. I gave him my most sincere hug. "Thank you, Jerry. I've got so much to learn."

He grinned and said softly into my ear, "No sweat. Us strays gotta stick together. Right?"

"Right!" He pulled away and went to his room, leaving me standing there with a heart just busting full of gratitude. "Grannie," I whispered, "wherever you are, I love you. Thanks for your help. I really like it here."

Chapter 7

When Thompson drove us back to Skin Dreams, I paid attention to the route he took. I wanted to get a clear picture in my head, sort of learn the lay of the land. He switched on the radio, not very loud, and we didn't talk much. I found myself feeling a little amazed at how fast things were progressing. It was only a little over twenty-four hours since I'd left home and already I'd found a place to stay. I knew that maybe it was temporary, but still it was a good place to be for however long I ended up being there. I'd made two new friends and I really liked them. Heck, I guess I'd made three new friends if I counted Joe, the truck driver. Maybe even six new friends if I factored in Honey, her old man, Ronnie and their pal Chet. I might never see them again, but maybe I would and they'd all three been real nice to me. In addition to the friends I'd made, I had also learned some things I never would've imagined about movies. How bad movies could actually be pretty good if you saw them from the right angle. And finally, I'd learned how to make pork chops in a crock pot. I hadn't tasted them yet, but I was pretty sure Jerry knew his chops and his spices. I imagined I'd be real satisfied with the way the dinner tasted later that night.

Thinking of this, I said out loud, "Jerry seems to know a lot about cooking. I think I'll learn a lot from him."

"Yeah. Jerry's not a bad cook. He gets a little heavy-handed with the garlic sometimes."

That brought a smile to my face.

Thompson parked the pickup in the same spot it had been the night before. He pulled a wad of keys out of his pocket and unlocked the back door. He punched some numbers on a little beige plastic box mounted to the wall.

"What's that?" I asked. I was trying to be as attentive as possible and learn quickly anything I might need to know in the future.

"I entered the alarm code to shut off the security system." He went in and sort of automatically started flipping switches on the computer, the overhead lights, the 'open' sign in the window. He unlocked the front door.

I was thinking I'd like to get to the point where he trusted me to enter the alarm code and take care of other responsibilities around the place. Of course, I kept that thought to myself.

Once Thompson had everything squared away, he turned to me and said, "Okay. What makes you think you want to be a tattoo artist?"

"Well," I said, gathering my thoughts. I knew it wouldn't do to tell him I'd plucked the idea out of thin air just the day before. I might choose to live that way, but I had no illusions that other folks did that. I called it living by faith. Other people needed to plan every little thing. They never really noticed most of their plans never amounted to diddly squat. They considered they were being responsible adults by thinking things through and putting in what Mrs. Richards called their 'due diligence.' If I'd tried to explain to Thompson about my faith, he would've just chalked it up to my being young and inexperienced. In his eyes, it probably would've pegged me as being immature. I sure didn't want that.

"I've always been pretty good at art. I'm not bragging, mind you. It's just I never was that great at anything in school. I did pretty good in art, though. So, I got to thinking; how was the best way to make a living from art? I'd heard that the 'serious' artists usually struggled for years. Lots of them never made a penny. I don't love art enough to starve to death for it. I just want to make my way in the world, you know? I figure a tattoo artist has a better shot of paying bills than a painter who wants his stuff to end up in a museum."

I'd let the words just flow slowly out of my mouth. I wanted to seem casual, but confident, even though, as my friend Kelly back at Terrell would've said, 'I was pulling this stuff out of my ass.' I left off and waited for a response from Thompson.

He pressed his lips together and nodded. "Okay. Seems like you've got your head screwed on pretty straight. A lot of creative people get too caught up in their own personal vision and don't seem to realize they need to have the support of others to make a go of it."

Score one for the little white trash girl! Inside I was overjoyed that he'd bought my explanation. Outside I was cool as a cucumber. Now, looking back on this I can see how my lying might seem like manipulation, something a criminal would do. It was no pleasure to lie to my new friend, my 'benefactor' as Jerry had put it. I may have been pretty much still a kid, but I'd sure noticed that the only truth that mattered in the real world was the one people believed. In other words, people act on what they think is true, even if it isn't necessarily so. I knew my ultimate intent was to be able to support myself and to be a good employee for Thompson. I determined it was in everyone's best interest to do and say whatever would open the doors to the fulfillment of my vision. I had other, more romantic, intentions as well, but I wasn't about to press those.

"How about you, Thompson? How'd you come to be in this business?"

"Well, it sure wasn't because I thought I was an artist. When I got back from Iraq I was pretty much disgusted with everything. With life itself. I went off the deep end for a while, started hanging with some rough characters. Bikers, drug dealers, you know. I gradually moved into the tattoo thing from that perspective. Everybody I associated with in those days wanted a tattoo. I had a ready stream of customers. One day I sort of woke up. I walked away from all that and came to Austin to start over."

"Where were you before?"

"Portland."

"Yeah. Your accent sure isn't Texan. I spotted that right away."

"Hey, like the bumper sticker says, *I wasn't born in Texas, but I got here as fast as I could.*"

"So, you like it here?"

"Well, it's like any place. You have to take the good with the bad. I don't believe in perfection. I can't vouch for the rest of Texas, but Austin's liberal enough to suit me. There's an underlying pragmatism that I like about the place."

"What's that?" As far as I could recollect, I'd never heard that 'pragmatism' word before.

"Pragmatism? I guess you'd say it's a sort of practical mindset. Pragmatic people don't have a lot of uncertain notions clouding their reasoning. They deal with life on its own terms, even if things are less than perfect. After all, nothing's perfect, right?"

"Right."

"Your ideas about why you want to be a tattoo artist are fairly pragmatic, I'd say."

"Thank you. That's the first time I've ever been called pragmatic and I hope it won't be the last."

That made him laugh.

I looked at all the many designs posted on the walls. "You say you don't consider yourself an artist, but these samples say otherwise."

Now, he laughed even harder.

"Oh, you think I came up with all of those?"

"Didn't you?" The way he asked the question made me feel foolish somehow.

"No. I can't take credit for those. Oh, there's a handful that I came up with on my own, but most of them came from free design sources." I must've looked confused, so he put his hand on my shoulder and said, "Come on, I'll show you."

He typed in some words and up popped a website with thousands of tattoo designs you could download for free. You could print them out in color to make displays or you could print out just the outlines.

"You look a little disappointed," Thompson said.

"Yeah. I guess I am."

"Pragmatism rears its ugly head again. Tattooing is a very competitive business. I need to be able to offer as much as anyone in order to compete."

"So, you still have to draw these designs on people anyway, right?"

"No. Sorry to disappoint you, Sadie. We transfer the image outline onto the customer's skin, then we just ink it in and fill it with color if they want that."

I just sat there frowning. It was a little like being told there's no Santa Claus. But, I was a pragmatic gal, according to Thompson, and I was going to make the best of this disappointing revelation.

"Well, you have busted my bubble. I have to admit that. But, I can see the value of this and I'd say it actually makes my prospects even better."

"There you go." He patted me on the shoulder and wandered away to open some mail. "Why don't you just look around at the designs for a while? That's a good way to begin educating yourself about the business."

"All right then."

I scrolled through the thousands of designs, wondering what it would be like to do my first actual tattoo on a real customer's body. What if I slipped and made a mistake? These things didn't wash off. Applying one on somebody's arm was serious business. My god, what about inking on a person's face? I was more than a little intimidated by the thought.

Time passed and nobody came into Skin Dreams. I'm no whiz with a computer, but I took in quite a bit of information about the tattoo business. When my attention began to wander, I looked up and saw Thompson kicked back in one of the comfortable chairs intended for the customers, reading a magazine.

"So, you were in Iraq?"

He lowered the magazine and stared at me in a way that made me feel pretty darn uncomfortable. "Yeah," he answered after that uneasy pause. I started to ask him a follow up question, but he cut me off. "I don't talk about it. I like you, Sadie, and we'll get along just fine as long as you don't ask me questions about Iraq."

"Yes, sir. I sure don't want to offend you for any reason."

His expression softened, then he even offered me a little smile. "You haven't offended me."

I didn't want to leave things on that note. I searched my mind for other lines of thought that would let me get to know him better. What popped out of my mouth was this: "Do you meditate a lot?"

That shocked him. A look of surprise swept over his face. "How'd you know about that?"

"That room you've got me staying in, the solarium; it just seems like a place for meditating. When I was lying on that little bed this morning, it just came to me that you probably used that room for meditation."

"You're very perceptive. Maybe 'in tune' is a better description. Or maybe even psychic."

"I get little nudges toward the truth sometimes," I admitted. I considered whether I should tell him about Grannie. I decided to leave that subject alone for the time being anyway.

"That's a special ability. A lot of people ignore their intuition."

"I try to pay attention to it." I didn't tell him my Grannie used to always say, 'The knowing's as much a curse as it is a blessing.'

"Good. Well, to answer your question; yes, I meditate most mornings in the solarium."

"My gut feeling is that meditation's something I should learn. Will you teach me?"

"It's not really something I can teach, but I'll be glad to communicate what I know. It's made a major difference in my life."

"I feel bad about knocking you out of your meditation spot this morning."

"Don't. I meditated in the park for a bit when I went for groceries."

I had thought he was gone a long time just to be buying food. "Good. I feel better then."

"Did you sleep okay?"

"Real good. I never saw a bed so low to the floor, but I was comfortable as could be."

That's when Thompson told me that bed down on the floor was called a futon. He spelled it for me and explained that most Americans call it a *foo tawn*. But, he told me, it's a Japanese word and should properly be pronounced *foo tone*. I made a note of that. So, the little white trash girl from Texas got her first lesson in proper Japanese. I was moving right up life's ladder of education, I'll swear!

He went back to reading his magazine. I was tired of playing on the computer, so I just looked out the window at the folks passing by on the street. After a minute I noticed there was a woman with long black hair standing near the spot where I'd sat before; the place where that homeless guy took my chips and tried to intimidate me. She was wearing sunglasses, so I couldn't see her eyes, but it seemed to me she was staring at Skin Dreams. Her dress was kind of gauzy and white and she wore lots of jewelry; multiple necklaces hung down between her breasts and both wrists had three or more bracelets. Lots of colorful stones. The first thing that popped into my mind was the word 'witch.'

As she continued to stare at the tattoo shop I began to think she was deciding whether or not to come in and take a look. On the off chance that she needed a little nudge, I made a beckoning gesture, even though I didn't know for certain if she could see me. I thought it would be a good thing if we got a customer in early in the day. I turned to Thompson to tell him we might have a prospect, but something about the way he seemed engrossed in his reading gave me pause. When I looked back out at the street, the woman was gone.

I had no way of knowing at that moment, but she was going to play a big part in the way my future shaped up.

Chapter 8

Around six o'clock a man came through the front door. He was nice and brown from working in the sun. His green eyes really popped out at you. By that I don't mean they were big. He didn't have what folks call 'pop eyes.' In fact, his eyes were kind of squinty, but the way those green eyes contrasted with his tanned skin was almost startling. He grinned all the time, like his face was just stuck in grin-mode. There was no reason for his grin, it was just his way of meeting the world. I liked him without knowing why.

"Hey, Thompson," he called out.

Thompson looked up and quickly gave the guy a grin of his own. "Rusty, how are you?"

"Doing fine. How's your life treating you?"

"I have no complaints. It's good to see you, man." Thompson stepped forward and grabbed Rusty's hand, then pulled him into a hug. "You just kind of disappeared. Where the hell you been?"

"I got a job painting a bunch of houses in Jefferson for a guy. I just camped out there in my van for a while. The guy hired me to do one house, but he just kept adding work. I been over there for four months. If I'd known I was going to be gone so long, I would've let you know."

"You have a cell phone, don't you?"

"Guilty. Okay, I got no excuse. But I am glad to see you!" He slapped Thompson's shoulder and looked over at me. "Who's this pretty young thing? Did you trade Lucinda in for a better model?" Now, I could tell Rusty meant this comment as a joke. Not to be taken seriously. This was the first I'd heard of Lucinda. Thompson frowned and both Rusty and I got the idea he wasn't real happy to hear that name.

"Lucinda's been out of the picture for a few months."

"Oh, man…sorry. I didn't know."

"No worries. It's all for the good."

Rusty noticed I was just sort of left hanging, so he took a step toward me and stuck out his hand. "I'm Rusty. Thompson may be too rude to introduce you, but I'm glad to know you."

"Sadie. Hi, Rusty." I shook his hand. His skin was rough from the work he did, but he had a gentle touch and a real positive energy about him. He was giving off good vibes.

"How long you been with Thompson?" he asked.

"Don't go getting the wrong idea…" I started.

"Sadie's not my girlfriend, Rusty. I just met her yesterday."

"Okay, I get it. Don't mind me. My feet are so big I can't find any place to put 'em except in my mouth." He laughed and winked at me. I laughed, too. I couldn't help it.

Thompson said, "Sadie wants to ink. I suppose you'd call her my protégé."

Now, I was uncomfortable because I didn't know what that word meant. As far as I could recall, I'd never heard it before. I felt like it had a sort of French sound and might've meant something sexy, since the French are known for their casual approach to sexual matters. But I was in the dark, not knowing if I should smile or be embarrassed.

"Well, you'd suppose wrong, because I don't know what a protégé is," Rusty said, cocking his head. Then, I laughed, glad I wasn't the only ignorant person in the room.

"I've taken her under my wing to train her. She's my student."

Rusty thought that over. "I see. Is she a good student?"

"It's too soon to tell."

"I'll be a good student. You won't regret teaching me," I chimed in. It was automatic and I think I surprised them both. The way they looked at me said they were giving me the benefit of the doubt.

"I believe you will," Rusty said.

"Yeah. I've got a good feeling about her," Thompson added.

I felt my cheeks warming. I'm sure I was red-faced.

"Well," said Rusty, "after four months of steady work, I'm caught up on all my bills and I've got some extra cash burning a hole in my pocket."

"You've come to the right place," Thompson said. "What'd you have in mind?"

"That eagle we were talking about the last time I saw you."

"Yeah, I sort of remember that. Which eagle was it?"

"That one." Rusty pointed at a huge eagle design. It had wings spread wide. Lots of detail and lots of color. It was a huge tattoo design. Rusty's arms were covered with tattoos and his shirt was unbuttoned low enough that I could see he had some ink there already; beneath the gold chain and the big medallion he was wearing.

"You got room for it?" Thompson asked, expressing just what I'd been thinking.

"Been saving my back for that bird." He pulled off his shirt and sure enough his whole back was clear.

"Since you're undressing, I guess that means you're ready to dive right in."

"Yes, sir. I've been wanting that eagle for years. Never could get far enough ahead to pay for it."

"Great. Not only do I need the money, but this will be a great one for Sadie to watch."

Once again, Rusty winked at me.

So, we jumped right into the process. Thompson showed me how to print out the design and after we got Rusty situated in a massage chair, so he could be comfortable for a good long while, we transferred the outline onto his back. Thompson took his time, making sure everything was just so, perfectly positioned and symmetrical. Once the outline was in place, he had Rusty sit up with his back to the mirror on the wall. We held up hand mirrors, so he could check out the reflection and approve the placement. Of course, he was fine with it. I got the impression a lot of his other tattoos had been put there by Thompson. There was a degree of trust there that a new customer probably wouldn't have.

Rusty settled back in and Thompson began the long process of inking in the outline. It was slow-going and little drops of blood had to be dabbed away sometimes. After a good long while, Rusty said, "I could sure use a drink."

"You know that's against the law," Thompson said, looking at me. I guess he was making sure I was paying attention to that fact. I nodded at him. "I can give you some ibuprofen if you like."

"Naw, I'll just tough it out," Rusty said.

Later on, he groaned. Thompson commented that the places where the skin was close to the bone were the most sensitive. He asked if Rusty wanted to stop, but Rusty told him to keep going. He groaned a few more times and Thompson stopped.

"Sadie, can you run down to the fried chicken place and get an ice tea with a straw in it?" he asked.

"Sure. Where's the fried chicken place?"

"It's at the end of the block on Fifth street. Shortest way is to go left down the alley, then turn right. It's right there. You can't miss it." He took a couple of bills out of the register and handed them to me.

"Anything else?" I asked.

"Nope. Just a large iced tea."

"Sweet or unsweetened?"

"Unsweetened," they both said at the same time.

"Okie dokie."

I followed his instructions and in no time at all I was headed back with the beverage. I was almost to the back door of Skin Dreams when I noticed that same woman I'd seen before. The one in the white dress with all the jewelry. I could have sworn she was staring right at me. But I didn't get any time to consider that much, because someone said, "Hey!" real loud and kind of hateful. I turned around and that old homeless guy was stepping out from behind Thompson's truck. He moved pretty quick and grabbed my throat with one of his grimy hands. He leaned in close enough that I could smell his nasty breath and he said, "You need to get out of here. You're not wanted here."

I didn't think at all. It was like I just acted automatically, like a machine. I kicked him as hard as I could right between the legs. The pants he was wearing were worn and flimsy and I connected hard with his private parts. The old guy's eyes widened with shock and he released my throat, falling down on his knees, holding his crotch with both hands. "You little bitch!" he growled.

"Thompson!" I screamed. I turned and rushed to the door and as I was laying my hand on it, I caught a glimpse of that woman in white walking away. I flung the door open and screamed Thompson's name again, but both him and Rusty were already running toward me.

"What?" Thompson was the first one out.

I pointed at the old man. He realized now that he was in deep shit. I could see the fear in his eyes when he saw Thompson and Rusty. "He tried to choke me," I said. "I kicked him hard in the you-know-what."

Rusty started laughing. "Way to go, Sadie!" He put a hand on my shoulder.

Thompson grabbed the old homeless guy by his shirt and pulled him up onto his feet. "You've done it this time, Gus!" Thompson shouted. "I've had it with you. You're going to jail, old man."

The old guy just groaned and looked down at his feet.

They called the police and held Gus there until the cops came for him. It was a whole big, long, drawn-out mess and I felt horrible about it all. I felt responsible. Here Rusty should've been getting his tat and because of me, they were having to deal with the police. The officers put handcuffs on old Gus and put him in the backseat of their car. They asked if I wanted to press charges. I looked at Thompson. He nodded, so I said yes. They asked for my ID and seemed a little suspicious when I said I didn't have one.

"She doesn't have a driver's license yet, but she lives with me." Thompson told them. He gave them the address. That seemed to satisfy them. Finally, they left.

"I am so sorry for all of that," I said when it was just me, Rusty and Thompson.

"Don't be," Thompson said.

"Yeah, it wasn't your fault," Rusty added.

"That old guy has been causing trouble around here for too long. He needs to be off the streets before he attacks someone else."

"I don't know why he did that," I said, wishing the whole thing had never happened. It was only then that I remembered the tea. "And I spilled your iced tea."

"Forget it," Rusty said. "Listen I'm going to walk down and get another tea and stop by my van to doctor it up. When I get back, let's keep working on this eagle. Okay?"

"Sure," Thompson answered him.

When he left, Thompson asked if I was okay.

"Sure. I'm fine. I'm not really hurt. It just took me by surprise."

Then, even though he'd heard me tell it to the police, he asked me to describe it all over again. I did and as I was going on about it, I started to mention the woman in white, but I couldn't really see how she was related to Gus attacking me, so I left her out of my story.

"Everyone'll be better off with Gus locked up. Including Gus," Thompson said.

"I guess so. Still I feel bad about it. I don't want you to start thinking I'm bad luck and want to get rid of me," I said. My voice cracked a little because my emotions got the better of me in that moment.

Thompson put an arm around me and gave me a sideways hug. "Don't worry about that. I'm not going to hold you responsible for some old nutjob's antics."

"Good," I said, trying hard not to cry.

"You and Jerry have already gotten to be good friends. I know he's glad you're around to help with the cooking. I'll give you a fair chance, don't worry. It'd take a lot more than this for me to kick you out. As long as you learn and do what's expected of you, you're welcome to stay."

"Thanks, Thompson."

"You're welcome. Now, don't give it another thought. Okay?"

"Yes, sir."

"Atta girl! Now, speaking of cooking, I thought we'd invite Rusty over to the house to eat with us tonight if that's okay with you. We have plenty of food."

"Sure, it's okay. I'd be glad to have him there."

"Good. He's spending a lot of bread with us. All in, that eagle's going to run about fifteen hundred by the time it's done."

I was shocked. "Really?"

"Yep. And that's with me giving him a substantial discount. I want him to finish it up as quick as possible, because we need the cash. So, let's treat him good. Like one of the family."

"You can count on me," I said. "I like Rusty."

"Yeah, he's a pretty good dude."

When Rusty returned, he had 'doctored' his tea with bourbon and he was sipping it through a straw. The liquor quickly made him even more jovial than he already was. After Thompson told him he was invited to dinner, he was pleased as punch.

"Y'all are just too good to an old, house-painting redneck!" he exclaimed.

"Us rednecks gotta stick together," I said, almost without thinking.

I saw my comment pleased Thompson and Rusty really liked it. "You're all right, Sadie," he said. "I don't care what they say about you." He was joking and I knew it.

"I don't care either," I said, sort of defiant like.

We all laughed.

No other customers came in that night and it was a good thing, because there was hours of work to be done on Rusty's eagle. By the time we locked up, the entire thing was outlined and a small portion of the colorful details had been inked in.

Chapter 9

Those pork chops that Jerry showed me how to make in the crock pot had filled the house with the most delicious smell. Right away my stomach started growling and I realized just how hungry I was. Rusty had followed us over and I could tell Jerry was a little surprised to see him, but not in a bad way. It seemed like they'd never met before. Rusty's just such an easy-going fellow that people can't help but like him. And it was no different with Jerry. Pretty soon they were exchanging jokes and talking like they were old friends.

Jerry came into the kitchen and helped me finish putting the meal together. We pulled the kitchen table away from the wall so the four of us could sit there. Jerry had heated up the oven and had some rolls with butter on top ready to pop right in. So, in just a short while we had green beans, corn, pork chops and hot, buttery rolls ready to eat. I don't think I've ever enjoyed a meal more than I enjoyed that one.

Rusty had been drinking since late afternoon, so he was pretty well drunk by the time we sat down to eat. He wasn't falling down or obnoxious, mind you, just a little louder and quick with a joke. He didn't say or do anything that was off-putting, but he was definitely the life of the party.

"Damn, these pork chops are the best!" Rusty said. The way he was shoveling food into his mouth I was fearful that we'd run out before everyone had their fill. I paced myself, taking little bites and chewing each one thoroughly. "Did you cook these pork chops, Sadie?" he asked with that big old grin of his.

Before I could answer, Jerry chimed in. "She sure did. They're great, aren't they?"

To Thompson, Rusty said, "So you didn't just get a helper ... excuse me, a protégé, at Skin Dreams, you got a great cook, too. You know how to pick 'em, Thompson."

Thompson smiled, but just kept chewing his food and shot me a wink.

"Now, I feel like I'm getting a bunch of praise under false pretenses," I said. "Jerry taught me this style of cooking pork chops, just this morning. I imagine I'll cook them this way pretty regular from now on, but I can't really take the credit."

"I thought I noticed Jerry's influence," Thompson remarked, "especially where the garlic's concerned."

Now, all of us laughed at that, including Jerry.

"I love garlic," Rusty said. "This is the best meal I've had in a long time, whoever's responsible for it."

After dinner, Rusty let it be known that he wasn't done drinking for the day. He insisted that Thompson join him at a local bar. He invited me and Jerry along too.

"No, thanks. I've got work to do," Jerry answered.

When Rusty glanced at me, I said, "I don't drink, Rusty. I appreciate the invitation, though."

Rusty went to the bathroom and Thompson quietly told me that he wouldn't be gone too long, but he wanted to make sure Rusty made it home safely. Rusty wasn't just a friend, he was also a big part of our income at the moment and Thompson wanted to be certain that the eagle tattoo got completed in a timely manner and we got paid in full. I told him to be careful as I stacked the dishes in the sink.

When they got ready to leave, Jerry and I walked out onto the porch with them and told Rusty goodbye. They climbed in Thompson's truck and pulled away slow, old Rusty hanging out the window like a big friendly dog. As huge and strong as that man was, I couldn't help thinking he'd be a handful to deal with if you ever got on his bad side, even if he did seem like an overgrown kid.

Jerry followed me back into the house. Without thinking about it, I said my usual blessing again. Just like the time with Thompson, it caught Jerry's attention.

"What was that?" he asked. He looked concerned. "Jesus, you're not a witch too, are you?"

"I said, 'God bless this house and all who enter into it, now and forever,'" I told him. "What is it with you two? Thompson asked me the same thing last night. It's just something I say that my grannie taught me. It's nothing to be afraid of."

"Oh," Jerry looked just a touch embarrassed, "sorry. Thompson's ex was a practicing witch. She was bad news and caused us a lot of grief before he finally got rid of her."

"Lucinda?"

"Yeah. So, he told you about her?"

"No. Rusty mentioned her name today and Thompson acted like he didn't want to talk about her."

"The less said about that bitch, the better."

"I guess it's good for me she's gone," I said, walking back to the kitchen. "Sounds like she would not have put up with me learning from Thompson, if she was still around."

"Oh, hell no! There was never a more controlling cunt on the planet."

I guess his use of the 'c' word must've raised my eyebrows, because Jerry turned red and said, "Sorry. That was uncalled for. Still, Thompson's a lot better off without her in his life."

I returned to the sink and began washing the dishes. Jerry grabbed a beer from the fridge and opened it as he sat down at the kitchen table. "Thompson's got such a good heart," he said, wiping his mouth with the back of his hand. "I don't have to tell you. He's always taking us strays in. Lucinda was one stray he should never have bothered with. That woman is not happy unless she's hurting somebody. Just a born trouble-maker."

As the sink filled with water, I squirted some dish washing soap in and watched the bubbles swallow up the plates and utensils. "Where is she now?"

Jerry shrugged when I looked up at him. "Who knows. The important thing is she's not here."

My curiosity got the better of me. "What's this Lucinda look like? Can you describe her?"

"I can do better than that." Jerry got up from the table and went into the living room. I heard him fumbling a bit in there as I switched off the water and began washing the dishes with a sponge.

He came back with a book in his hand. He opened it and took out a photo that was tucked between the pages, holding it up for me to see. "That's Lucinda."

In the picture Thompson was smiling and had his arm draped over a dark-haired woman's shoulder. Thompson looked genuinely happy, but something about the turn of the woman's mouth seemed more like a smirk than a smile. She was holding the black cat in her arms and I was pretty damn sure she was the woman I'd seen outside Skin Dreams earlier that day, first across the street and later at the end of the alley.

"Is that Satan?" I asked.

"Yeah. I don't know why she didn't take him with her."

The first thing that popped into my head was that Lucinda was not far away and that she'd been sending Satan to keep an eye on Thompson and Jerry. I imagined the cat had told her about me. Crazy. Yes, I understand how that sounds. But I can also tell you for a fact that there's a lot more to this world than most folks imagine.

I told Jerry about Gus attacking me in the alley. I told him I'd seen Lucinda hanging around.

"Holy shit!" Jerry's eyes bugged and he almost spit his beer out. "Did you tell Thompson?"

"No. I didn't know who she was or if she had anything to do with it until just now."

"Well, I'm going to tell him when he gets home."

"Are you sure it's a good idea?" I asked him. "I don't want to be the cause of trouble for y'all. I'm terribly grateful that you two took me in and are giving me a chance to earn my keep. I don't want anything to ruin that. I got nowhere else to go." That last admission caught in my throat and I started crying. Maybe it wasn't the absolute truth. I suppose I could've gone back to the group home, but I'd already decided I'd rather die than return there. That place was an island of lost souls. I didn't belong there. I didn't deserve to be forced into the kind of life they wanted me to live.

Jerry jumped up, all startled like and came over to me. He pulled a paper towel off the roll and offered it to me. "Here," he said. "Don't worry, Sadie. Thompson's not going to kick you out. Heck, even if he did, I wouldn't let you end up on the streets. I have friends. There are places where you'd be welcome to crash and I'd go with you to make sure you were okay."

My heart was touched by the sincerity in his eyes. "You'd do that for me?"

"Of course, I would."

I couldn't stop myself from giving him a big hug. "You're a good friend, Jerry!" I said, squeezing him hard as I could. "I don't know if I deserve your friendship. Not yet anyway. But, I'm going to do my best to be worthy of it."

"No worries," he said, patting my back awkwardly with one hand. "Everyone deserves friends. I don't want you to feel insecure. I have a good feeling about you and I don't intend to let anything bad happen to you if I can help it. I'm certain Thompson feels the same."

"I hope so," I said, letting him go.

"But we have to tell him about Lucinda. We can't let that witchy bitch get away with this. All right?" He looked into my eyes. He put his hands on my shoulders and I knew he was just wanting to reassure me.

I nodded.

"Good," he said, clearing his throat. I could tell this little display of emotions was as uncomfortable for him as it was for me. Maybe even more so. "Okay, then …"

"Thanks." I dried my eyes with the paper towel.

"No problem." He gulped down the rest of his beer, tossed the can and grabbed another from the fridge.

"I need to finish washing these dishes."

"Why don't you let me do those?" He stepped forward to take my place at the sink, but I held up my hand to stop him.

"No. I want to do this. It'll help me get over my little crying jag. Really."

"Okay," he said, unsure about it. "If you're certain."

"I'm certain."

"Okay. Well, when you're done, let's watch a movie, if you're up for it."

That put a smile on my face. I barely knew Jerry, but I was certain he was my friend and that was what I needed most at this juncture. "I'd like that."

Jerry went into his bedroom and I could hear him pecking away on his keyboard, writing something for his book on B-movies I imagined. I washed all the dishes, then dried them and put them away. Thanks to Rusty, there were no left-overs to put away. When I was done, I went to the bathroom and washed my face and brushed my teeth. Then, I went to the door of Jerry's bedroom and rapped on the wall with my knuckles.

"I'm ready for that movie if you are."

"Sure thing." Jerry finished typing a sentence, then bounced off his chair and into the living room. "I have a movie in mind that I think you may get a kick out of." He scanned the shelf, running his finger along the row of DVDs. "Here we go." He handed me the case. It was a garish cover with a couple of pale-skinned zombie-like folk; a man and a woman. They looked like farmers from the way they were dressed and the man was holding his own severed arm in one hand.

I read the title. "Bloodsuckers from Outer Space?"

"Yep."

"Sounds interesting." I just started laughing and Jerry joined me.

"It's another home-grown Texas flick. Some whackjob named Glen Coburn wrote the script in three days."

"That seems pretty quick," I said, frankly impressed.

"Yep. It is quick. I think you'll find it a very endearing little piece of schlock."

So, Jerry slipped the disk into his DVD player and started it rolling. The first scene took place at early morning on a farm. It seemed kind of peaceful and brought back some memories of my childhood, like when I'd go with Grannie to buy chickens and eggs from her friend Mort Stubbs. Pretty soon the farmer in the movie seemed to get caught up in the middle of a whirlwind and he just swirled around like he was dancing with the Devil, all confused and maybe a little helpless. The whirlwind faded away, but what the farmer didn't know was that it was an invisible lifeform from outer space that had swept him up and, in a few seconds, he was down on the ground puking out all his blood. Once the blood was all out of him, he crouched and growled and held his hands up like they were claws and he was an old angry bear. That's when the credits started playing accompanied by this catchy little rock tune.

Jerry paused the movie. "I'd say this calls for some popcorn. Do you concur?"

His mock serious tone and expression made me laugh. "Yes, sir," I said, "I concur whole-heartedly."

"That's what I wanted to hear. You stay put; I'll be back shortly." He went into the kitchen and I could hear him open up a pack of popcorn and start it in the microwave. There was the sound of the fridge door and the snap of a beer can opening. "You want something to drink, Sadie?" Jerry called out.

"I guess I could take a soda," I answered.

"Coke or Dr. Pepper?"

Neither one really sounded all that good because I was full from dinner. Still, I answered, "A Coke, I guess."

"On the way."

A couple minutes later, Jerry nestled back onto the sofa. He put the big bowl of popcorn between us and switched the movie back on. Between swigs of beer and handfuls of popcorn, he gave me his take on the movie. One gag might suggest the influence of a film called *Dr. Strangelove,* another might have been a nod to Japanese monster films from a company called Toho. I tried to take in everything he said, thinking I'd learn something that could help me later, but most of his comments were really over my head. I'd never seen *Dr. Strangelove* or *Psycho* or any Kung Fu flicks, so I just filed his narration away in the back of my mind, intending to refer back to it later if need be.

The movie sure had its funny moments. We laughed a lot and Jerry got more and more manic with his observations, the more beer he drank. By the end of the movie, I'd say Jerry was pretty drunk. He wasn't staggering or anything, but his speech was slower, a little more particular, like it was an effort for him to assemble sentences. And that wasn't like Jerry at all. He's pretty eloquent in his normal state of mind. As he prepared to head off to bed, we both noted that Thompson wasn't home yet and we hoped he wasn't too drunk to drive.

Jerry was sleepy.

And I was horny.

There was some silly sex stuff in the movie; nothing that would really arouse a person, but just seeing naked bodies made me realize it was a long time since I'd come. I thought about Thompson and what it would be like the first time he made love to me. Yeah, I was getting ahead of myself, but I knew that time would come. I was certain of it. I slipped off into the solarium, slid between the sheets on the little futon. My hand slid down my belly and into the warm, wet spot between my legs. I imagined it was Thompson's hand instead of mind. I remembered the way he smelled when he drove us home from Skin Dreams. I knew in my heart that before long we'd be in this bed together, his warm strong body on top of mine and his hard cock sliding into me. I painted these exciting and comforting pictures with my mind and touched myself until I was satisfied.

Afterwards, I just relaxed in the bed, ready to fall asleep. But I heard a sound and saw Satan creeping along the window sill outside my room. I would have thought nothing of it, but all of a sudden Grannie was there with me. *Get up and follow the cat*, she was telling me.

I was tired. I wanted nothing more than to roll over and fall asleep. But Grannie was persistent in a way only she knows how to be. Her instruction couldn't have been more urgent if she'd been flesh and blood in the room with me, poking me in the ribs with her broom handle.

"Okay, Grannie, okay!" I whispered, pulling on some clothes.

Hurry child, she insisted. *Hurry!*

I slipped quietly into the kitchen and went out the back door without a noise. Wherever Grannie was leading me, I hoped she'd get me back before Thompson came home. I didn't want to think about what could happen if he found me gone in the middle of the night. How would that look? Especially, if he was drunk?

Chapter 10

I came out of the kitchen door into the backyard and saw by the light of the moon that Satan was walking the top of the wooden fence. He paid me no mind as I moved toward him. Then he hopped down and out of sight into the alleyway that ran behind the house. The gate leading into the alley was old and the hardware on it was rusty. I figured no one had used this gate in a good long while. It took a couple of stout tugs to get that latch undone and then another hard pull to get the gate open wide enough that I could slip through. It screeched on its rusty hinges like an injured bird. I hoped Jerry was sound asleep and wouldn't notice. The whole time Grannie was poking and prodding my mind. If I said I was just damn nervous, that'd be a major understatement. I had no idea what my grandmother was up to, but I knew better than to disregard her instructions. She had never steered me wrong.

In the alley I felt the crunch of gravel and broken glass under the soles of my sandals. I tried to step quietly on account of I had a strong sense that I shouldn't draw Satan's attention to the fact and let him know I was following him. He headed straight down the alley, paying me no mind at all, almost like he didn't know I was there. That, in itself, was a little strange, considering cats are usually pretty aware of every little thing. Sneaking up on a cat is generally a tough thing to do. But Satan just padded along to the mouth of the alley. He paused for a second, then headed off to the right, out of my line of sight behind a big old red-tip bush.

A great wind shot down the alley and hit me with such force that it stopped me in my tracks. Now, that was odd because it hadn't been breezy at all before then. The wind carried a message and it wasn't a pleasant one. It was a reminder of the dark gulf, the abyss. The place where souls can become lost in darkness. It was like the wind was a strong laugh out of the mouth of someone or something that wanted all souls to be lost. There was something personal about that wind, like the force behind it was mean-spirited and enjoying playing with those it considered weak and defenseless. People like me.

Grannie seemed to be pushing and pulling me at the same time. *Get a move on, girl!* I reminded myself who I was, remembering that never, ever in and out of lifetimes had my soul ever been drawn into that darkness. I stumbled forward. When I came to the street, I thought for just a second that I'd lost the cat called Satan. Then, a movement caught my eye and I saw him moving quickly through a yard across the street and down at the next corner. I wanted to run to catch up, but I felt Grannie telling me to just keep an eye on the cat and walk steady after him.

Following a good two hundred paces behind Satan, keeping him in my sight as he darted in and out of the shadows, I moved slowly forward. About half way down that block he veered off to the left real sudden and ran between two houses. Now, here I was walking the streets in the middle of the night. I felt mighty uncomfortable about going right up between two houses, not even knowing the people who lived there. What was I going to say if someone came out and found me creeping around in the space alongside their house? *Sorry, sir, I'm trying to catch my cat? Sorry, ma'am, my dead grandmother told me to sneak between these two houses?*

Grannie was surely with me. She urged me on but led me to understand that she was watching over me and would do all she could to protect me. I smelled smoke when I stepped into the narrow space between the two houses. Then, like a brick wall, another hellacious wind just rose up out of nowhere. You can't imagine the force of that ungodly wind. It took every last ounce of my energy and willpower to stay on my feet. I knew without a doubt this was a spiritual thing, not a gust of wind, but a definite intention placed into motion by dark forces. It wasn't some freak weather anomaly or the like. It was a conscious force and it wanted to stop me. Realizing that, my blood ran chilly on me, because I knew that for someone or something to want to stop me, it had to be aware of my presence. All my sneaking around wasn't going to add up to diddly squat. The darkness, the master of that ungodly wind was watching my every move. I imagined it looked down on me the way a woman watches an ant on her kitchen floor. I'd been spotted. It ... whatever it was, knew I was chasing the cat. I was sorely tempted to turn tail and run, but Grannie took hold of my shoulders and held me in place. After what seemed an eternity, that wind faded away. I breathed deep and imagined myself surrounded by a tornado of white light.

When the rushing drone of the devil's breeze left my ears, I came to recognize the sound of a fire crackling and that smell of smoke grew stronger. I inched forward until a chain-link fence with a gate in it blocked my path. Leaning on the fence and craning my neck a bit I could see into most of the back yard. There was a brick patio with a fire pit. A good-sized fire was just blazing away in that pit. There were big oak trees in that yard and the flicker of the flames made an illusion of movement in the leaves, like they were crawling alive with something, like ants in a hill or bees in a hive. Against the flames I made out the silhouette of Satan creeping along a low wall that ran in a ring around the patio.

Then I saw the woman. She was just a silhouette, too. She was wearing a gauzy robe and the firelight made it possible to see right through. Her naked body, all slender and sexy was revealed in a glowing halo as the light from the flames was diffused by her robe. I held my breath. It seemed she didn't know that I was watching. Her back remained toward me. She shifted back and forth like she was being rocked by unseen arms.

Softly at first, then gaining volume she started talking. More like chanting, I guess you'd say. I strained my ears for all I was worth, but I couldn't make out a word she was saying. I reckon it was some other language I'd never heard before. I don't know if maybe it was German or Arabic, but it had those kinds of harsh sounds. Like an old man clearing his throat to spit. There was a rhythm to it, too. I can't say for sure if there was any rhyme in the words, but there was a pattern ... what do you call it? A cadence. That's it. There was a cadence to her words. Her voice just moved on in the night, with a real purpose to it. There was some solid intent behind the sounds. Grannie always said words have more power than most folks are willing to take responsibility for. In that instant, I sensed the woman by the fire was going way out on a limb, maybe taking more responsibility with her words than a human soul ought to take. She got louder, then just dropped dead silent. It wasn't just her voice she dropped, but her robe, too. There she was naked as an ivory stature, her skin glistening and glowing around the edges with the flickering of the fire.

When her hand came up high above her head, there was an unexpected flash of light. That flash was a reflection off the blade of a knife. A big old butcher knife. That startled me and I let out a little gasp. I couldn't help it. I threw a hand over my mouth, but that was a foolish move. Too late. Her body went rigid at the sound of my gasp. But she didn't turn. Not yet anyway. Her other hand came up slowly and hung in the air alongside her head. Then the knife came with a dreadful deliberateness to the palm of that hand and sawed a gash into the palm. No play-acting about this woman's witch ritual. I could see the blood falling in huge red drops from her hand and running down her arm to trickle off her elbow onto the bricks below. That blood glowed an unearthly red, all lit up by that fire consecrated to some dark intention I didn't even want to consider.

Grannie wrapped herself around me. I felt she was creating a shield to protect me. I felt her leaning seriously into my consciousness as she whispered a single word. *Evil.* Now, my heart was pounding in my chest like a calf at a slaughterhouse trying to break out of its pen. I wanted to run, but my feet were planted in the earth. I couldn't move.

The woman muttered a short phrase. Maybe three words. I can't say for sure because that language was foreign to me. Not just foreign in sound, but foreign by intent. The hair on my neck bristled and I knew those words carried more evil bound up in a tiny package than a whole army of mortal men slaughtering their enemies. There was hate in those words that didn't belong to this world. It was incredibly dense, like, I am told, the matter at the center of a black hole would be. I needed to vomit and I probably would've, but at that instant the woman turned and looked at me with an unbearable haughtiness. Her expression told me she held me in utter contempt, like I was a bucket of guts or a pile of shit.

When I saw her face, I knew for sure what I would've already guessed. That naked witch was Lucinda.

Then, like some kind soul had taken pity on me and opened the door to my cage, I was released from the horror that was holding me and I ran with all my might. I ran faster than I'd ever run before, down that street, back down the alley and into Thompson's back yard. When I got into the kitchen and closed the door behind me, I felt like I was on safe ground, but my heart was still racing and I wanted to throw up.

Trying to be quiet, I rushed to the bathroom and vomited in the toilet. I rinsed my mouth out at the sink and looked at myself in the medicine cabinet mirror. I felt dirty, like there was little unclean things crawling all over me. In my mind's eye, I saw the expression on Lucinda's face and felt the burden of whatever curse she'd directed at my soul. Shucking my clothes, I climbed into the shower and scrubbed my body from head to toe just trying to lose that filthy feeling.

I got myself a glass of water and went to the futon in the solarium. I sat up in bed with my back against the wall, drawing on all the spiritual resources I could muster. Grannie's presence was still evident, but she seemed remote like. The idea hit me that she was nearby but engaged in defending me. Like I was a kid in the principal's office and she was in the next room arguing with someone, but I couldn't quite make out what she was saying. I said a prayer of protection and did all the things to wrap myself in light that Grannie had taught me long ago. It was a long time before I could fall asleep. Desperately, I wanted to tell Thompson and Jerry what I'd seen. How would I tell them? How would they react? I didn't know. I felt I was on real shaky ground. There was no doubt in my mind that Lucinda wanted me out of this house and out of Thompson's life.

When I made the determination that I was going to fight that bitch with everything I had, then the terror in my soul lightened. I felt like Grannie had come back in the room with me and I was able to fall asleep.

Sometime in the night, I heard Thompson come home. He was noisy, clumsy, so I knew he was drunk. He swore under his breath a time or two as he dropped his keys and bumped into furniture. I was tempted to go and help him to his bed, but I felt Grannie say no. Thompson went to the bathroom and took the longest piss I've ever heard. Then he stumbled on to his room and dropped like a bag of rocks on his bed. It was not long before I heard him snoring.

Laying on the futon, I tried to imagine what exactly I would say to Thompson and Jerry. It was a good thing that they both already knew she was a witch and did not like her. Still, this whole thing happening so fast did not place me in the best light. Would they think I was a witch too? They'd already suspected as much. Would they get it in their heads that me and Lucinda were just two witches fighting over Thompson?

"Grannie," I whispered, "don't leave me. Stand watch over me tomorrow and help me choose my words."

I will, sweet girl, now sleep.

And I wanted to sleep, but could not for a long, tedious time.

Next thing I knew, I was waking up to a room full of sunlight.

Chapter 11

I was rested. The strangeness I'd gone through the night before was still with me, I knew it was a serious concern to be faced, but I wasn't nearly so scared in the morning light as I had been. It was late; 10:35. Jerry's bedroom door was still closed and I didn't hear a sound coming from that direction. I could only suppose he was still asleep. I knew Thompson was still asleep, because I could hear him snoring. On tiptoe, I went to his bedroom door and pulled it shut.

I made coffee. Looking out the kitchen window, I could see I'd left the gate open, so I went out to close it. It took me some serious shoving to get the thing back the way it had been before I opened it the night before. The hinges needed oiling. While I waited for the coffee to brew, I took the bottle of cooking oil outside and spilled a generous portion on the rusty hinges. Then I opened the gate again and moved it back and forth a few times to allow the oil to get down inside those hinges. It worked pretty good and I was a little proud of myself for thinking of it. I poured more oil over the latch. After closing it and opening it three or four times, the gate was behaving the way a gate should. Not like new, but way better than the first time I tried to pass through it.

As the coffee maker sputtered that way it does when the water's all gone down into the pot below, I took a mug from the cabinet and poured myself a good portion. Just sitting at that table, with my hands wrapped around a warm mug, felt good. Really good. I promised myself there and then I'd do whatever it took to preserve my place in this house. Grannie had brought me here and she would not have led me astray. I belonged.

"I smell coffee."

I jumped, I'll admit it, because I'd been so caught up in my own thoughts. It was Jerry. Seeing him put a smile on my face.

"Yes, sir. Fresh coffee. Help yourself."

"Sounds like a good idea."

He was wearing a nearly worn-out robe and his hair was tangled and twisted like a small bush on his head. Jerry looked pretty comical at that moment, but I'd never laugh at him to his face. It wouldn't be friendly. Even so, his comical look cheered me and made me feel a bit more normal. A little braver.

After fixing his cup, he came and joined me at the little kitchen table.

"Coffee's good. Thanks."

"My pleasure, sir."

"I must've had more beer than I realized last night. I feel like I've slept in a barn. Maybe a haystack or something." He stretched and worked his shoulders and neck. Probably, he'd slept all wrong and now had the aches and pains to prove it.

I laughed.

"What?" He looked at me with a puzzled expression.

"Well, you do kind of look like you slept in a barn."

He sighed and smiled with half his face. "I'm not surprised. How many beers did I drink last night?"

"I didn't count. Didn't realize you wanted me to keep tally."

Shaking his head and fluttering his eyelids, he sipped his cup of joe. "Thompson still asleep?"

"Yes. I didn't see him, but I heard him come in last night. It was really late and from the sound of it he was pretty drunk."

"Yeah. I vaguely remember hearing him."

"Jerry, I'm worried about Thompson driving when he's drunk. It's dangerous and not just to him."

"Did he drive? That's not like him. He'll usually Uber it home."

I didn't know what Jerry meant. Up to that time, I'd never heard of Uber. He stood up and went to the front door, pushing the curtains aside on the window next to the door. After looking out for just a second, he came back to the table shaking his head. "He didn't drive when he was shit-faced. Truck's not in the drive way."

"Good. I feel better about that."

"Yeah. Me too. Thompson's a pretty responsible sort of guy."

I nodded, agreeing with him. "You hungry? I can make you some bacon and eggs."

"Aw, you don't need to do all that. I can just fix myself a bowl of cereal." Those were his words, but his eyes told me a whole different story. They lit up at the mention of bacon.

"I'd like some bacon and eggs," I said. "And it's no more trouble to make enough for two ... or three. Scrambled okay?"

"Sounds great."

"You're okay, Sadie. I don't care what they say about you."

His words were familiar, because I'd heard the same line from Rusty the day before at Skin Dreams. But he seemed to enjoy playing at being clever, so I acted like I'd never heard the phrase.

"What they say?" I put my hands on my hips and pretended a defensive response.

Jerry just burst out laughing. "Got you," he said. "It's a joke, Sadie. Besides, who do I know that could possibly say anything about you?"

"Nobody. For sure." I laughed with him. "Where'd you learn that kind of joke?"

"Thompson. It's the sort of thing guys in the military say to one another. Especially, if they're drinking."

"Yes, I can imagine that." Surely Thompson and Rusty had been using that line for years. It was the sort of mildly annoying banter that helped guys bond with one another. "Think I should make enough for Thompson, too?"

"For sure. He'll be hungry when he gets up. That could be a good while from now, but he will be hungry. You can just cover it and leave it on the stove top for him."

"I will."

I was not much of a cook to speak of at that time, but I'd been scrambling eggs since I was an itty-bitty girl. That was one meal I could do just fine. I fried the bacon and set it on a plate with a paper towel under it to soak up the extra grease, then I cracked six eggs and mixed them with milk in a bowl, whisking them up real good and frothy. I tossed in some salt, pepper and powdered onion, because that's the way Grannie taught me. I poured the eggs into the bacon grease. That smell of salt, pepper, eggs and bacon is just a heart-warming experience no matter how often it happens to me. I feel so close to Grannie *and* my mother when I smell breakfast cooking.

"Damn, girl. You said you couldn't cook. I can tell by watching, you know what you're doing."

Jerry's compliment made me laugh and probably put a little color in my cheeks. "Well, it's true, I can scramble eggs. That doesn't win me any blue ribbons."

"I'll be the judge of that. Smells heavenly. You are a sweetheart to cook me breakfast. Here, I'll make some toast for us, just to show I'm not a complete slug." He started to get up, but I put a hand on his shoulder and pushed him back into the chair.

"Sit. You drank too much beer last night. Drink your coffee. I can put bread in the toaster. You just keep being a slug."

"Yes, ma'am. So, I'm a slug?"

"Not at all. I don't care what they say about you."

"Zing!" Jerry laughed. "You're a fast learner."

"Thanks. And I think you're a good teacher. That's a good thing because I have so much to learn."

He winked at me and I dropped bread into the slots of the toaster.

"Damn, that was good!" Jerry said, a short time later, pushing his empty plate away. "Sadie, you're the best."

"Glad you liked it," I said, just the way my grannie and my mother used to do.

"Want to watch a movie?"

That offer was tempting, but I shook my head. "No. I think we should be as quiet as possible and let Thompson sleep until he wakes up on his own."

"Yes. That would be the considerate thing to do. Good call. And if the smell of the bacon and coffee didn't bring him around yet, then he truly is beat. Alcohol will do that. Particularly, if you're in the company of a world class drinker like Rusty."

"I got that impression."

"Being quiet's no biggie. I've got plenty of work I could be doing in my room, but I hate to just leave you alone to twiddle your thumbs."

"I was thinking I might read something. I've never been much of a reader, but I think it's time for me to start. And right now's a good time to do it while I'm in a house with lots of books and with a friend who writes for a living." I could see Jerry was pleased by my words.

"Okay," he said, standing up from the table. He put his dirty plate in the sink and poured himself another cup of coffee. "Come to my room and we'll pick something out for you."

I followed him into the 'inner sanctum.' That's what he called his room. There were probably hundreds of books; on shelves, on his desk, on the nightstand, stacked on the floor. The bed was unmade and I had the strong impression it stayed that way. The air in the room was musty. It smelled like Jerry and a bit of incense. I hope the look on my face didn't make him think I was judging him. The place was a disaster. The entire house was a bit untidy, but this was ten times worse.

"Forgive the condition of my room," he said. "I fired the housekeeper for her insolence." This last part he said with a pretty convincing British accent like you'd hear on one of those movies set in the 1800s.

I thought to myself, *Yeah, this room's enough to make a housekeeper insolent.* I did not say that, though. It might have been too sharp a joke, barbed with too much truth. What I said instead was, "I'm sure she deserved it, your lordship." *Your lordship.* That's what the servants always seemed to call the men of the house in those movies. I knew this because Mrs. Richards loved to watch programs about Sherlock Holmes and poor women who married well.

Jerry appreciated my cleverness. He patted me on the shoulder. "Sadie, you will never know how much I appreciate your presence here." He was sincere. There was not one speck of doubt in my mind. And I was so grateful. I wanted to just give him a big hug and tell him how totally grateful I was to be there. But it did not seem the right time or place for that. Instead we just got quiet and I think we both got a little uncomfortable in that silence.

After clearing his throat, which made him seem as nervous as I felt, Jerry said, "What's your reading level?"

"Level?"

"Yeah. That'll help us decide on a book for you."

"I honestly can't say," I told him.

"Most Americans read at a fifth-grade level or below with poor comprehension."

"That sounds bad."

"Yeah. Kind of hopeless, since fewer and fewer people are even attempting to read. And here I am trying to make a living as a writer."

"I want to try to be one of those who reads and understands."

"And I think you will. You may not have a lot of schooling, but you seem pretty sharp to me." I would've let him know I appreciated that compliment, but he quickly continued talking. Maybe he was afraid of another uneasy silence. "I have an idea. Just look around the room. Read the titles on the spines of the books. We'll trust the gods to guide you to the book that's right for you."

"Gods?"

"Not to be taken literally, dear. We'll trust that fate, or your subconscious, or whatever you want to call it, will direct you. Look around."

There were so many books. The first one that caught my eye was a big, thick white book. The reason I noticed it was the title; *White Trash*. We'd just recently watched movies with the same title, so naturally I made a connection in my head. I picked it up and read the words on the front cover. *White Trash. The 400 Year Untold History of Class in America. Nancy Isenberg author of Fallen Founder.*

"This is a very big book. White Trash? Like the movies?"

"That's not light reading, Sadie. You're welcome to read it if you like, but it's more historical than entertaining."

"Are you reading it?"

"Yes. Research. Not everything I write is movie related. I do the odd academic magazine article now and then."

I opened the book and read a few sentences. Right away I saw that I would have difficulty wading through the language and catching the drift of the author.

"I can't read it," I said, "but will you tell me a little about it?"

"Sure. It's an examination of class in America. We have a popular myth regarding American exceptionalism. There are supposed to be no class divisions here as there were in the old world. The pilgrims seeking freedom, the noble American experiment, all that was dreamed up years after the fact for the history books. To teach kids a way of perceiving what it means to be an American, to get them to salute the flag and all that. Basically, England emptied its cities of the white trash and sent them here to clear the land and do the grunt work, so the class of land owners could benefit. Basically, the only time the underclasses were offered land ownership was when their masters wanted to expand westward. Once the territories were tamed, these same masters set about taking the land away from them."

"Wow! That's a mouthful. You sound like a teacher, Jerry." I put the book down. "It sounds depressing."

"Yeah, it is a little depressing. America is not about equal opportunity. Never has been. That's a PR campaign designed for school kids."

"I'll keep looking," I said, returning my eyes to the books all around me.

"Any ideas what kind of story you'd like to read? Space men? Warriors? Detectives? A love story maybe?"

"A love story should be easy to understand."

"Okay, that might be a good choice." Jerry went to a shelf near his bed and dug around for a few seconds. "Here you go. Yeah, this may be the ticket." He came back to me, grinning, and pushed a paperback book toward me. I took it from him.

The title was very colorful on a white background and there was a black and white photo of a young couple in the lower left-hand corner. It was a number one bestseller; *Love Story* by Erich Segal. Next to the photo, near the bottom of the cover, it said, 'Now a Paramount motion picture starring Ali McGraw and Ryan O'Neal.'

"Is it good?"

"I'll let you be the judge of that. It sold a lot of copies all over the world and was on the New York Times Bestseller List for 41 weeks."

"When was that?"

"1970."

"Before I was born."

"Yep. Is that a problem?"

"No. I guess not."

"Good. Why don't you start reading it and see if it tickles your fancy? If not, come back and we'll find something else. In the meantime, I'll try to get some writing done."

"Okay. Thanks, Jerry."

"My pleasure. Thank you for the kick-ass breakfast."

"That was *my* pleasure."

I let him sit down at his desk and I went to the sofa to read. I'm not a great reader. I imagine I turned pages a lot slower than most would have. But I liked the story well enough. Not many of the words gave me a huge problem. I asked Jerry for a dictionary to look up the really tough words. There weren't that many of those. The dictionary stayed on the sofa beside me while I read. Some situations a dictionary doesn't help with anyway. Like on the second page when he's talking about going to the Radcliffe library and not just to check out the 'cheese.' Looking up the word 'cheese' in a dictionary isn't going to tell you that's sort of old-timey slang for attractive women, especially their nice-looking legs. Jerry had to explain that one.

I didn't know what a 'preppie' was either. It just wasn't information that would come up in the world I was from.

Even though I was not a part of the crowd that understood all of Erich Segal's references, it was clear to me that most of what he wrote was intended to point out his clever way of looking at stuff. And I think the book was supposed to make me wish to be a part of the world he described. If I'd had more education, maybe it would've had that effect on me. I just didn't see the appeal. It was a different world he was talking about, but not really a better one. People in that world frowned on those with less money or social standing. That was something I could relate to. I remembered the three girls who made fun of my backpack down on 6th Street. I thought about it and realized there are two ways to respond to that kind of snobbery. You can let it shame you and motivate you to become like the people who are looking down on you, or you can decide to take a different path and refuse to be influenced by those thoughtless judgments. I felt the second path was the one for me. Letting mean people turn you mean just seemed like perpetuating a problem. Solving problems, finding a better way, that seemed best to me. The last thing in the world I wanted was to make someone else feel bad because they weren't exactly like me.

Chapter 12

It was close to three in the afternoon when I heard Thompson tromp like an elephant out of his bedroom and go to the toilet. He didn't close the door all the way and once more I got to hear him take a crazy long piss. It went on forever. I was thinking, how is it possible a man can hold so much piss inside him. Truth be told, I was feeling a little embarrassed, like maybe he was going to catch me listening to him. Not likely, but I'm sure you get my drift.

Finally, he flushed the toilet. As he came out of the bathroom, Jerry shouted out, "Ladies and gentlemen, the gold medal for freestyle pissing goes, once again, to Thompson!"

I couldn't help myself; I just broke out in a giggle fit.

Thompson, still in his clothes from the night before, all tossed and wrinkled-looking, stopped in his tracks and just shook his head. He frowned at me.

"I'm sorry," I said, trying to stop laughing, "but, he's right. I never knew a man could piss so much."

"Well, I'm glad I could provide the morning's amusement," Thompson said, flexing his jaw and tongue like maybe he was going to cough up a hairball.

"Check again, big guy," Jerry said, stepping out of his bedroom, his coffee mug in his hand. "It hasn't been morning for hours." Even with his worn robe and his crazy hair, Jerry looked a sight better than Thompson in that moment. He glanced my way and gave me a wink. I think he was gloating a little, maybe, because it was a rare occasion that he compared favorably to Thompson.

Thompson sighed, then nodded with a sense of having lost a fight. Like he was giving up or something, but not really that big of a surrender.

"How you feeling, bro?" Jerry asked, patting Thompson on the shoulder.

"Like hammered shit," Thompson grunted.

"Which, coincidentally, is exactly what you look like," Jerry grinned.

I felt like I needed to jump into this mix. "No, you don't look *that* bad! Don't listen to him."

"Thanks," Thompson said. He gave me a half-smile, weary-looking and maybe just a hint embarrassed.

"I made you some breakfast," I said.

He grimaced, like food wasn't the most appealing idea right then.

"She made a damn good breakfast for all of us," Jerry said. "You'll love it, once your appetite kicks in. In the meantime, why don't you get a shower, buddy. We'll start some fresh coffee for you." He winked again in my direction.

"I'm on it. Fresh coffee coming up." I unfolded my legs from under me and set my book face down on the sofa.

Thompson disappeared into his room.

After I made the coffee, I went back to the sofa and settled back in. I took up my book but didn't really look at it. I was remembering the strange things that happened in the night and puzzling on the best way to tell it to Jerry and Thompson. Things had fallen into place so easy for me here. Thompson took me in and Jerry hit it off with me real quick. So much good had happened in such a short time. I wished that the bad stuff had waited a while longer before showing up.

I must've been frowning, because I heard Jerry say, "That's an awfully serious face you're wearing, Sadie."

"Oh," I looked up at him. His smile warmed me a bit and I guess I smiled back.

"You worried about Lucinda?" he asked.

At first, I thought he somehow knew about what I'd seen in the middle of the night. Then I remembered that I'd told him about seeing her in front of Skin Dreams and at the end of the alley when that old homeless guy attacked me. "Yeah. I'm troubled," I said.

He came over and sat beside me.

"Don't worry." He patted my knee. "Thompson's not going to hold you responsible for anything that crazy bitch has done."

"Good to hear. I hope you're right."

"Of course, I'm right. We'll figure out what to do. Don't worry." He stood up. "Coffee's smelling good. I'm going to get a warm up. Want some?"

"No. I'm about coffeed out for today."

"All right. Relax. After Thompson's had his breakfast, we'll sort this out. Okay?"

"Okay."

He glanced at the book on my lap. "How's the book?"

"I think it's pretty good," I said, picking it up and studying the cover. "I'm not that far into it, but I'm pretty certain I'll finish it. Eventually." The truth was, there were other times I'd started reading a book with the best intentions but lost my follow-through somewhere along the way. I wanted to be someone who not only started books, but finished them, too. So far, I'd made it to the part where Oliver's talking with his father about the Peace Corp. I guess that was a big deal back then. I don't think many people even know what the Peace Corp is anymore.

"Hang in there," Jerry said, ambling toward the kitchen. "Take your time. Savor it. You'll be glad you did."

Sounded like good advice.

After his shower, Thompson came into the kitchen. Me and Jerry were waiting for him at the table. He smiled at us and went to the coffee pot. "Just what I need." He poured a cup and sat across from me. "Is that bacon, I smell?"

"Yes, it is. Shall I heat it up for you?"

"Not yet." He held up a hand to stay me from rising. "I never feel like eating right away and for sure not today."

"So old Rusty made you tie one on, did he?" Jerry asked.

Thompson nodded and sipped from his coffee. "Damn, this tastes good."

"Where'd you leave the truck?" Jerry asked him.

"It's at the Cherokee Lounge."

"Couldn't have picked a seedier spot." Jerry laughed.

"I know. I hope it's still in one piece when I go back for it."

"Rusty loves his dive bars, doesn't he?"

"That he does." Thompson gulped some more coffee before saying, "Bad news is, I'm in no shape to open Skin Dreams today. Good news is, Rusty gave me a check for payment in full on the eagle tattoo. He can come back whenever he likes to finish it up. We've got enough to catch up on all the bills."

"Hallelujah!" Jerry waved his hands in the air.

"I think it was that great meal you served him that made Rusty decide to pay in advance," Thompson said looking at me and nodding.

"Well, thanks. That's kind of you to say, but it wasn't that special."

"Just being treated like family means a lot to Rusty. Most of the time he's out and about, sleeping in his van, eating hamburgers, working hard. He appreciates being made to feel welcome here."

"Rusty's a good dude," Jerry chimed in.

"Yes. I can tell he's a good man," I said.

"*Good* may be overstating it, but his heart's in the right place. He's a predictable sort." Thompson got up and poured himself another cup of coffee.

When he settled back down in his chair, Jerry surprised me by saying, "Speaking of predictable, Sadie's got something to say about our most predictably fucked-up acquaintance."

They stared at me and I felt super uncomfortable. Then I felt the presence near my ear. Grannie was beside me. "Well," I cleared my throat to buy me a second of time to think about what I would say. Then, all sudden-like I felt confident and I just jumped right in. "Yesterday, at Skin Dreams, I noticed a woman standing across the street just staring at the place."

Thompson cocked his head in anticipation. Maybe he was already figuring out who I meant.

"I started to point her out to you, Thompson, but your attention was on something else and pretty soon she was gone."

"Lucinda?" Thompson was looking at Jerry when he spoke her name. Jerry just nodded. Thompson looked back at me.

"Then, when that old man Gus attacked me; she was standing at the end of the alley."

Thompson sighed, heavy-like and dropped his mug on the table with a thump, shaking his head.

"Man, I told you to expect more trouble from that bitch," Jerry said.

"Are you sure?" Thompson was talking to me. "How do you know it was her?"

"Jerry showed me her picture last night."

Now, a very strange expression appeared on Thompson's face. I'm sure he was wondering why the hell Jerry would be dragging out pictures of Lucinda. He glared at Jerry, waiting for an explanation. Jerry quickly told him about me saying my prayer at the front door and everything that followed.

Thompson drew a deep breath. "And you're sure it was her?"

I nodded.

"I regret the day I ever laid eyes on that woman."

"Amen," Jerry said, rising and getting a warm up for his coffee.

"There's more," I said. I clasped my hands together and imagined Grannie was holding my hand.

Jerry turned from the coffee maker and gave me a surprised look.

"What is it?" Thompson asked.

"Last night, before you came home, Satan was outside my window."

"Uh oh …" Jerry said, his voice trailing off.

"Something told me I should go out and get him." That wasn't exactly the truth of the matter, but I sure didn't feel comfortable telling the two of them about my dead grannie watching over me. Not yet anyway. "I followed him down the alley."

Thompson tilted his head and looked at me sideways like maybe he didn't want to hear what I was going to say. Grannie nudged me.

"I followed him to a house just a couple blocks away."

"God damn it!" Thompson hit the table with his fist.

"I told you it was weird that she didn't take the cat!" Jerry said, his voice all shrill and agitated.

"Anyway, Satan ran into the back yard of one of the houses. I was nervous about following him late at night like that."

"What happened?" Jerry sat back down and sipped from his cup.

"There was a pretty big fire burning in the back yard. This woman was standing by it, saying some things I couldn't understand. I think she was talking another language. Then she cut herself with a big knife. Sliced right into her hand and let the blood flow. I was scared, surprised. I must've made a noise, because she turned and looked right at me."

"And you're sure it was Lucinda?" Thompson's jaw was set in a defiant way, like he was accepting an offer to fight.

"Yes. It was her."

Jerry rocked back in his chair, grabbing the edge of the table with both hands. "This is about as trippy as anything I've ever heard!" he said. "So, what do we do now?"

"We go pay her a visit," Thompson said, standing up. "Jerry get your street clothes on. The three of us will go together."

I saw a flash of fear pass through Jerry's eyes. I couldn't blame him for that. My own stomach was twisting with dread.

"Okay. Give me a minute," Jerry said, leaving his cup on the table and going to his bedroom. I could hear him muttering to himself as he opened and closed drawers and shuffled around in there.

When I looked back at Thompson, he was shaking his head. I felt about two inches tall and scared to death that he was going to kick me out over all this mess. Not today, but soon. I couldn't stop myself. I started to cry.

He got a surprised look on his face. "Sadie, don't cry. I'm sorry you had to get all mixed up in this."

"Thompson, I was feeling so lucky to be here. Things were going so good. Now, this. I was afraid you'd blame me and want me to leave. Truth is, I'm scared."

"Don't be." He reached his hand across the table and I took it. He squeezed my hand very gentle like. "I'm sure this will all work out okay for all of us. But, it's high time to get Lucinda Gooch out of our lives once and for all."

I jerked when he said the name Gooch. That was, after all, the name of my real father. The Reverend Archibald Gooch, pastor of the Zion Hill Church of Redemption. What were the odds that it really meant anything? Slim to none, of course, but the sound of it still unsettled me. "Her name was Gooch?"

"Yeah. That's what she told us. But, based on her track record, that could be a lie too. Where Lucinda's concerned the odds are fifty-fifty."

His words hit me like a punch in the stomach. Here I was enjoying his hospitality and most of what I'd told him was a lie. He didn't know my real name. Didn't know that I'd been pretty much raised inside the crazy house at Terrell. For now, Thompson was on my side, but how long would that last if he knew the truth? The whole truth?

Jerry came back in the kitchen wearing jeans and a Walking Dead t-shirt.

"Lead the way," Thompson told me.

"All right." I stood up and went out the door into the back yard. It looked a lot nicer in the sunshine. It needed mowing and a little straightening up, but it was mostly pleasing to the eye. I found myself thinking maybe we could have a cook-out sometime. That might've been me grasping at ordinary run-of-the-mill things, so I wouldn't have to think about witches and magic and the possibility of losing my new home.

When I opened the gate to the alley, Jerry said, "Wow! You make that look easy. I always have to tug on that thing."

"It was pretty rusty, so I oiled it," I said.

"That figures," Thompson said, sort of under his breath, shooting a look in Jerry's direction.

"Yeah. I've been talking about doing that for months and you're here a couple of days and you've already taken care of it." Jerry admitted, not looking at Thompson.

"Trying to be helpful," I said, like it was no big deal, which it wasn't.

"Thanks, Sadie," Thompson said as we passed into the alley.

"Okay," I said, walking toward the mouth of the alley, "I just followed the cat up to this next street and he took a right around that big bush there." We walked the rest of the way over to the house without talking. When we got there, I hesitated just a bit making sure it was the right spot.

"This it?" asked Thompson.

"Yeah, I think so. Everything looks a little different in broad daylight." I walked up between the two houses and peeked over the chain link gate. There was the patio and the fire pit. I caught the faint smell of ashes. "Yep. This is it. She was standing right over there when she cut herself." I pointed.

There was a padlock on the gate, so we couldn't just walk right into the back yard.

With a grunt, Thompson turned and went around the house real quick to the front door. Me and Jerry just followed along behind him. Thompson knocked hard on the door, but as I'd imagined, there was no response. He looked in through a couple of windows.

"The house is empty."

"Empty?" Jerry acted like this was a surprise to him, but I wasn't surprised at all.

"Not a stick of furniture in the place," Thompson said.

He left me and Jerry standing there and began knocking on neighbors' doors. He got no response at the first couple of doors he tried. I guess they were at work. On his third try, at a house directly across the street, a nice-looking older lady answered his knock. Jerry and I watched from in front of the vacant house while he talked to her. After a bit, Thompson turned and headed back toward us. The woman kept watching after him as he crossed the street to where we were waiting. Finally, she closed the door, but I saw a rustle in the drapes in one of her front windows, so I figured she was curious about the three of us and couldn't resist peeking at us from behind her curtains.

"What's the scoop?" Jerry asked.

"Lady says a moving van came yesterday morning and took everything out of the house."

"What do you think?"

"I don't know. Maybe she's finally gone for good, but I'm thinking we should call Rita."

Jerry looked at me, then gave Thompson a serious nod of approval. "Agreed."

Chapter 13

Rita, it turns out was a little, short brown-skinned lady. She was kind of box-shaped. Her body had an unusual squareness to it. And her head was sort of square, too. Her eyes were bright and she spoke with the accent people have when Spanish is their first language and English is their second. I liked her right away. She was 'a bright light' as Grannie used to say, meaning her soul was crystal clear. Rita smelled of lavender.

Thompson had let her into the house. I came out of the kitchen drying my hands on a cup towel, because I'd been washing the breakfast dishes. I stopped in my tracks and just bathed in the light from that woman's smile. We had a moment there, I guess you could say. Though, I don't believe I could put it into words exactly, our souls exchanged a lot of information in that first few seconds. My heart swelled with the kind of joy usually only triggered by my grannie.

"Rita, this is Sadie," Thompson said.

"I see." The little woman took one step forward and sized me up from head to toe. Her scrutinizing was friendly, but no-nonsense. She made a half frown when her eyes connected with mine again. "Sadie, huh? That's not what I'm getting."

Thompson cocked his head and looked from Rita to me then back at her.

If I knew anything in that moment it was that you cannot lie to women like Rita and Grannie. If I tried to lie to her things were a hundred percent guaranteed to end up in a bad way.

"Sadie's just a nickname I gave myself, because I liked the sound of it," I said. That was the truth. Now, how much truth did I need to tell right then and there? That was the question. Rita continued staring at me with expectation. "My real name is …"

"Liza," she said. She continued looking at me with kindness, but it was a serious kindness. Her look let me know that she wasn't going to go along with any monkey business. I don't know exactly how deep she dug into my personal history right then, but I had a keen sense that her intentions were good and I'd do well to shoot straight with her.

"Is that right?" asked Jerry. "Is that your real name?"

I nodded. "It is."

"I'm glad you called me," Rita said to Thompson.

"Me too," Thompson said, eying me kind of sideways. I felt pretty darn uncomfortable. I started to say something, but Rita smiled real big and spoke before I had the chance.

"Here's what we're going to do; we're all going to sit down and enjoy the beverage of our choice. If you've got hot water, I've got my own herbal tea bags." She patted the black purse that was hanging from her shoulder. "You boys have a beer or coffee. And Li …

Sadie will probably have a coffee. I see she doesn't drink alcohol. That's a good thing for someone like you, dear."

"Thank you, ma'am," I answered.

"So, when everyone has their drink, we'll begin our discussion."

I started heating water on the stove for Rita's tea. I heard Thompson say, "Where would you like to sit, Rita?"

There was a long pause before the little woman replied. In my mind's eye, I could see her carefully taking in everything, weighing the pros and cons before making her decision. Picking a place to sit wasn't a mindless choice for her. Like my grannie, I could tell she was keenly aware of energies all around us and I felt she wanted to maximize the potentials of those energies. Grannie used to call it, 'letting the chair choose you.'

"Why don't we sit at the little kitchen table? That seems like the best place for a serious family discussion. It's cozy."

That phrase 'family discussion' brought a smile to my lips. I felt like part of a family here. I wanted that sense of belonging to continue.

"All right." Thompson came in and pulled the little table away from the wall, so the four of us could take a seat around it. I looked at him and smiled, but he just gave me a blank look. I couldn't tell what was going through his mind. But I'll wager Rita knew what he was thinking; what all three of us were thinking. This woman was a clean vessel, with clear vision.

I gave Rita Jerry's owl mug for her tea. It just seemed appropriate. Jerry took a beer. Me and Thompson kept going with coffee. We all settled in at the table and Rita said we should all hold hands and spend a moment in silence blessing ourselves, the house and the sacred space we were creating. We closed our eyes and just sat there. There was a sudden noise from the living room area, like maybe a few DVDs had fallen from the shelf.

"Hold the circle," said Rita, quietly, but quick and serious. Then she added, "We're just balancing the energy here."

We carried on like that a good while longer than I expected. Finally, she said it was okay to release hands and open our eyes. When I opened mine, she was smiling at me with what seemed powerful kindness. I felt my cheeks turn red, but I didn't break eye contact with her. Not since my grannie died had any living person made me feel so accepted.

"We'll start with you, Sadie. Tell me what you know about Lucinda." When she said the name, there was another cascade of falling DVDs in the other room. "Don't let that bother you. By the time I leave today, we'll sweep this house clean of any lingering darkness." Her smile made me believe that was exactly what would happen.

"I don't know much about her. I didn't even know her name until yesterday." As I said this, I could hear Rita thinking, 'and these two didn't know your name until today.' But she kept smiling and I tried not to feel ashamed. "When I said my prayer of blessing at the door, both Thompson and Jerry thought I was saying a spell. That's how I came to know she was a witch."

I had the brief feeling that Rita disapproved of the word 'witch.' I'm not certain that's how she felt, but the thought shot across my mind. Maybe she considered herself a witch or something like it. She just kept smiling, bathing me in that love light. I knew what she was doing and I appreciated it. Witch or not, she knew about the power of love and she was using what she knew to create a better world. That may sound a little Pollyanna-ish, but I swear, that's exactly what she was doing.

"It's good that you bless the house when you enter and depart," Rita said. "Keep that up." Then she nodded, like telling me I should keep talking.

"The cat, Satan, made me think something was up. I really didn't give it too much thought. I was just happy Jerry and Thompson were being so good to me."

"They are both good men." Rita said that real matter of fact like.

"Outside Skin Dreams I saw her standing across the street. I didn't know who she was, but I wanted to point her out to Thompson. He was busy, so I just let it go. Later that day, Thompson sent me to buy some iced tea. When I came back, I saw her again just before Gus tried to choke me."

"She was using Gus the same way she used the cat," Rita said, taking a sip of her tea. More DVDs fell with a clatter.

Jerry couldn't take it. "What the hell?"

"Easy." Rita placed her hand on top of Jerry's and he calmed right down.

"When are we going to be done with that bitch?"

Rita raised an eyebrow. I think it was Jerry's language.

"Sorry," he said, "No offense."

"It's all right. In answer to your question; today. This house and the three of you will be clear of her today, by the time I leave."

"Good," Jerry answered.

"Amen," I said. Rita looked at me like she expected me to keep talking, so I did. I told her about following the cat over to the other house, about the powerful wind and what I'd seen Lucinda doing in the back yard.

Rita looked at Thompson. "You should have told me when you realized the cat was still around."

"I thought it was strange, but it just seemed like another thoughtless, unkind thing she would do; leaving the cat behind."

Rita nodded. "Do you two have anything to add? Anything I don't already know?"

Thompson shook his head.

"I don't think so," Jerry said.

"All right." Rita placed her hands on the table in front of her with her fingers interlocked. "Before I perform the cleansing, I feel like there's something I need to say." She looked at me. "It's a very good thing this young lady is here. It's good for her and it's good for you, Jerry and Thompson. As bad an influence as Lucinda was, just that much and more, Sadie here is a positive influence. She carries powerful spiritual energy. She's had a hard time of it in this lifetime. Maybe someday she'll tell you something about all that. That's up to her. You can trust her, though. She's a powerful ally. She took a new name because she was making a fresh start in life. She deserves a new start."

I was grateful for her words, but I was twisted up with emotion and fought to keep from busting out in tears. Thompson looked at me sort of serious but reserved. When I looked at Jerry he seemed to be sort of in awe. "Thank you," I said. I bit my lip to keep from crying.

"Let's clean house," she said with a big smile, clapping her hands together with a loud smack.

Most of the time Rita was doing her cleansing, I just sat at the kitchen table. I felt like I'd been pushed out of my comfort zone a little. I'd been exposed as a liar to the two people that suddenly mattered most in my life. I knew in my heart that a comfort zone built out of lies wasn't worth a damn anyway. Taking stock of my blessings, I saw that even if Thompson and Jerry asked me to leave, I was still way better off than I had been just a few days earlier. Things had happened real fast for me and in a good way. We get attached to the pleasures and avoid the pains, so they tell me. The trick for all of us is to take the bad with the good, keep moving toward our goals whatever those may be and to not discount our blessings when we encounter hard times.

As I was thinking these things, I realized maybe it was Rita's influence that my thoughts were spinning off in that direction. I recognized in Rita a good soul. She was a lot like Grannie. I could call her another person on my team in a sense. Sitting at that table, I made up my mind that I was going to make an effort to stay in touch with Rita, try and make a real friend out of her. I wanted her to be more than just a passing bright spot in my life. If she saw as deep into me as I thought she did, then she probably was interested in being my friend, too.

Rita had taken a few things out of that black purse of hers. I think there was some lavender, some little bundles of sage and some salt in a special container. I didn't follow her around to see what she was doing, but the house isn't that big and I could easily hear most of what she said. Rita's not a quiet person. That helped. She's a big soul packed into a small body and her personality shines like the morning sun. Her voice almost seemed too big to be coming out of such a small human.

Piecing together the bits I heard, it seemed like she was using the salt, lavender and sage to gather all the dark energy into one central location in the house. She prayed a little here and a little there, calling on a higher power to provide a fresh spiritual start in our house and to prevent any negativity from the past intruding on our future. I say she talked to a 'higher power' because I don't exactly remember her using the word 'God.'

Maybe she did, I don't know. I was only half paying attention to her. The other half of my mind was saying my own prayers in hopes I'd get to stay and finish what I'd set out to do; become a tattoo artist and build a good life for myself.

While she was in Jerry's room, I heard Rita say, "You know, Jerry, that weed you smoke is not a bad thing. It's like anything else, just a neutral tool in this world of ours. But I can tell you without a doubt, you will be far more productive if you don't use it so often. That's not a judgment, it's just an observation. It's not for me or anyone else to say how productive you should be. It's your life. You have a brilliant mind and I'm certain many people would like to read the things you write. Also, the cannabis is a lot better in every way if you ingest it. Smoke of any kind is not good for your lungs. You don't have to be a genius to figure that out."

Jerry answered in a really timid voice, like a small boy who'd been caught stealing an extra cookie. "Yes, okay, I'll keep that in mind."

That exchange made me giggle just a little. And it warmed my heart. Rita really was trying to do all the good in this world that she could before it came her time to leave. I wanted to be like her.

She moved slowly through the house, sweeping up the negativity and piling it up in the living room near the front door. Seems she was timing her work to finish up right at sunset. As the sun disappeared below the horizon, she opened the front door and swept all the old dirt into the gathering night, leaving a positive clean environment for us to live in. I wondered for just a moment if it was a good thing to release the negativity out into the world. Most folks would think of it as something that needed to be boxed up or destroyed. As if she was reading my thoughts, and maybe she was, I heard Rita say to Thompson and Jerry, "Energy is just energy. Just like matter, it transforms readily from one form to another and can never really be destroyed."

I understood her to mean that the negative energy was like a big cow patty or a dog turd. You don't want it in your living space, but if you put it out in the world, bury it or use it to fertilize a garden, it breaks down into components that feed the stream of life. That idea warmed my heart. I mean it resonated with me. It was a truth I already knew, deep down, but one I needed to be reminded of. The complications of life make us lose sight of the bigger picture. I wanted to stay focused on that bigger picture.

After the completion of Rita's ritual and some chit chat between the three of them, she called out to me, "Sadie, child, would you please join us?"

I went into the living room and was blessed with another one of her big smiles. Naturally, I smiled back.

"Let's join hands again," she said. She placed us boy, girl, boy, girl in a ring in the center of the living room. "Thompson," she stared hard at him and spoke in a stern tone, "are you ready to relinquish all that has gone before? All mistakes, all errors in judgment, all temptations, all willing infractions of your moral code made for selfish reasons?" I had the impression that she started with Thompson because he was the head of the household, the leader and the one most likely to be feeling a sense of righteous indignation. To get shed of the past we all had to acknowledge our own mistakes and the part we'd played in creating the trouble we were trying to put behind us.

"I am," Thompson said, simple, straight-forward and without hesitation.

Next, she asked me the same questions. Then she asked Jerry. Of course, we all said we were ready to do those things. This was the surest path to defend ourselves from any dark influences from Lucinda or anyone else. She sealed our agreement with a blessing and concluded by saying, "So it is." Her expression went instantly from serious to joyful and I felt my heart sailing upward in the direction that she'd sent it.

"Time for me to go," she said.

Thompson quickly went to his bedroom and came back with a wad of cash that he pressed into her hand. "Thank you," he said.

"And thank you." She turned to Jerry and took his hand. "Jerry, I expect great things from you."

"I'll try not to disappoint you," he answered. It was amazing to me to see the difference in Jerry's personality when he was talking with Rita. He seemingly went from a cocky jokester to an awestruck kid.

"You won't disappoint me. You will do all you were born to do. I would remind you that sooner is better than later." She faced me. "Sadie, will you walk me to my car, dear? I'd like a private word with you."

I wondered how Thompson and Jerry would react to her request, but I saw they took it in stride. Neither of them seemed to pay it any mind at all. "Sure. I'll walk you out." I followed her to the door.

Before passing through, she said in a voice loud enough so that everyone could hear, "God bless this house and all who enter into it. Now and forever." She winked at me.

We stepped onto the porch and she pulled the door closed behind us. "It's nice out here," she said. "Let's sit on the swing a while."

"Okay."

She took my hand and led me to the swing. Her hands were soft, gentle. When a breeze passed over us, I could smell the scent of lavender. "I love porch swings, don't you?"

"Yes, ma'am, I do." I said, sitting next to her.

She pushed slightly with her little short legs and gave us a bit of movement on the swing. "Please don't call me ma'am. It makes me feel old." she said, giving me that dazzling smile of hers. Rita's features were not what anyone would normally call beautiful. Most would say she was a downright homely woman. When she smiled she was beautiful all the same. "Call me Rita."

"Okay."

"I want us to be friends." She reached into her purse, fiddled around a bit and pulled out a card and handed it to me. Instinctively, I held it up to my nose. It was heavy with the scent of lavender. She laughed. "You like that?"

"I sure do."

"Good. That's a good sign. You know, Sadie, I feel very good about you and I want you to feel good ... comfortable with me."

"I do feel good about you."

"Fine." She eyeballed me a bit. Maybe she was choosing her words with care. "I sense you know more about what's really going on here than most people."

"Going on here?"

"Yes, here. This world, the planet, this plane of existence." She may have expected me to say something then. When I kept my mouth shut, she went on. "Those men in there are good men. They are both doing the best they can with their given level of understanding. I'd bet they'll both blossom into men of understanding. With time. But you ... you seem to have been born with a better understanding than most adults."

"I don't know what to say." I felt uncomfortable, even though I realized she held nothing but love for me in her heart.

"You don't have to say anything, child. I see that your purpose here stretches way back, in and out of lifetimes and encompasses spiritual matters in ways that would be more appropriate to a saint than a tattoo artist."

I felt exposed. Loved, but exposed.

"Saint Sadie, our lady of ink." She liked her joke and she laughed. Loud and long and finally I joined in a little. "I want you to remember that no matter what seems to be going on around you, you will always have the upper hand if you can view matters with a sense of humor and joy."

"Yes, Rita, I believe you."

"Good." She patted my hand to reassure me. "Now, I know you've been through a shit storm already in your life." I must've looked surprised by her choice of words. She stopped and burst into laughter again. "I said that for your benefit. Remember. Sense of humor. It helps keep things in perspective. What's the trouble of one lifetime compared to an eternal existence that spans the universe and multiple dimensions?"

Now, I'd never thought about it in those words, but I knew exactly what she meant. Rita saw that I understood. I nodded.

"When a rescue worker has to go into a sewer to save a child who's fallen in, he's going to have to wade through some nasty stuff. Now, just because he ends up with shit on him, that doesn't mean he belongs in the sewer. It doesn't mean he *is* shit. You follow me?"

"Yes, ma'am …"

"Uh unh!"

"Rita. Yes, Rita, I understand."

"Of course, you do. Now, all that went before has not sullied your soul in the least. It has no impact on the job you came here to do. You know that. I know that. Given half a chance, Jerry and Thompson will know it, too. It may be hard for you to share the facts of your past with them. That's understandable. It's only going to get harder with the passage of time."

I nodded. I knew she was right.

"It's clear to me you've taken a shine to Thompson."

"Is it that obvious?"

"He may not have really noticed it yet, but he's a man. He will notice. What I want to say is this; it would not be fair of you to get involved with him ... you know, sexually ... before he knows the whole truth, even though that may seem like the safer route. He wouldn't kick you out once he's taken you into his bed. Has that thought occurred to you?"

I was a little ashamed to admit the truth. "Yes. I have had that thought."

"Well, just like you have the right to prove you are the shining star I see you to be, Thompson has the right to demonstrate that he's the good man we both know him to be. If you keep secrets from him ... and from Jerry ... you do them a disservice. Nothing good, nothing lasting is built on secrets."

"I understand. I will tell them the truth."

"Good. Choose your time carefully. You have the right to do that. But, sooner is better than later."

"Okay."

"I am going to watch with great anticipation to see how your life plays out, Sadie. I want to stay in touch. Keep that card in a safe place and call me whenever you feel like it. You don't have to have a reason to call. If you're thinking of me, chances are I am thinking of you. Call me."

That invitation made me feel so good, I just leaned over and gave her a great big hug. And the tears started rolling down my cheeks. When I pulled away from her, I wiped the tears from my cheeks. "Sorry," I said.

"No. You're not. Those are tears of joy, not sadness. Those are always welcome. That's what your grandmother is telling me to say."

"Grannie?" I let out an odd little sound, half laugh and half cry.

"Yes. I like your grandmother. She seems to like me."

"That makes perfect sense."

"We both want you to know that you're not alone. You're strong, but you don't have to carry all the burden by yourself. We are here for you."

I hugged her again.

"Now, it's time for me to leave. And it's time for you to get back inside and start weaving your future."

"Okay." I said, looking into her bright, dark eyes. I loved her.

"Today is the first day of the rest of your life." Rita said, with a big grin. "A cliché, but it's true."

I walked with her to her car. Once she was behind the wheel, she winked at me. "See you soon." She backed her car out onto the street, waved at me, then drove away. I stood there until her car was gone out of my line of sight.

"Grannie," I said, "I know you're hovering around nearby. I reckon you had a hand in this, too. I am truly grateful for my new friend."

Chapter 14

Things were different for a couple of days. The guys weren't cold or distant. They certainly weren't mean. Still, the thing I'd witnessed with Lucinda and the spiritual intervention of Rita just kind of made everybody step back and take stock of what was going on. They did not distrust me, but I *was* the newcomer. Jerry and Thompson realized they really didn't know much about me. Rita had told them to expect some revelations, but only when I was ready to spill the beans.

Truth be told, I guess I felt a little stand-offish, too. I went to the shop with Thompson. He had me spend a lot of time on the computer. I read all about the history of tattoos on the internet and everything I could find about the business end of skin art, too. I think the freedom I felt was making me grow up a lot faster. Like I was having a mental growth spurt. I felt like I was getting smarter. This set me to really thinking about it.

Was I getting smarter because I felt like I had to grow up? That seemed to be the truth of it. I knew if I was back in the group home I'd be herded around by Mrs. Richards and the other well-meaning adults. They weren't doing anything wrong. I saw that real clear-like. They were doing what they felt was best for all the girls they were charged with caring for. They were protecting young women with uncertain mental processes from the big, bad world. I couldn't speak for anyone else, but I knew that in my case they were turning me into a cripple. Crippled emotionally and potentially. They would've led me down a path where I would have few expectations other than shelter, food and a boring avoidance of pain. Maybe that was the best way to keep us girls from becoming a danger to ourselves and others. Surely, they thought so. But, now, out here in the real world I could see that wasn't the way things worked at all.

I saw real clearly that life was and had always been a matter of survival. We had all these modern-day comforts that were supposed to convince us life had become something else. The radios, refrigerators, super-markets, washing machines, televisions, computers and, yes, the drugs, too; all those things were meant to lull us into a false sense of security. The men and women who were in charge of policies and decisions that affected every last one of us didn't believe that way. They knew the world was still a jungle. Life was no safer than it had ever been. At the push of a button, thousands of people could die. With a phone call, people could be rounded up and put in jail with no explanation given. The foolish masses were supposed to get their world view from the TV. They were supposed to believe abuses of force and power were a thing of the past.

I didn't want to be one of the fools. And I damn sure didn't want to be a fragile little pet cared for by the state. All of this weighed heavy on my mind and heart.

These thoughts percolated up from within me, but I'd be lying if I said I wasn't influenced by ideas from Jerry and Thompson. Thompson rarely spoke of his views, but his actions said he was in charge of his own destiny and he wasn't going to trust anyone else to put a frame around reality for him. Jerry was a lot more talkative about his ideas. He was kind of like a college professor. I mean he had good reasons for his positions on things, but it was all presented in theoretical terms. See? There's his influence right there. How many times would I have used the word 'theoretical' if I wasn't living under the same roof with Jerry? Probably never.

A few days after Rita's visit, Thompson asked me if I was ready to do some real ink on real skin. I wanted it. Real bad. Even so, it came as a surprise. A shock really.

"You're going to let me tattoo a customer?"

He laughed. "Whoa, there, spitfire. You really think that would be a good idea at this point?"

"Of course not. That's why I'm asking."

"I knew you were a sensible girl." He grinned and I had a real sense that he was warming back up to me, the way things had been before Lucinda's bullshit. But I would've preferred that he call me a sensible *lady*, rather than *girl*. He called all our female customers ladies and I wanted him to think of me with that same respect.

"Thanks. So, you want me to do an actual tattoo on someone. Who?"

"Well, we could catch a stray dog and shave him. Tie him down, drug him and let you have at it." He said it with a straight face, but of course that was just his warped sense of humor. I slapped his shoulder. Pretty hard, actually. He knew I'd never hurt a defenseless animal. And for the record, neither would he. He was just yanking my chain.

"Really," I said. "What'd you have in mind?" Suddenly, I got the idea that he trusted me enough to add some ink to his heavily tattooed body. "You? You want me to tattoo you?"

He looked surprised, then burst into a laughing jag that took him a good while to overcome. He grabbed his sides and every time I thought he was going to stop laughing, he'd look at me and start right up again. By the time he finally finished getting his jollies at my expense, I felt pretty foolish.

Thompson reached out and gently touched my cheek. "Sadie, sweetheart," he said, "I do trust you. A lot. But there is no way in hell, at this juncture, I would let you tattoo me. You're going to learn the same way I did."

That sounded encouraging. At least he was being fair with me. "Okay. What's that?"

"Yourself. Choose a spot on your body where you can easily give yourself a tattoo. That's step one. Step two is choosing a design of the appropriate size. Third, and most important, choose something of lasting significance. Something that has deep meaning to you and will still have deep meaning fifty years from now. I don't mind putting anything the customer wants on *their* skin. It's their body and their decision. But I do not understand or agree with a permanent likeness of Sponge Bob or some other lame bullshit immortalized in flesh."

What he said made a huge impression on me. "Good. Yeah. That sounds right," I answered, nodding. If I was going to have art on my skin, it was going to represent ideas that were deeply rooted in my soul.

"In addition to eliminating any liability, inking yourself'll give you firsthand knowledge of the pain involved."

"The pain," I said. Yes, that was a real consideration, too. I wasn't afraid of the pain, but I think Thompson got the idea that the word 'pain' intimidated me.

"Not so much pain as discomfort," he said.

"Now, you sound like a nurse," I told him. I remembered nurses saying, 'You may feel a little discomfort,' when they gave us injections at Terrell. And the dentist. He used the same words.

"All right, then, doctor patient." He was right about that. I would soon be both. "What I want you to do is choose a place for the tattoo. I'd suggest the thigh. It's meaty. You'll feel less pain there."

"Discomfort," I corrected him with a big smile.

"Yes, doctor, less discomfort. And you can easily hide it from view if you fuck up somehow."

Now that idea brought a frown to my face.

"Not that you're going to. My guess is that you'll do a perfect job, first time out. But shit happens and it's best to allow for the unforeseen."

"You're right."

"So, let's approach it this way; you pick out three fairly small designs that you really like. Once you've done that, let me take a look. Be prepared to give me a detailed explanation of the appeal that each one holds for you. No bullshit. Just heartfelt connection. Okay?"

"Why would I bullshit you about this?"

"I don't think you would. I just want to understand your rationale. It's a choice that will last a lifetime and I want to be certain that you've given it the weight it deserves. Agreed?"

"Yes, sir!"

"Sir?"

"I didn't mean that. I'm just excited."

"Good. But we're going to make sure that excitement has cooled down to a solid resolution before you start injecting ink into your skin."

"I agree completely," I said.

Thompson gave a shrug and gestured toward the computer and the many designs hanging on the walls around us. He didn't have to say another word. I scanned the walls for a good thirty minutes or so, then I logged onto the computer and spent the rest of the day searching.

When we got home that night Jerry had ordered pizza, so we all just chowed down on that and I didn't have to cook anything. I shared my excitement about choosing a tattoo with Jerry. For some reason or another we were all just lounging around in the living room with our plates and beverages, instead of sitting at the kitchen table.

"Nice," he said. "Have you picked it out yet?"

"I'm still considering a few choices," I told him. "I'm not going to get in a hurry." When I said that, Thompson winked at Jerry. Jerry smiled real big and nodded. "I saw that, Thompson," I said. "You're not as slick as you think."

"Easy. I'm just playing with you. Everybody gets excited about their first tattoo. It's only natural."

That made sense. I turned to Jerry. "How about you, Jerry? What was your first tattoo?" He didn't answer right away but held up a finger as his mouth was stuffed with pizza. When Thompson started laughing, I sort of knew what was about to be said.

He swallowed and washed it down with a swig of beer. "I don't have any tattoos."

"Not one? That surprises me. What's the matter? Thompson wouldn't give you a break on the price?"

Thompson guffawed. "Hell, I'd do it for free!"

"You're not afraid, are you?" I didn't mean to embarrass him. There was no mockery in my question.

Jerry cleared his throat. "I wouldn't say that exactly. It's just that tats are really permanent. I've thought about it. More than once. I've just never settled on an image I wanted to wear on my skin for the rest of my life."

Thompson laughed again. "It's got nothing to do with the pain, right buddy?"

"You mean the discomfort?" I said. I couldn't help but join in the fun just a little. If a young gal like myself could endure it, I couldn't see why Jerry wouldn't be able to.

"That is a consideration," He admitted, taking another bite of pizza.

Thompson made a sound like a chicken and sort of flapped his arms in a hennish fashion. Now, that may seem a little cruel, but I don't think it was. Not really. We'd all been on egg shells since the thing with Lucinda. This was just the tension finding a way to release itself.

"Hey," Jerry shouted. It was more of a mumble-shout because his mouth was so full of food, but he didn't care. "I'm not into pain, like some people. Know what that makes me? Normal! That's what." He swallowed his food, then stuck out his tongue at both of us.

"Some say normal's just a setting on the dryer," Thompson commented. It was a bit of a taunt.

"Yeah," I chimed in, "a setting nobody uses!"

Then, we were all laughing. It was the perfect collapse of all the tension that had lingered over us.

When we all settled back down, I said, "Hey, why don't we watch a movie together. It's been a while."

"Sure. I'm up for it," Jerry answered.

I looked at Thompson. He's not nearly the movie person Jerry is and I was afraid he might beg off and go to his room. "Well?" I prodded him.

"Sure. Why not? Let me make a pitstop and grab another beer and I'll be glad to join you."

"Good!" I was genuinely glad and couldn't help clapping my hands together. "Pick us a really good one," I said to Jerry.

"All righty." He stood up, plate in hand and went to the DVD shelves. He pushed his glasses up on his nose and gave the matter some serious consideration. In a few moments, he said, "Aha!"

"Aha what?" I asked.

"Since you seem to have such a keen interest in the whole white trash thing, I think this might be the perfect movie." He held the DVD up for me to see. It was *Sling Blade*, starring Billy Bob Thornton.

That was the first time I saw or even heard of *Sling Blade*. It's not the sort of picture they encourage people from Terrell to watch. I have to say that movie affected me more deeply than any film I'd seen before. It had humor and it had tragedy. It was like real life in that regard. Of course, there's the whole murder and mental hospital connection that brought it close to home for me. When the film ended, I just sat there a little stunned.

Jerry switched it off and ejected the disk. "Well, what do you think?" He turned and saw me deep in thought. Maybe he took my serious expression as disappointment or maybe he thought I was offended for some reason. "Hey," he said. "You okay? You look a little spaced out."

"I'm fine." I held up a hand as I collected my thoughts, then I gestured to the place where he'd been sitting. "Sit down, Jerry. I have some things to say." I looked at Thompson. "To both of you."

Thompson just nodded and Jerry sat back down looking a tad apprehensive.

"I have a lot to say and it'll be a lot easier for me if you'll just both hear me out. If you interrupt me or start asking a bunch of questions, I'm liable to bust out crying and I don't want that to happen. Not if I can help it." Truth was I felt like crying already.

Thompson, again, nodded. Jerry leaned forward with his elbows on his knees. "Sure thing," he said.

"Y'all know my name's not Sadie. You know I've got a past. Rita warned you about that. Now, I'm just real fortunate to have found good friends like you two. You both deserve to know the truth and there's never going to be a better time for me to tell it than right now."

Grabbing my hands together in front of me and not making eye contact with either of them, I jumped right in. I told them about Dan McWhorter and how he introduced me to sex. I told them what happened when my mother found out about it. I told them about the house burning down and me being blamed for it, though I couldn't remember anything about that. I mentioned my grannie and how she was a lot like Rita, but I didn't tell them I still feel her around me a lot. I sort of skimmed over my years at Terrell. Then, I finished up with the group home and how I just couldn't see myself going along with the life they wanted me to live. I told them I believed I deserved better than that.

"God's given me what feels like a shot at a pretty good life here," I said. Tears were running down my cheeks, but I'd managed not to break out bawling. I counted that as a minor victory. "I've never had such good friends as the two of you. I'm grateful and indebted to you. I hope you still want me for a friend, now that you know the whole truth."

Only then did I risk looking either of them in the eye. Thompson was quiet. He nodded when I looked at him and I could tell he accepted me as I was and appreciated the fact that I'd laid it all out on the table. When I looked at Jerry, I could tell his head was spinning. I guess he was experiencing information overload. I don't know what he'd thought my past might be, but whatever he'd imagined, it clearly had not come close to the truth of the matter. He was pressed back into his seat, one hand gripping an arm rest, the other squeezing a beer bottle so hard that his knuckles were white.

"Are you okay, Jerry?" I asked, wiping the tears off my face.

"Whew!" he said. "I would never in a million years have guessed any of that."

"You all right with it?"

"Oh, sure. Yeah. Of course. It's not your fault, what happened." His words were awkward and I felt like he was trying to convince himself more than anything.

"You sure?" I asked.

He looked me in the eye. "I think you're a good person," he said. "It breaks my heart to imagine you going through all that. I'm just stunned."

I smiled. I felt like I understood him and I was confident that our friendship would continue and grow stronger.

"They let you out of the hospital, right? I mean you didn't escape or anything. Right?"

"Jerry!" Thompson shook his head.

"It's a fair question," I said, holding a hand up to Thompson. "If I was in your place, I suppose I'd be wondering the same thing."

"Okay," Jerry said. "Good. No offense. They said you're good to be free and not a danger to yourself or others and that's good enough for me. I just want to know I'm not going to wake up some night and find you standing over me with a lawnmower blade in your hand. Something like that would never happen, right?"

Thompson sighed heavily. I could see he was embarrassed by his friend's fears. Thompson had been to war. Jerry never had. It was only natural that they'd each have their own distinct way of looking at this.

"Never happen. Right?" Jerry repeated.

I don't know what got into me. Until that very second, I would never have imagined myself doing what I did. I lowered my voice and did my best impersonation of Carl from *Sling Blade*. "If you behave yourself, I reckon not. Mmm hmm."

In an instant we were all laughing so hard we couldn't breathe. That was the very first time I ever imitated Carl. Since that time, it's become a regular thing for me. Jerry calls it my 'Carl schtick.' It always seems to diffuse a tense situation. By the time we'd all caught our breath and stopped laughing, I knew I was home and that these two men were going to stand by me.

Chapter 15

For my very first tattoo I chose a triskelion. It's an ancient symbol with three spirals radiating out from a central point. Some say it's a Celtic symbol, some say it originated in ancient Greece. No matter where it was first drawn, I think it touches a lot of folks in the depths of their hearts and minds. It's what Jerry calls an archetypal form. That means it comes up out of the depths of our consciousness, like a tool that all of us have hidden away in our subconscious minds. I like the look of it, the simple beauty and the way it makes me feel.

"Nice choice," said Thompson, when I showed him the version I wanted to use. "Why the triskelion? Why would you want to wear this on your skin for the rest of your life?"

I'd given it a lot of thought, so I had no problem at all answering his question. "First, I think it's beautiful. Second, it's got the three spirals all connecting in the middle. Right now, that seems like you, me and Jerry.

Each of us has our own life, but we're all connected by our friendship. You two are about the best friends I've ever had. I'll never forget you, no matter what. I'd love to have a permanent reminder of how I feel about you. When I'm eighty years old, all I'll have to do is look down at my thigh to remember everything that's happening right now."

He didn't say so, but I could tell Thompson liked what I'd said. Words were unnecessary. It showed clear enough in his eyes.

"If you're certain, then, let's get you set up and you can start working on it."

"Mighty fine." I was beaming.

Thompson got me everything I needed to do the job. He helped me to be certain of the position and apply the transfer to my leg. He offered a few pointers and told me not to be intimidated by the process. I needed to just jump in and discover what it was all about for myself, he said.

"Remember the immortal words of Bob Ross," he said. "There are no mistakes, only happy accidents."

I laughed. We'd watched Bob Ross's show a few times at the house while we were eating. I think he and Jerry just liked having it on for background noise, but I felt like I was really gaining some valuable information from that guy, with his funky hair-do. He provided me with some perspective, even if his style of art was not something I'd ever shoot for.

Thompson put up a screen, so I'd have a little privacy while I worked on my tat. That first moment when the needle penetrated my skin was a revelation. There was pain involved, but not much. I could see the wisdom in having me do it myself. We all know it's easier to endure pain we are applying to ourselves than the pain others are putting on us. I chewed a stick of gum while I worked and that seemed to mellow things out a bit for me.

Shortly after I started, I heard the phone ring. Thompson picked it up and exchanged a few words with somebody. I wasn't paying all that much attention. I was too excited about both giving and getting my first tattoo. After he hung up the phone, he called out, "Sadie, I need to talk to you for a minute."

I put the needle down. "Okay. What's up?"

"Can I come behind the curtain?"

"Sure." I lowered my dress so the tattoo would be hidden from sight. I wasn't ready for him to see it just yet. I could tell by the tone of his voice that whatever it was he wanted to talk about was serious business. "Come on back."

He stepped around the screen into my private area. "That was the police department."

"Police department?" The words were out of my mouth before I gave it any real thought. Then, after I'd spoken, I realized it had to be about Gus and me filing charges against him.

"Yeah. They were calling to let us know there won't be any follow up on your charges against Gus."

That didn't seem right. My first reaction was to feel a little indignant. The guy had tried to strangle me. If that wasn't reason enough to bring charges, I couldn't imagine what was. "Why not?"

"He's dead."

"Dead?" The irritation that had been rising inside me vanished instantly.

"That's what they said."

Now, instead of indignation, I felt sad. The old man was nuts and he had attacked me, but I didn't hate him or want him dead. "How?"

"He died in jail. They said they couldn't reveal any more than that because it's under investigation."

A lot of things went running through my mind. Like, don't they take away anything you could hurt yourself with when they put you in a jail cell? Would the police have any reason to hurt that crazy old man? And, of course, was it possible that Lucinda had anything to do with it? The knot in my belly told me, yes, she very well could've had a hand in it. But, part of me didn't want to think that's the way it was. I hated to think of anyone, even Gus, locked up and unable to run away, becoming prey for a dark soul like Lucinda.

"How's this make you feel?" I asked Thompson.

"Uneasy."

"Yeah, me too. Is there anything we should do?"

"There's nothing we can do for him now," Thompson answered. "Except maybe say a prayer for his soul."

"I'll do that."

"Me too."

We stared at each other for a few moments.

"Okay, I'll let you get back to your tattoo," he said, going back out to the front part of the shop.

"Yeah."

This news of Gus's death had put a damper on something that had been a cause for joy and excitement; my first tattoo. I said a silent prayer for the old man's soul and wished him safe passage to wherever he was headed. Unlike some of the teachers I'd had at Terrell, I did not assume he was headed for a dark place or a place of punishment. I did not feel that was justified, besides, like I said before, I think hell and heaven are states of mind. I wanted Gus, whatever remained of him, to be healed, patched up and sent on his way to a new and hopefully better existence. His hard times in this life had damaged his mind for sure. As for attacking me, I was certain he'd been a helpless puppet under the influence of Lucinda. I forgave him.

Once I'd settled down again and distanced myself from the emotions I felt over Gus's passing, I picked up the needle and started working on my tat again. It wasn't long before I heard Rusty come in. It had taken him a while to get back for a second session.

"Now a good time?" he asked Thompson after they'd said their greetings.

"Sure, Rusty. Anytime you like since you've paid in full. My wish is your command."

"Stop. You're smelling the place up with your bullshit." I guess he heard my needle going behind the screen. "Got another customer ahead of me?"

"Oh, no," Thompson answered. "That's just Sadie."

"She's giving tats already, eh?"

Thompson laughed. "You could say that. Hey, Sadie, Rusty's here. Say hi."

"Hey, Rusty," I called out to him.

"How you doing, sweet pea?"

"Just fine. And you?"

"Here to get some ink applied."

"You and me both."

"What's that?"

"I'm doing my first tattoo."

"On yourself?"

"Yep."

"Ooh, I want to see."

"Would you mind waiting 'til I'm done? I'm a little nervous and I'd rather show it to you when I'm finished."

"Oh, sure, sure. I understand."

So, Rusty settled in and Thompson continued that massive eagle on his back, while I pecked away at my tiny little triskelion, slowly but surely filling in all the lines.

After about an hour, I heard Rusty say he could use a drink.

"Want to take a break?" Thompson asked him.

I was ready for a little break myself, so I called out, "Hey, Rusty, I'm ready for a little break myself. How about I run down the ally and get us some ice tea?"

"You sure? I don't want to put you out."

"You aren't putting me out. I could use some tea myself." I stood up and let the sundress I was wearing fall down over my ink. Then, I stepped out from behind my screen.

Rusty was face down while Thompson worked on him. He looked over one shoulder at me. "So how about that tattoo. You going to show me?"

"When it's done, I will. I'm just taking a break."

"Okay. I understand."

Rusty looked tired, kind of worn out. There were big bags under his eyes. He just didn't seem nearly as lively as he had that first day I met him. I worried that if he wasn't working, painting and earning money, he might just be spending his days getting drunk. Nothing'll age a man faster than demon alcohol. Like Thompson sometimes says, 'It's not the years, it's the miles.' Rusty looked like he'd been logging miles like a long-haul trucker. Getting him ice tea, so he'd have something to mix his whiskey with, might not be doing him a favor at all.

"You okay, Rusty?" I asked. "You look a little tired. Haven't been sick, have you?"

Thompson set his needle aside and shot me a warning glance. I knew he wanted me to be real careful with my words when talking to our best customer.

"Aw, no, honey. I'm fine. It's just that I've been having trouble sleeping."

"Why's that?"

"Bad dreams. It's the damnedest thing. I've never been prone to nightmares, but lately it seems like that's all I have."

"I'm going to run get our tea, but when I get back I'd like to hear about your dreams. If you want to talk about them. I've always been interested in dreams." I went to the register and took out some cash. "You want anything, Thompson?"

He thought it over, but only for an instant. "Sure. Why not? I'll have a tea. Unsweetened, of course."

"Of course. I'll be back in a jiffy." I went out the back door and pretty soon I was back with the three teas. No witchy interference and no attempted strangulations in the alley.

Rusty went out to his van to 'fix' his tea.

"I don't know if it's a good idea to have him talking about his nightmares," Thompson said.

"Oh, okay. I won't mention it again. But if he brings it up, I want to hear it. Sometimes it helps to talk about scary dreams. Okay?"

Thompson just shrugged. I understood where he was coming from. Years of being in business had taught him to keep a leash on his questions and curiosity. I don't think it was that he didn't care. I think he just wanted to give folks their privacy. There were things he didn't like talking about. Like his time in the military. It was only natural that folks had subjects they were sensitive about. I was pretty sure this was different. Rusty didn't have to mention his nightmares if he didn't want to talk about them. And he was a big boy after all.

Rusty came back into the shop, sipping at his whiskey-fortified tea. Before he laid down on his belly again, he took a seat. I suppose he was welcoming a break. We sat in silence for just a short time, then he said, "You like talking about dreams, do you?"

"I do. My grannie paid a lot of attention to dreams."

"Like I say, I've never had any trouble with nightmares. None I remember. Most of the time I don't recall my dreams at all, good or bad."

"Grannie used to say that dreams are road signs sending us messages about what lies ahead in our lives."

Rusty laughed. "I don't know about all that, but this dream seems to be hanging in there, chipping away at me, keeping me from sleeping."

"Same dream over and over?"

He considered my question. "Not exactly the same. It varies. But, the setup is always pretty much the same. I'm out in the boondocks hunting. It's twilight, all shadowy and hard to make things out. I'm looking for deer. Sometimes the branches look like antlers and I'll squeeze off a shot. I'm thinking it's too dark to be hunting. But you know how dreams are. I just keep right on going. I hear things in the distance."

"What kind of things do you hear?" I was glad to see Rusty getting so involved in the telling of his dream story. I hoped that getting it out in the open would help him let go of it and sleep better.

"Like a distant horn. The kind of horn hunters used in the woods long ago. In some of these dreams I look up and see a castle on a hill in the dim light. You know, like a ruined castle that's been empty for hundreds of years, all crumbling and overgrown with vines." He seemed to be examining this image with his mind's eye. Then he said, "Sometimes it looks more like a Greek ruin with the pillars jutting up into the sky, but no roof. Like I say, there's no rhyme or reason to it."

"What else do you remember?"

"Then, a lot of times, I'll hear a noise nearby. Sometimes I look up and see what I think is a deer moving in the brush. I shoot and I hear a woman scream. I run over and see it's not a deer at all, but a naked woman." Rusty seemed to pull out of the dream he was focusing on and he looked me in the eye. "Don't think less of me. Like I'm a pervert or something. I'm just telling you how it goes."

"No worries," I said as gently as I could. It was my intention to let him just get it out and maybe find an answer to what it was that was causing his distress.

"So, it's this naked woman lying on the ground bleeding. And she does have antlers on her head. Not growing out of her head, but like a primitive head dress. You know, like a native American might wear in a ritual dance. Something you might see in a documentary on TV."

I nodded to let him know I was getting a clear picture of everything he was describing.

"I kneel down beside her and, when I look in her eyes, I get scared. Real scared. She's evil. Like the devil. She's got a knife in her hand and she goes to stab me in the heart. That's when I jolt awake. After that it's a long time before I can get back to sleep. Sometimes I just lie there until the sun comes up."

"You poor thing," I said without thinking. The look he gave me let me know he was not the sort of fellow who appreciated pity. "I just mean, going without sleep has got to be a bitch."

"It is," he agreed. He sipped his tea.

"You said it's not always the same. You feel like sharing anything else?"

"Okay. Sometimes when I look over, I see she's tied to a tree. Like someone intends her for a sacrifice. A human sacrifice. Those times I go over to set her loose. When I get close, she looks in my eyes and I know that she's been raped. Not just once, but a lot by a whole bunch of men. And maybe some women, too. It's sick. I don't understand it. I just want to help her, but she looks in my eyes like she's judging me. It's like she's telling me I'm one of the gang that raped her. I know that's not true. I want to make her understand that it wasn't me. I'm scared of her and I feel like if I untie her, she's going to go berserk and kill me. She sort of jumps out of her body. That sounds crazy. It's like her spirit jumps out of her body and tries to get inside me. She wants my body. I know I can't let her do that. I'm terrified and I wake up."

The poor guy. He just sat there all hunched over, looking beat up and worn down. I wanted to help him. But, what could I do? Then Rita came to mind. I asked myself, what Rita would do in a situation like this? What would my grannie do? Next thing I knew, I was saying, "Rusty, it's not my intention to meddle in your business, but I have to ask you; would it be all right if I said some prayers for you the next few days?"

This took him by surprise. So much so that I don't think he knew what to say. He looked from me to Thompson.

Thompson said, "Nothing to be afraid of, Rusty. It's just her way. She says little prayers every time she comes in through the front door."

"Just some things Grannie taught me when I was a little girl," I said.

Rusty let out a big sigh. I had the sense that, somewhere along the way, something had happened that put him crossways with churches and religion. "I don't see how it could hurt anything," he said, finally.

"Okay, then. I'll do it." I looked over at Thompson and he gave me a wink.

"I guess we better get back to applying your eagle, then?"

"Oh, hell yeah!" Rusty said in that big voice of his, looking just a tad embarrassed.

"And I'll get back to my own tattoo," I said.

After I was behind my screen and working away again, over the sound of my needle and the sound of Thompson's, I heard Rusty say, "I really like her. Sadie's got a good heart. You know that?"

Well that just about made my heart melt. I kept right on working because I didn't want him to know I was paying any attention to what he was saying with Thompson. But I can tell you, I was glowing with the best kind of feeling.

"Yes, she does," Thompson answered him.

And that made me feel fine, too.

When I finished my tattoo up, my thigh was a little sore. I could only imagine what Rusty's poor back felt like. I decided to let them continue working without any interruption from me. I pulled out the copy of *Love Story* that Jerry had loaned me and continued reading. I was just getting to the part where Oliver Barrett III is asking Dean Thompson for a scholarship when I heard Rusty say he thought he was done for today. His voice was weary and I felt for the poor guy.

"Yeah, that's fine. We've gotten a lot done today, Rusty. Want to take a look?"

"Sure."

When I stepped out from behind my screen, Rusty was standing with his back to the wall mirror holding a small mirror and angling over his shoulder to check out Thompson's handiwork. It was looking pretty spectacular.

"Damn, Thompson! You sure do pretty work."

"Thank you for giving me the chance to do a nice big piece with a lot of detail. That doesn't happen every day."

"Nice bird, Rusty," I said.

"You like it?" he asked, grinning at me and looking a little more alive than he had all day.

"Sure do."

"How's yours coming?"

"It's finished, but it's not a work of art like yours."

Rusty looked at me a minute, his eyes roaming up and down my body. I think he was considering to ask me to show it to him. Then, he thought better of it. The dress I was wearing was sleeveless and not that long. I'm sure he figured out it was in a kind of personal spot and he didn't want to make me uncomfortable. "What'd you choose for yours?" He finally asked.

"It's a triskelion. Something simple for my first time out."

"Happy with it?"

"I think so. It's seeping a little. I'll give it a day or two to dry out, then I'll decide if it's good enough."

"And if it's not?" Rusty chuckled.

"I guess I figure out a way to cover it up with more ink." I was just saying that to make conversation with him. I knew it was good and the lines were clean. I'd been super careful.

"Speaking of seepage," Thompson said, "let me clean you up a bit."

Rusty sat down and let Thompson pad off the blood with some gauze. He lightly rubbed on some anti-biotic ointment. Then he reached into a cabinet under the counter and pulled out a brand new white T-shirt.

"Here you go. Slip this on. It's a double x. Should be big enough to fit loosely. It'll keep you from getting blood on your shirt or the upholstery in your van."

"Thanks, bro." Rusty slipped into the big white shirt. Even though it was a double x, it wasn't exactly loose on him. "What do I owe you for the shirt?"

"On the house. You paid in advance, which was a great help to us. Just keep that tat clean and put some antibiotic ointment on it. No infections allowed."

"Will do."

"Would you like to have dinner at our house, Rusty?" I hadn't talked to Thompson about the invitation. I just blurted it out when the idea popped into my noggin. I could tell Thompson was pleased. He smiled at me.

"No, sweetheart. I'm just going home. I'm beat. Maybe I'll get some sleep tonight."

"I hope so." I said.

"Say those prayers for me. I'm sure I can use them."

"I will."

After a couple of false starts—you know what I mean, where you say goodbye but the conversation veers off into new territory and you just keep talking a while longer—he finally walked out the door.

"What do you say we close up early and head home?" Thompson asked.

"You're the boss, apple sauce."

"Good. I'm hungry."

We locked up and drove home. When we got there, we found a note from Jerry. He said he'd be out late with some friends at a movie meeting of some sort. It was rare for Jerry to leave the house for an evening.

"Looks like I'm cooking for two," I said. "What sounds good?"

"Mexican food."

I must've looked surprised, because Thompson started laughing. I'm sure he knew I'd never made so much as a taco in my short career as a cook.

"Let's go to Playa Azul," he said. "They're cheap enough. We can enjoy a good meal without having to do any dishes."

"You sure?" I asked. I knew we were on a budget and the house was full of groceries.

"Yeah. Mexican food suit you?"

"Right down to the ground."

The food was great. I haven't eaten a whole lot of Mexican food, but the enchiladas they served me were very tasty. Thompson had beef tacos and some beer. When we got back home again, we were both satisfied and happy.

"Want to watch a movie?" he asked, closing the front door behind us.

I thought about it. "No, let's just sit and visit a bit."

"Visit?" He sounded like he thought I'd used the word inappropriately.

"Yes. You know, conversation? You and me don't get that much time to just talk. At work we're doing work stuff and when we're home Jerry does most the talking."

"That's for sure."

"And I'm not complaining. I love Jerry and I've already learned a bunch just by listening to him. I want to just talk for a while. With you."

"Sounds good," he said. "Want anything to drink?"

"No. I'm stuffed."

I plopped down on the sofa and he scooted off into the kitchen for another beer. When he'd returned and sat himself down, he asked, "Anything in particular you want to talk about?" He poured beer into his mouth.

"You."

"Me?"

"Let's talk about you. You know pretty much all there is to know about me now. And I know more about Jerry than I've ever known about another living person. I know his preferences, his dislikes, where he was born. I'm sure I'll learn a lot more about him before it's all said and done, but I'd like to know a little more about you."

Thompson was thoughtful, quiet for a minute. He studied the label on the beer in his hand, then he looked up at me with a real gentle kind of a smile. Seemed like he didn't really want to venture off into talking about himself, but he was willing to do it for me.

"Anything in particular you want to know?"

"Nope. Just whatever you feel like telling. I know there's things in your life that are private and I don't want to cross any boundaries." That was me remembering Mrs. Richards. She was always going on with us girls at the group home about the need for setting boundaries. "Just share whatever suits you."

He thought, but not long. "I was born in Mobile, Alabama. My dad was an electrician for a defense contractor. My mom was a stay-at-home mother. We lived for a while in a big old house right on the bay. It was nice. I don't mean nice, like fancy or well-appointed. Our dining room table was a sort of picnic table my father built from 2 x 4s. The big old house was pretty much empty. We couldn't afford furniture. The yard was great for a little boy who liked to climb trees. I climbed all of them, except for the pine trees. All the women in the family went on about how wonderful the magnolia tree smelled. I climbed that one and stuck my nose in a big blossom and sniffed." His face told me the little boy version of Thompson had not enjoyed that experience. "Never have liked the smell of magnolias."

His eyes got a faraway look and I could tell he was playing memory movies in his mind. "We had a pier that went way out into the bay. We fished almost every day. Crabs and flounder were a big part of our diet. My dad made me a raft out of two inner tubes and an old door. I paddled around in the bay on that thing. I was so tanned, my grandmother said I looked like a little blue-eyed Mexican boy. I'm not sure that was a compliment. The folks were pretty, you know … racist."

I said nothing, just smiled and nodded. Now that he'd opened the door to me, I wanted him to just go wherever his fancy led him. He talked for about an hour. That's a long time for a man like Thompson who doesn't take pleasure from talking. Jerry would've been just warming up. He looked at the clock on the shelf by the television, then he looked at his unfinished beer. I'm sure it was warm. He downed the rest of it anyway. "Have I talked enough for one sitting?" he asked me.

I nodded. "Thank you for sharing the stories of your childhood." I'd learned so much about him. His first car was a red 1971 Pontiac Firebird in perfect condition. He'd played guitar as a teenager but hadn't picked one up for years. His folks were alive and living in Washington state somewhere. He didn't talk to them much. He hadn't exactly come out and said it, but I thought there was friction between him and his dad over his bad feelings about the military after his time in Iraq.

He got up and went to the kitchen. "You want anything?" he called out.

"No. I'm fine."

I heard him toss his empty beer and pull another one from the fridge. He joined me again in the living room. "How's the tattoo feeling?"

I wasn't expecting that question after the other stuff he'd been talking about. Kind of took me off guard. "It's okay. A little sore."

"Feel like your first tat is a success?"

"I think so. I was awfully careful."

"Good."

"I'll show it to you, if you like." It was my turn to surprise him. He wasn't expecting me to make that offer. He was quiet for a second. "Want to see it?"

"Sure. If you don't mind."

I slid my dress up and started peeling back the cotton pad I'd taped over it. He came over and sat beside me on the sofa. There it was, revealed for the first time, my triskelion.

"Nice job," he said right away. "Spirals aren't the easiest thing, but you did a really clean job of it."

"Thanks." I was a little self-conscious, but really glad he was taking an interest. It felt good to have him sitting so near.

"Sore?"

"A little."

Without asking, he touched his cold beer bottle to my tat. It felt good. Sent a shiver running through my body and started a fire between my legs. When he raised his eyes to meet mine, I was praying he'd kiss me. And he did.

Right away we were squeezing each other, our mouths hungry for one another. Then we were peeling our clothes off, full of the fire that we'd started. When I was completely naked in front of him, he paused and took me in with his eyes.

"You're beautiful," he said.

I didn't respond with words, just pulled him to me as we fell back longways on the sofa. Thompson's muscular body felt good under my hands and pressing against me. His skin was warm and smooth and rippled with muscles. When he touched me between the legs it sent a shudder through me. I wanted him like I've never wanted anything. Drawing him nearer, I kissed his neck. I felt him entering me, hard and huge. He was bigger than I'd expected, but I was so wet there was no cause for concern. Just sweet pleasure. He filled me with hot passion. It seemed impossible that he could fit, but he did, pressing up against the secret places inside me and making me crazy. I gushed. The warm juices just poured out of me. I wanted to absorb him, to just pull him into me and become one big soul together. Then I was crying out. Not with pain, but with an aching joy I'd never known. I squeezed him into me even harder. Then he sort of froze and let out a real heavy breath. I felt every drop as he exploded inside me.

He just lingered there. And that's what I wanted. We were both breathing heavy and coated in sweat. Finally, he pulled away and looked in my eyes. He kissed me, first on the lips, then on my forehead. With a slight groan, he pulled back further and sat up, still between my legs.

"I hope this wasn't a mistake," he said.

"Don't think that." I scooted up into a sitting position. "I wanted that. More than anything."

He didn't say anything. He just took me in his arms and held me real tight for a long time. I kissed his shoulder and his neck, enjoying the salty taste.

Chapter 16

After we had, I guess you'd say 'consummated,' our relationship, we took to sleeping together. I suppose Thompson had a talk with Jerry explaining how things were. I don't know for sure. Jerry just took it all in stride, not a raised eyebrow or any sign that anything unusual had happened. The main thing was that he didn't treat me any differently than before. He was still my good buddy, watching movies with me and sharing information. I have to say he's probably the best teacher I've ever had in this lifetime. He's always eager to answer any of my questions, even when I suspect he thinks the answers should be obvious. Never has he made me feel stupid or like I was bothering him. I owe a lot to Jerry.

And I owe a lot to Thompson. In the world of tattoos and business, he's been just as patient with me. He's very carefully instructed me on all the dos and don'ts. I can honestly call myself a tattoo artist, now. I owe that to Thompson. That spur-of-the-moment dream I had the day I escaped the group home and my life as a poor mentally ill ward of the state became my reality. And because of that I've come to trust my intuition more and more. What seemed like a momentary fantasy at the time was actually a blueprint, or at least the first step on the path, for the life I was intended to live. I couldn't be more grateful.

Thompson taught me much more than just tattoo knowledge. Once we were sleeping in the same bed, that meant the solarium was available for meditation. He encouraged me to join him in the mornings before we went to work. I felt awkward at first, but there was no good reason for that, it turned out. Meditation came kind of natural to me. It was probably because of my experiences with Grannie and the fact that I'd had so much time to just think back at Terrell.

"Just empty your mind," Thompson said. "Take a deep breath, relax, inhabit your body with mindfulness."

These phrases seem unusual compared to the mental postures most modern folks assume. We're all in the habit of filling every minute with some sort of noise. If it's not the radio, it's the television, or the computer, or just jabbering to another person. If there's no one to talk with, most of us just jabber away with ourselves in what Thompson called the 'internal monologue.'

He also called it the 'monkey mind.' That sort of resonated with me. I was already convinced that I'd lived many times before. I didn't have to unlearn that this little Liza McWhorter or Sadie Richards was all there was to me. I'd experienced the vastness of my own consciousness a time or two and I'm sure that helped me accept and access the state of mind we call meditation.

"Empty the mind," Thompson would say, softly.

For most of us that's a little like saying, 'don't think of an elephant.' The vast majority of folks have never even considered going beyond the habitual clutter of thoughts. Until you've really given it a shot, you can't begin to imagine the benefits. Once I was entering that state of mental stillness on a regular basis, I found I could concentrate better on normal tasks. My mind became more receptive to new experiences. Learning seemed easier. The books Jerry shared with me became less of a chore and more like simple pleasure to read.

In all of nature, resonance plays a big part. It's the same with our minds. Because I was willing to resonate with Thompson's understanding, I quickly got comfortable with daily meditation. In no time at all it seemed a day without meditation just felt weird.

One day shortly after we made love that first time, he said to me, "So, do you want to be a Sadie or a Liza?"

I looked up from the computer. I didn't really know what to make of the question. Clearly, I wanted to be Sadie. I'd chosen the name. That's what they were calling me. "What are you getting at?"

"If there's any chance your past could show up and wreck your new life, I think we need to take precautions." He sat in the chair next to mine.

"Precautions? What kind of precautions?"

"I've been thinking we should get you some identification that shows you to be Sadie Richards. You can pick any birthday you like, but I don't think it should be your actual birthday."

"Are you serious?" This sounded like something from one of Jerry's spy movies.

"As a heart attack."

"You know how to do that?"

"I know people."

"Have you really thought about this?"

"I've given it a lot of thought."

"Isn't it dangerous. Like false identity … that's a pretty big crime isn't it? Don't people go to jail for that?"

"They do."

"Well, then …"

"Hear me out."

I nodded. "Okay."

"People do go to jail, but it's usually because they've created a fake identity in order to commit crimes. You're not a criminal. This would just be an added layer of protection. A wall separating you from your past. Like Rita said, you deserve a fresh start."

I leaned forward and hugged and kissed him.

"I've given it a lot of thought," he said.

"I trust you, Thompson. Let's do it."

A couple of weeks later Thompson handed me a brown envelope.

"What's this?"

"Your new life," he said.

Inside the envelope was a birth certificate and a social security card. "Sadie M. Richards," I read off the card. "What's the M stand for?"

"I don't know. Look at the birth certificate."

I unfolded the paper and read my new name. "Sadie Marie Richards. Marie." I said my new middle name a few times, just trying it on for size.

"That work for you?" Thompson asked.

"Yes. I kind of like the sound of it."

"I had them make you three years older," he said.

"Three years older? You rushing me into an early grave?"

He laughed. "You're twenty-one now. You're legally an adult."

"Wow!" This was all pretty exciting. Sort of made my head spin.

"Liza McWhorter is dead," Thompson said solemnly. "Long live Sadie Richards."

"Anything else we need to do?"

"Next step is driving lessons."

"I'm not sure I want to drive."

"Well, I'm not going to force you to drive. Still, I want you to learn how to drive well enough that you can pass the driver's test. You need to have a driver's license. Pretty much everybody has one. If you don't get one it'll be just a little glitch that draws attention to you."

"I see. Okay, I'll try."

That night before bed, I took out the envelope again and thought about my new identity. It felt good. I liked being Sadie Marie Richards. I put everything back in the envelope and placed it in the little cardboard box where I keep my important stuff in the top drawer of the dresser Thompson got for me. I say important stuff. Not really important with a capital 'I,' but things that are meaningful to me. Like a copy of the menu from Playa Azul, the Mexican restaurant where we ate that first night we made love. Some other little trinkets. When I was in the box I noticed the two business cards I'd stashed there; Rita's card and Joe Farrell's. I held Joe's card a moment and thought about how kind he'd been to me, giving me a ride and forty dollars that first day I struck out on my own. I made a mental note to ask Thompson if I could call him and ask him to come by for a tattoo next time he was passing through. I put both the business cards on the night stand next to Thompson's bed. *Our bed. The night stand next to our bed.* That way I'd see them in the morning and remember to follow through.

As I figured, he had no problem with me calling Joe Farrell. Thompson said he'd like to meet the guy, shake his hand and thank him for his kindness to me. Turns out the call to Joe was the very first call I ever made on the cell phone Thompson bought me. My very first cell phone. Nothing special, just an android from Metro PCS. Nothing fancy, but it does everything a more expensive phone will do and I get unlimited everything. Not that I use it for a lot of internet stuff. We have the computers for that. I do absolutely love being able to take pictures any time I want. That's a bonus for sure.

I punched in Joe's number. It rang maybe five times before it rolled over into his voice mail.

"You've reached Joseph Farrell and Farrell Transport. Please leave me a message at the tone." Short and sweet.

After the beep I said, "Hi Joe. I hope you remember me. This is Sadie. You gave me a ride to Austin a while back. I told you I wanted to be a tattoo artist. Joe, it was real nice of you to help me out the way you did, giving me the forty dollars and all. I'm just calling you, like I said I would, and inviting you to stop by next time you're in town. The name of the shop is Skin Dreams." I gave him the location and said bye. It felt good having that behind me. Joe had been the first person to help me on the road to my new life. I considered myself pretty darn blessed and I looked forward to repaying the man in some way.

After disconnecting from my call to Joe, I called Rita. I made a point of adding her to my contacts right along with Thompson, Jerry and the number to the shop. I think those were the only numbers I had in there at that point, though I may have had the number to Italia. That's the pizza place the guys like to order from.

Just one ring and Rita answered. "Hello, Sadie, I'm so glad you called me."

I was taken back a bit with her knowing it was me and everything. I was still getting used to phones, I guess. "Oh, hi! Yes, I've been wanting to call you."

"Well, I'm so glad you did. It's good to hear your voice, sweetie."

"Good to hear yours, too."

"So, tell me how everything's going."

Now, to me that just seemed like a formality. As connected as Rita is, I knew darn well she already had a good idea of how things were going. I also knew that talking was something friends did just because it felt good. And I was glad to consider her a friend. "Things are going so good. I don't really know how it could be better. I'm so happy, Rita! I keep thinking I'll wake up and find it was a dream."

She laughed. "Merrily, merrily, merrily, merrily, life is just a dream," she said. "It is a dream, child, but it's a dream you deserve and I think it'll last a long time."

"I sure hope so."

"Count on it. You've squared everything away with Thompson and Jerry? No more secrets?"

"Not a one. I can't think of anything I haven't told them. Rita it just feels so good to be accepted. The both of them are like family now. I'm lucky."

"Blessed. It's not luck. It's your destiny and you deserve it."

"Thanks. I'd like to think so."

I was confused when she said, "Please just have a seat and I'll be right with you." Then I realized she was talking to somebody else, that she was working. That was probably one of her clients waiting on her.

"Oh, you're working," I said, "I better let you go."

"I do need to go, but now that I have your number, I will call you soon. I'd like to have lunch with you so we can take our time and really visit."

"I'd love that."

"How much advance notice do you need?"

"Not much at all. Could you make it somewhere close to Skin Dreams, though? I'm not driving yet, but Thompson says he's going to teach me."

"Great. I'll call you in a couple of days and we'll set it up."

"Okay. Bye, Rita."

"Bye, dear."

I hated having to let her go, but I was totally excited about the idea of having lunch with her. Just like you see women doing in all the shows on TV. Silly, I know. It's such a little thing, but this was going to be my very first lunch with a lady friend. That's a far cry from lunches in the cafeteria at Terrell or us girls crowded around the dining table at the group home. I felt really great!

Long story short, Joe called back and seemed thrilled that I'd followed through on calling him. That made me feel almost as good as my future lunch plans with Rita. He said he'd stop by in a week or so.

I had my lunch with Rita, which was fantastic. She picked me up from the shop and took me to a tea room in an antique mall that she was fond of. "I love the old stuff," she told me. "I never know who or what I'll find hovering around a piece of antique furniture." She shared some true stories with me about ghosts that I actually found pretty frightening. Then she reminded me that Grannie was a ghost. I loved being exposed to her open-minded perspective on everything.

The meal at the tea room was served in courses, which was new to me and seemed pretty fancy. Our first course was a little salad of mixed greens with feta cheese and walnuts with balsamic vinaigrette dressing. Listen to me spouting off the menu like I was a waiter or something. But, that's how big a deal it was to me. When I was in Terrell or at the group home, I hadn't imagined I'd ever be having a nice lunch in a fancy little restaurant with a wonderful friend like Rita. I was in hog heaven as Grannie used to say. I watched Rita carefully, so I'd know how to do everything. Napkin on the lap and all that.

"So, life is good, little one?"

"Life is so good, Rita! I feel like I've died and gone to heaven."

She laughed. "You deserve everything you're experiencing. Remember that."

"I will."

"Are you making any new friends?"

"Well," I had to think about that, "I suppose so. I meet lots of folks at the shop."

"Are any of them people you'd actually consider friends? Like the two of us are friends."

"Rita," I said, "I think I could search the world over and have a hard time finding another friend like you."

She beamed. I could tell my assessment of her had warmed her heart. "I feel the same way about you, dear. I do want to stress the importance of friends. You need your own circle of friends, Sadie. People you are comfortable with and just enjoy being around."

"Next to you and Thompson, I've got to say Jerry's a really good friend. He's so smart and he encourages me to think about things I haven't considered before."

"I'm glad you have him in your life." She sipped her tea and eyed me thoughtfully. "Do you have any opportunity to meet young women? Girls … women your own age?"

Most of my acquaintances were older. I just seemed to get on better with older folks, though I hadn't given the matter a lot of thought until then. "Most of the women my age seem kind of …"

"What?"

I searched for the proper words, but didn't really find an exact fit for what I was feeling. "I don't know. Kind of empty-headed."

Her eyes widened and I could tell my comment had surprised her. "Really?" she asked. "How so?"

I gave her a quick rundown of the experience I'd had with the three girls who'd made fun of me my first day in town. "Everyone's got their eyes on their smart phones. They're texting about nothing much to people who don't really seem to be their friends. They watch silly videos and laugh about them. All their attention is focused on noise. Just plain noise. I don't see a lot of meaning in all that. Don't get me wrong. I'm glad to have the phone Thompson got me. I don't want it to be the only thing I think about all day long, though." I asked myself what words Jerry would use to describe what I meant. Then it came to me. "Superficial. I guess all that behavior just seems superficial to me. Like the waste of a mind. The waste of a lifetime. Does that make sense?"

Rita nodded. "You're an exceptional young woman," she said. "Most would just follow along with the crowd in order to have friends. Monkey see, monkey do."

"Monkey mind. Thompson's got me meditating. I think I see all that nonsense for what it really is."

"Yes. You see it clearly. Still, you need some friends your own age. We need to come up with a strategy to find you some friends who are as thoughtful as you are."

"How do we do that?" It seemed like a tall order. Until recent times, I'd had my whole life ordered and scheduled by people who thought they knew what was best for me. I was pretty proud of what I'd accomplished on my own so far, but I had no clue where I could find anyone like me. And I didn't want to gather a bunch of empty-headed girls around myself just for the sake of having friends. That was no better than the group home.

"I'll give it some thought and let you know what I come up with."

About that time, the little round lady who was serving us came and took our salad plates. Next, she put a couple of bowls of soup made from butternut squash in front of us, along with some warm sourdough bread and butter. It all smelled so good and tasted even better. I could see why Rita loved coming here, but I also saw right away that if I ate like this on anything approaching a regular basis I'd soon be as big as a barn. It was nice for an occasional treat, so long as it remained a rarity.

Rusty finally finished with his eagle tattoo after a couple more sessions. God, was it a thing of beauty! He joked that he was going to have to get a taxidermist to mount it in a frame after he died because it would be a crime to bury such a masterpiece. I could tell that made Thompson proud.

Joe showed up and let me put a small tattoo on one of his arms. He seemed so genuinely happy for me and Thompson. Thompson liked him, too. He wasn't just being polite. They had a lot in common and had no trouble at all keeping a conversation going for a good long while. When they realized both of them had a thing for deer hunting, Joe said he was going to invite us along next season to hunt on a deer lease he kept. I wasn't that thrilled about the prospect of going out in the woods to shoot defenseless animals, but I could tell Thompson really appreciated the offer. It was good to see us being an actual couple and accumulating a circle of friends. I started feeling right grown up and a little proud about it all.

Time passed. The seasons changed. I developed a group of my own clients, people who requested me as their artist of choice, even though Thompson had tons more experience. Now, I have to admit a lot of them were big, mannish lesbians who hoped they had a chance of bedding me. I tried to be friendly without misleading anybody. Thompson told me, in business you've got to use any and every advantage you have. Not that I had anything against girl on girl action, mind you. I'd had my own flirtations with the same sex thing, as I've already said. But I was happy with Thompson. I sure couldn't see any advantage in straying away from what I knew was a good thing to experiment with what was supposed to be forbidden fruit.

"You just haven't been with the right woman, yet." That was Dana Morales that said that, but I'm sure she wasn't the only one who'd thought it. Dana was a brick-layer who'd come in one day with a friend of hers. She'd taken an immediate shine to me. Sometimes she'd stick her tongue out at me in ways that I suppose were meant to arouse, but really only embarrassed me. Embarrassed me for myself and for her. I guess she was about half drunk most of the times she came in. Still, she had me do about five different tats for her. Dana was a good customer. She probably didn't realize me and Thompson were an item. We never did express any physical displays of affection at work. We were just strictly business. That was the best way to avoid any complications.

In general life was good. Thompson said a few times that I was the easiest woman to get along with that he'd ever met. Not that we didn't disagree sometimes. We did. I was careful not to let any disagreements get out of control. I still had those early childhood memories of Dan and my mother fighting. Not all the time, but often enough. And that had ended about as bad as any fight ever could. I was careful to choose my battles with Thompson. When it was something real important to me, I'd stand my ground. I think he respected the fact that I never turned a dispute into a shouting match. I think regular talks with Rita helped me keep everything in perspective.

Months passed and I kept right on adding art to my skin, my body gallery, my walking, talking art museum. These are all phrases Jerry used to describe what my physical appearance had become. Sometimes I'd stand in front of the mirror completely naked and examine my tats, remembering the rationale for each one, admiring each design and frankly trying to remember what my body had looked like before I was covered in ink. I knew I'd get old someday. My tits would sag and my muscles would turn to flab. I'd be just another wrinkled old woman covered with tattoos. Would I be repulsed by them, then? Not likely. I'd chosen each and every design with the utmost care and all of them held a special significance to me.

"Better slow down, darling," Thompson said. "If you fill up your whole body with tats in the first year, what're you going to do for the rest of your life? Suppose you get an idea of something you'd like ten years from now, but don't have an inch of skin left?"

Grudgingly, I admitted he was probably right. I tapered off a bit. Even so, I was what most would call a heavily-tattooed young lady in fairly short order. I was particularly fond of the tat I called my mandala. It was a ring that made use of signs from the zodiac and other mystical symbols. I was a little surprised one day to realize I'd been with Thompson for almost a year. I was happy. *We* were happy. Jerry, too, I think.

Chapter 17

I don't recall how it all came together exactly, but when deer season rolled around, Thompson, Rusty and Joe committed to a hunting trip together. Jerry hadn't seen his mother for a good long while and she lived in a town called Albany in Shackelford County, not far from Joe's hunting lease, so he decided to go along. The hunting lease was on some ranch land out in the middle of nowhere. Joe said the nearest town was a tiny place called Draper, Texas. While the others shot defenseless animals, Jerry figured he'd spend some time with his mom, take her out to eat and just try to be a good son for a while. I think Jerry felt a little guilty about not staying in closer touch with his mom and not being a little further along financially so he could help her. Her name was Clara. I kind of like that name, Clara, but I couldn't really say why.

I just assumed I'd stay home and keep the shop open while the boys had their fun.

But one night when we were lying in bed, before we fell asleep, Thompson said, "Sadie, would you come with us?"

"On the hunting trip?"

"Yeah."

"I don't think it's a good idea. I might be able to make some money while you're gone. I'm not keen on the idea of killing Bambi."

He frowned. "I don't expect you to understand. I can't really say I understand it myself, but it feels good to be out on the land. It makes me feel connected."

I had an insight I hadn't considered before. "Is hunting something you used to do with your father? When you were a boy."

His expression told me my question took him off guard, which was not my intention. "Yeah," he said. Just like a whisper.

"I'm not judging you," I told him, putting my hand on his shoulder. I smiled at him, but his eyes were distant and sorrowful. "I accept it's got a meaning for you that it doesn't have for me. That's all right."

"I know." He began to reminisce about some childhood hunting experiences. The stories were about things that happened on hunting trips, but the point behind the stories, what Jerry would call the subtext, was that he'd been real close with his old man and it still pained him that they weren't speaking to one another. I just let him talk and he covered a lot of ground, including his ideas about genetic memory and the chords of consciousness that are struck in men when they go out to kill animals. He talked a long time, then he fell silent.

"Why do you want me to go?" I asked him after a bit.

"Joe says Kathleen's coming along." I hadn't considered the possibility that Joe's wife might be there. "And when Rusty found out that Kathleen was coming, he said he wanted to bring his new girlfriend, Trisha."

"Oh." Now I had a clear picture of the whys and wherefores.

"You absolutely don't have to come," Thompson said. "I really don't want you to do anything you don't want to do. I think you might appreciate camping out under the stars and you'll probably enjoy getting to know the ladies. I know they're older than you, but ..."

"I'll go."

"You will?"

"Sure. I think it'll be a good experience for me. I've never camped in my life. And you're right, I would like to get to know these women. What do you know about Trish? This is the first I've heard of her."

"I don't know much at all. Rusty's only been seeing her for a few weeks. He's not one to talk a whole lot about his girlfriends. Maybe that's because he's had so many."

"Yeah. Well, count me in. You're right, I will enjoy sleeping under the stars. I guess I'd better do some research on cooking over a campfire?"

He smiled and kissed me. "I don't think you need to worry about that. By now, I'm sure Kathleen's an old hand at cooking outdoors. Besides we have gas cook stoves, so it's not that different from cooking at home."

"Easy peasey," I said, snuggling in close to him. "I'm sure I'll learn a lot from Kathleen."

"I love you." I'm not sure if his feelings came forward because I'd listened patiently to his childhood stories or if he appreciated me for being willing to go along and eager to learn from a new experience. I don't suppose he really needed a reason to say it and it's not like he'd never said it before, but he doesn't say those three words all that often.

So, now I was part of the hunting party.

I called Rita the day before we left town to let her know we would be gone a few days. She didn't answer, so I left her a voice message. "Hi, Rita. I guess you're with a client. Thompson's asked me to go along on his hunting trip, so I'll be out of touch for a few days. Let's get together next week so I can tell you all about my first time ever camping out. Bye."

I helped Thompson load everything into the truck and the next morning, after a good breakfast, we set out on the road. Thompson's truck is one of those extended cab things, so I sat up front with Thompson and Jerry sat behind us with his little bag, his laptop and a paper sack with a few books in it. We'd been driving a little while, just listening to the radio and all when I noticed Jerry was looking a little worried or maybe anxious is a better word.

"Hey," I said, "what's wrong?"

"Hmm?" He turned away from staring out the window and stared at me in a way that just wasn't like him. "Me? Nothing's wrong. Why?"

"You just don't seem yourself." He didn't say anything, but his jaw was working, muscles flexing and I would not have been surprised to hear his teeth grinding. "Come on, this is me, Jerry. You can be honest."

He smiled, but he had to force himself. It wasn't the usual Jerry smile. "I don't know what it is. I just feel unsettled. Worried."

"About what?"

"I just told you, I don't know. I'm feeling like something bad might happen."

"Aren't you happy about seeing your mama?"

"Sure. That's not the problem. I'm looking forward to hanging out with Mom."

"Well, this is a hunting trip. Accidents sometimes happen. Are you worried about the guns?"

He thought about it. "No. I don't think so. My gut is just all snarled up."

"What normally makes you feel that way? When was the last time you had that sensation?"

He took my question seriously and, again, he thought it over. "What comes to mind is being sent to the principal's office or getting pulled over by a cop."

"Clashes with authority." I was using a method of self-examination that Rita had taught me for getting to the bottom of unexpected emotions.

"I guess so, but I don't really think that's it. I suppose my mom's an authority figure. Not so much anymore. I'm really looking forward to visiting with her. It's not like she's got any axes to grind with me. It's something else."

"Any deadlines you've put off?" Jerry was pretty bad about procrastinating and turning in articles and such at the eleventh hour.

"No. I'm caught up."

Thompson cleared his throat in a way that sounded a lot like an expression of disbelief.

"No shit!" Jerry insisted. "I truly am caught up."

Thompson smirked, but I said, "I believe you. So, it's not that. What else could it be? Are you nervous about leaving all your books and DVDs behind? I know how much they mean to you."

A big smile came across his face. "You might have something there. It is hard to be away from them. I really hadn't realized how much I exist in the world of words and images, but I think you may be on to something."

"You'll just have to make do with the real world for a while, I suppose."

"I guess so." He winked at me and looked back out the window at the wide-open spaces slowly drifting by. "Maybe I'm becoming a little agoraphobic."

That was new one on me. "What's that?"

"It's a person who's pretty much afraid to be anywhere but their own home. They like their own little space and become anxious when they have to go out."

"Sounds like you," Thompson said. But he said it with a joking tone. I don't think he was serious.

"Naw. I don't think that's you, Jerry. You spend more time in your own head than most of us, but I think you enjoy people and new experiences." Again, I was using what I'd learned from Rita. *Thoughts are things.* She says that a lot. It's a good idea to counteract a person's response to a negative suggestion with a more positive suggestion. We live in the world we create with our ideas and emotions. I believe these things to be true.

"Thanks," Jerry said. He knew what I was up to and he was grateful that I cared enough to offer a positive spin. Smiling, he seemed like he was finding his way back to his usual happy self.

"And another thing; I'm glad you're so into the books and movies. Because of you, my education regarding the real world has moved along a lot faster than it would've otherwise."

"Real world?" Thompson was teasing. Like maybe none of us were living in the real world, the normal world, the setting on the dryer that no one uses.

I put on my Carl voice. "I reckon I meant life outside the nervous hospital. Mmm hmm."

We all laughed.

Settling back in to our own quiet thoughts we drove on for a while. Thompson's always fine with silence. For him a road trip's no different than any other time in that regard. He pretty much only talks when it's necessary. Unlike me and Jerry, he doesn't get any pleasure from talking just for the hell of it. Jerry and me could talk for hours about a bunch of stuff that doesn't amount to a hill of beans, just because we enjoy it. Thompson never does that. I'm pretty sure even the thought of doing that would make him weary. So, he was fine with just steering the truck and peering out at the prairie lands all around us. There wasn't much to interest the wandering eye between Austin and Albany. Jerry took out one of his books and started reading, so I figured I'd do the same. I'd brought along an old copy of a book called *The Elementals* about a wealthy family in the deep South that go on vacation to some remote houses they own. One of the main characters has a sort of weird relationship with his daughter and some dark spirits are trying to destroy the family. I'd read seven books since Jerry had loaned me *Love Story*. I don't suppose that makes me a certified bookworm or anything, not like Jerry for sure, but I was proud of my accomplishments and I could tell the reading was changing the way I thought and the way I talked.

We stopped in a little town called Santa Anna because everyone was ready for a break. All of us hit the restroom and Thompson topped off the gas tank mainly because he felt obligated to buy something since all three of us used the facilities. That's the business man in him. He doesn't like it when people wander into Skin Dreams wanting to take a piss, so he figures no one else likes it either. I guess you call that integrity.

I'd noticed earlier we'd driven through some areas where there was no cell phone reception. After I peed, my phone chirped. I guess we were near a cell tower. It said I had a new voice mail. While I waited for Thompson and Jerry I listened to the new message.

"Hi, Sadie." It was Rita. "I am so sorry I missed your call and even sorrier I didn't get to talk with you before you headed out. I have a feeling. I don't like to use the word 'bad.' You know that, but I feel you need to be extra careful on this trip. I've tried and tried to get a fix on what it is that's setting off the alarm bells, but I'm coming up blank. It's almost like something is blocking me. Anyway, this thing that could happen feels very, very serious. I sense you'll be fine, but it could be a very rough time. Wish I could tell you more, sweetheart. Keep your grannie close to you. And call me as soon as you're back in town. Bye for now."

Now, that troubled me. She was trying to put the most positive spin on it, but it was clear from the sound of her voice that this feeling was causing her real distress. I sat down and said a prayer of protection I'd heard her use. Then I said, "Hey, Grannie, you with me?"

"Yes, darling," was the response I got back, but it had a faraway feel to it. It felt like the way words come to you when someone's talking to you from the other end of a tunnel.

Thompson walked out of the store about then and caught me cogitating. "What's wrong?" he asked.

"Oh, I got a message from Rita. She said she had an uneasy feeling about this trip. She wants us to be extra careful and be alert for potential problems."

"Any specific kind of problem?"

"No. She couldn't really pin it down."

"The guns, I guess."

"Hunting accidents do happen. Even with experienced hunters."

"I'll be super careful."

"Good."

Jerry came out of the store with a big bag of cheese puffs. "Snack?" he asked, holding the open bag in front of me.

"Sure," I said, grabbing a handful. I love those things. They're addictive. Once you chew them up, they pretty much break down to a mouthful of nothing. I guess that's because they're mostly air, hence the name 'cheese puffs.'

"Thompson?" He poked the bag in Thompson's direction.

"Naw."

"How can you turn down cheese puffs?" Jerry seemed sincerely puzzled as he munched away like a hamster filling his pouches.

"Yeah. They're the best," I agreed, grabbing more from the bag.

"I don't want to get orange stuff all over my steering wheel," he replied, walking toward the truck. "And I'd appreciate it if you two would try to be careful. Did you grab any napkins?"

"Nope. Didn't think about it," Jerry said before sucking the orange stains off his fingertips.

Thompson watched him with a touch of disgust. "See what I mean? Now you'll be getting orange crap mixed with your spit all over the cab of my truck. It's gross."

Jerry stared, dumbfounded, like a kid who couldn't understand why he was being scolded.

"I'll get some napkins," I said. I popped back inside the store and came back with a healthy handful of white napkins. I gave Jerry half.

When we were back in the truck, I said, "You're not really upset by the fact that we're eating cheese puffs are you?"

"No. Not really. Just keep the mess to a minimum, would you?"

"Sure. I know you love your truck and I will personally clean every surface of any residue."

"Good."

I leaned over and gave him a kiss right on the lips. Which he appreciated, but then he checked himself in the rearview mirror, licking his lips to be sure he had no orange crumbs.

"Give me some more." I reached over the seat and filled my hand with a nice pile of those delicious cheesy air-filled snacks.

Thompson groaned, rolled his eyes and we hit the road again.

Jerry's mother's house was a small gray square-looking thing with those old-fashioned asbestos shingles all over the outside of it. It had a narrow driveway leading into a carport, but there was no car. I wondered how she got to the grocery store or church or the doctor. I suppose she had friends who helped her out.

As we pulled in, she came out on the porch. That's something I remember Grannie doing back when she was alive. I suppose that was common back in the days when most folks lived on farms. It's pretty rare now for someone to come out on their porch as soon as you pull up. I imagined she was eager to see Jerry. It had been a while.

Jerry grabbed his stuff and went directly to her. Setting his stuff down on the porch he gave her a big hug. Jerry's not what you'd call a big man, though he's pudgy, but he sort of engulfed his little mother with that hug. She was tiny and frail-looking. Her glasses were of a style I'd only seen on one of the cafeteria ladies at Terrell. The lenses were thick, and magnified her eyes to an unnatural size.

"How are you, Mom?" Jerry asked pulling away from her and giving her the once over.

"I'm fine. I'm just so glad to see you. I've been anxious for your visit."

"It's good to be here."

By this time, Thompson and I were approaching the porch.

"Hi, Clara," Thompson said.

"Thompson, how are you?" Her eyes rested on him for just a minute, then she was taking me in. She scrutinized me from head to toe. I reckon she was wondering why a girl my age had so many tattoos.

"I'm doing good," Thompson told her. "Clara, this is Sadie."

"Hi, Clara." I gave her a little wave.

"Sadie. Pleased to meet you." Her head bobbed in a way that was probably as automatic as her words. I didn't think for a second that she was actually pleased to meet me. More like a little nervous. Maybe she was afraid I'd steal her silverware or something. I didn't hold it against her. I just smiled and tried to send her positive energy the way Rita says to do. "Won't y'all come in and have a glass of iced tea?"

Jerry looked at us. "You two got time for a visit?"

Thompson shrugged in my direction. "Sure. I'd love a glass of tea."

"You bet," I said, smiling at Clara.

She led us into the tiny living room and told us to sit on the sofa.

"I'm just going to put my stuff away," Jerry told us before he disappeared into another room.

The place was tidy. That's what Grannie would've called it. There were little handmade doilies on the arms of the sofa. All the furniture in the room looked to be antique. I felt like I was sitting down in a room from another era, like maybe we'd gone back in time to 1920 or something. The smell of mothballs had settled into everything.

Clara came back from the kitchen with a pitcher of tea and four glasses filled with ice cubes on a tray. She put these down on the coffee table in front of me and

Thompson. There was a sugar bowl and some long-handled teaspoons on the tray, too.

"Thanks, Clara," Thompson said, pouring one of the glasses full of tea. He handed the glass to me and poured another for himself.

Jerry came back in the room and sat in an old brown chair that made a funny noise when he put his weight into it.

"How was your drive?" Clara asked, pouring the other two glasses full of tea.

"It was pleasant," Thompson answered. "No problems. Just smooth sailing."

"Well, I'm glad to hear that." Clara turned her magnified eyes toward me. "Are you a deer hunter, too?"

I laughed. "No ma'am. The other hunters were bringing their ladies, so I decided to come along."

"I see," she said it quietly. I wasn't sure if she was judging me for coming along or not. From her style of clothing and the looks of the house I'd say she was just following in the pattern established by her mother before her. Like she never had an idea of her own or an inclination to update anything. Maybe it was as simple as she just never had the money to do anything different. That can happen. She looked pretty old to have a son Jerry's age. And I'd never heard Jerry say anything about his father. I was curious and made a mental note to ask Jerry some questions in the future.

"What's the latest news in your world, Mom?" Jerry asked, taking a sip from his tea.

"Oh, nothing too interesting. You know things here in Albany just toddle on like they always have. Greta had to have cataract surgery." With a little gentle steering from Jerry, Clara filled us in on the ailments of her friends and the new minister of music at her church. The old supermarket she'd shopped at for years had closed down and now she had to drive farther and pay more for her groceries. A former classmate of Jerry's had been elected mayor of the town. After about half an hour I knew more about the goings on in Albany than I ever did about current events in Austin.

"That was a fine glass of tea," Thompson said. "I think we'd better be moving on."

"So soon?" Clara asked, but that, too, seemed like a formality. She wanted some one-on-one time with her boy, I expected.

As we moved toward the front door, I noticed her old-fashioned telephone on a little table near a window looking out on the street. Then I saw an old photograph hanging on the wall above the phone. The picture showed a group of women gathered around a table with a bunch of hand-made quilts laid out in front of them.

"Are you a quilter?" I asked Clara.

She seemed surprised by the enthusiasm in my voice. "Not so much anymore, but I used to quilt quite a bit."

"Mom won some ribbons for quilting back in the day," Jerry said.

"Do you quilt, hon?" she asked me.

"No, not yet. But it's a skill I intend to learn sometime. My grandmother used to quilt."

"It does bring a great deal of satisfaction," Clara commented, staring at the photo on the wall.

"Where was this picture taken?"

"That was at the quilting contest at the county fair back in 1978."

Looking at that picture, my heart was filled with a surge of positive energy. Love. My heart was filled with love. Clara patted me gently on the shoulder as I stepped past her and out the front door. "Come back and visit when you can," she said.

"I will, Clara. I'm looking forward to it."

Walking to the truck I was just beaming.

"You seem to be in a fine mood," Thompson said. "You must've enjoyed talking with Clara."

"I did," I said. But I couldn't tell him the real reason I was walking on air. That photo on the wall. The woman in the center of the group, the one holding up the first-place blue ribbon over her quilt, that was my Grannie.

Chapter 18

Driving out of Albany, we headed north and passed through the little town of Draper. I was still experiencing the high I'd gotten from seeing Grannie in the photograph at Clara's place. Then I got hit by another completely unexpected blast from my past.

On the outskirts of town was a big billboard encouraging everyone to attend the Zion Hill Church of Redemption. There on that billboard, probably ten feet tall, was a likeness of my own biological father, the Reverend Archibald Gooch himself. The sight of that billboard put a lead weight in my stomach just as fast as that picture of Grannie had made my spirits soar. So, this was my hometown, where the strange journey of my life had begun. Funny, but for the life of me I never could've told you I was from Draper, Texas. How is it I could forget a thing like that? I just wanted to push that fact along with all the unpleasant memories out of my head, I expect.

Thompson picked up right away on my change of mood. "What's wrong?"

I didn't answer him straight off. How much did I really want to talk about the man who made my mother pregnant? The man who wanted nothing to do with her. Or me. I was committed to being truthful, transparent and sincere with Thompson, just like Rita had suggested, but I didn't really want to do or say anything that would put a damper on our weekend trip.

"Come on, Sadie. What is it?"

I opted for the truthful approach, knowing I'd be glad I did later, even if it brought up some negative emotions in the short term.

"That billboard back there."

"Yeah?"

"It was for the Zion Hill Church of Redemption. That big old fellow on it was Archibald Gooch, my real daddy."

Thompson glanced over at me, eyes wide and uncertain. Seemed like he didn't know what to say at first. "So, this is where you're from? Draper? This is where you ... where everything happened?"

"Yep, 'fraid so."

"Well, I'll be damned."

"Don't talk that way," I said. "You know what Rita says about choosing your words carefully."

"Sorry," he said. He pulled his truck over onto the shoulder and put it in park. "You going to be okay?"

"Sure."

He looked at me, a little doubtful.

"Yes, of course, I'll be fine. This doesn't change anything. Besides that's all ancient history."

"I guess this is what Rita was picking up on?"

"I suppose so." I hadn't come around to thinking about that until Thompson said it.

"Sadie, I'm sorry I pushed you into coming on this trip. If I'd had any idea about this, I would've insisted you stay home."

"All in all, I believe this trip is for the best," I said. Then I told him about seeing Grannie in that photo at Clara's place.

"No shit?" He grinned. "This really is something, you know?"

"Yes, it's the universe's way of tying up some loose ends, maybe. That's what I think Rita would say anyway."

"Mmm hmm. How wild that a friend from Oklahoma would have a deer lease in Texas; just the very part of Texas you were born in! Crazy."

"Crazy," I agreed.

"You want to look this guy up? Introduce yourself?"

That was one prospect that had never entered my mind. "No! Why would I do that?"

"He's your father. Maybe you want him to know. I think a lot of people in the same situation would want to have a face to face with their father."

"Maybe so, but not me."

"You sure?"

"Pretty sure, Thompson."

"Well, if you change your mind ..."

There was a loud squawk from behind us. We both looked back and saw a police vehicle had pulled in behind us.

"What the hell does he want?" Thompson muttered. Then he fished out the wallet from his hip pocket, anticipating that the officer might ask for it.

The man in his blue uniform and dark sunglasses approached the driver's side window as Thompson rolled it down.

"Hello, folks," he said, lowering himself down a little so he could get a good look at both our faces.

"Everything okay?" His eyes lingered a long time on me. Something about his grin was off-putting, but I just smiled.

"Oh, yeah. Everything's fine."

"Can I see your driver's license, sir?"

"Sure." Thompson handed him the license.

The deputy looked at it a good long while. "What brings you to Draper?" he asked.

"Deer hunting. Our friend Joe Farrell invited us out to his deer lease for the weekend."

"Farrell. All right. Just sit tight for a minute."

"Is there a problem?" Thompson asked.

"Just sit tight," the man repeated.

He walked back to his cop car and got on his radio.

"I guess he's running our plate number just on general principles."

"We weren't doing anything wrong, were we?"

"No. He's just trying to let us know who's boss in this town."

"Let him be boss," I said. "Don't say anything to ruffle his feathers."

"I won't."

The officer came back and pushed the driver's license through the open window. "All right, Mr. Travers," he said. "You folks have a safe weekend."

"Thank you," Thompson told him, sliding his license back into the billfold.

The grinning cop leaned down and looked at me. Pointing a finger, he made a clicking sound with his mouth. Then he turned and walked back to his car.

"Jerk," Thompson muttered.

"That wasn't so bad," I said, touching the back of his hand.

"No. Just typical. These backwoods cops have too much testosterone and a lot of time on their hands. Not enough brains."

"Let's just get back on our way."

"Yes, ma'am." Thompson pulled back onto the highway. I kept my eyes open for more signs featuring brother Archibald Gooch. There weren't any more. But I did see three billboards featuring a toothy red-headed politician named Terry Trumbull. He was running for the State Senate and wanted to make the great state of Texas even greater.

By the time we made it out to Joe's deer lease the others had been there a good long while. Their tents were set up and a smoking grill sizzled with a lot of great-smelling cuts of meat. We got out and everybody introduced themselves all around. Joe's wife Kathleen made me feel real welcome by giving me a big hug and fussing over me a little, more like a mom or a big sister than a friend. Rusty gave me a hug, too and introduced me to Trish. Trish was friendly enough, but not as out-there with it as Kathleen. She was in her late thirties I guessed and based on the lines in her face and her overall vibe I'd say she was a pretty heavy drinker, in the same league as Rusty. Of course, that made perfect sense. It wasn't likely that a sober lady would hook up with a man like Rusty. I was just glad that he had someone now. Even alcoholics need companionship, you know.

Joe and Rusty helped Thompson set up our tent while I did some small talking with Kathleen and Trish and anything I could to help fix dinner. By the time the sun had set, we were all huddled around the table with a plate of good food. Everybody else was drinking beer or some other style of alcohol. I just had a bottle of water. The fresh air, friendly company and great food did a lot to lift my spirits back up. The darkness settled over us and I could see more stars than I'd ever seen before.

"The stars. They're so beautiful," I said. "I don't think I've ever seen so many."

"Yeah. We're in a pretty good dark sky area," Joe said. "I should've brought my telescope. Out here you can get a really good view of Mars and Jupiter."

"Really?" I would've liked to look at those planets for sure.

"Next time you all come out here I'll make a point of bringing the telescope."

"I'd like that."

We stayed up a good long while chatting about this and that. Trish wanted to know about the tattoo shop, what it was like working there. She seemed impressed that I was a skin artist. I guess I felt a little flattered. I quizzed Kathleen about the seasoning she'd used on the meat. It truly was delicious. The men talked about hunting and told a few jokes. Finally, we split up and crawled into our separate tents.

It wasn't long at all before we could clearly hear Rusty and Trish 'getting frisky' as Thompson put it.

"You think they know everyone can hear them?" I whispered.

"As much as those two drank, I think they're beyond caring," he answered. Then he kissed me and pretty soon we were getting frisky ourselves. Plenty of passion, but not nearly as noisy as Rusty and Trish. The cool, fresh night air seemed to make my skin just that much more alive and sensitive to his caresses. When he nibbled at my nipples, I felt this fine tingling all through my body. He turned me on my side and slid himself inside me using a position we'd never done before. It felt like he was deeper in me than was humanly possible. I buried my face in my pillow and bit my cheek to keep from crying out. But I didn't want him to stop. And for a long time, he didn't. I was drenched and making wet little noises as his body slapped against mine and my labia tugged at his shaft. Then he let out a gasp and I felt his muscles going from tense to relaxed. He gave me one final wet kiss, then curled up around me. The smell of us and the scents coming from the natural countryside gave me a sense of well-being like I can't even describe.

Soon, I could tell by his heavy breathing that he was deep in sleep. I don't think it was long before I followed him into slumber.

I am at the river, tending my fig trees. That's the way it usually starts. The smell of the water and the trees and the sense of fulfillment I get from growing figs is hard to explain to a modern human. I pull a ripe fig from a tree and taste it. Sweet. Heavenly. I look around me and experience a sense of pride that all the trees within eyesight are mine. Golden light falls like a shimmering blanket across the landscape, making the leaves on the trees explode with a surreal greenness. The spirit of the earth is palpable. The harvest is a good one this year.

Then I hear the blast of trumpets. War horns to the north. When I look, I see the sky is red with flames and I know I must go toward the blaze of firelight. The golden sunlight transitions to darkness, except for the flickering red glow on the horizon. I walk toward the north, experiencing a growing sense of dread with every step. The cries of men, women, children and animals fill the air, broadcasting their torment. I hear the clash and clang of weapons; I can smell blood in the air and I sense the lust for killing that is sweeping through the land. The finer desires of humanity have been swept aside by this powerful dark force hungry for death and destruction.

First there are one or two at the roadside, then many. Eventually, I am wading through the carnage of a great war. I come to a rocky gully filled with bodies of civilians and soldiers, all tangled and heaped together. In places I see groups of souls hovering over the bodies. They have not yet realized they are dead but stand in powerless confusion.

Harsh crying to my left. I see children being led away to slavery. As I make eye contact with each one, I peer into their futures and wince at the perversions to which they will be subjected. I cover my face and cry.

A comforting hand falls on my shoulder. I open my eyes to see Amos. He smiles at me. I am him. He is me. He is me from then, comforting the me from now. Then I see both of us standing on a hill overlooking the bloody plain below where thousands of ghostly soldiers are acting out a battle of incredible savagery. A spirit, dark and malevolent moves over the place, reveling in the destruction it begets by manipulating the minds of men. The torment, the pain and the hopelessness of the victims of war are delicious in the mouth of the beast.

"Is this the way it was?" the now-me, Sadie, asks Amos, the then-me.

"This is the way it *is*," I answer myself.

An enormous dark mouth with shark teeth swoops down from the sky, swallowing everything as far as I can see. I turn to run, but Amos holds my arm tightly. He forces me to wait, to stand my ground. I am like a frightened animal, frantically trying to break free from a cage. Amos smiles and holds me even tighter. The darkness falls over us and we are sucked into the hungry mouth of evil.

I jump awake.

Thompson was kneeling beside me in the tent.

"Shhh," he said. "Seemed like you were having a bad dream."

"Yeah." I hugged him tight.

"Are you all right?"

My mouth was dry, my mind foggy, the fear I'd experienced still present in ghostly form, but fading fast. "Yeah," I repeated.

"It's time for me to head out with the guys," he said. "I should be back by mid-morning."

"Where will you be?" I rubbed the grainy dry things from the corners of my eyes.

"We'll hike about a mile north of here. Not far really."

"Okay." I kissed him. "Sorry my breath stinks," I said noticing my morning breath.

He kissed me again. "You taste fine to me."

"Be careful."

"I will. If you hear a gunshot, don't be scared. That'll probably mean we've got a deer."

"Poor Bambi," I muttered.

He laughed. "Okay, sleepy head. Why don't you try to get some more sleep?"

"Is Kathleen awake?"

"Yeah. She made some coffee for us, but I think she's about to lie back down."

"Okay. I love you," I said, falling back among the blankets in our tent.

"Love you, too, sweetie." Then he was gone and I was left there smelling the cool damp air of the night.

Chapter 19

I woke for the second time that morning to the sound of gunfire. A single shot. I remembered what Thompson had said, so I wasn't bothered. I stretched and crawled out of my tent. Kathleen was seated at the table, sipping coffee.

"Morning, hon," she said. "Want a cup of coffee?"

"I sure do."

Kathleen poured me a cup and I sat down across from her.

"Thanks."

"Don't mention it. Sleep well?"

Actually, I had slept pretty well despite my nightmare. I wasn't inclined to tell my new friend about it. If I mentioned being the reincarnation of Amos, the biblical prophet, before you could whistle *Dixie*, I'd be telling her about the nervous hospital and all that mess. Somehow, I didn't think an imitation of Billy Bob Thornton as Carl would make everything okay. It was just too much to deal with before I'd even had my first cup of coffee. So, I said, "Yeah. How about you?"

"Oh, yes! I love it out here. I always sleep like a baby."

"It is nice. There are so many smells. And that cool breeze last night."

She seemed pleased that I was tuned in to the pleasures of camping. "A little bit of heaven, wasn't it?"

"Mmm hmm."

"Joe and I talk about retiring out in the country someday."

"That sounds nice."

"Yeah. I hope we're able to make it happen. I'd like to be in the mountains somewhere. Maybe Colorado."

"How about Trish?" I asked. "She up yet?"

Kathleen lowered her voice. "She's feeling a little under the weather. She got up a while ago to pee, but I could tell old man alcohol had put a hurt on her."

I nodded.

"I gave her some aspirin and she went back to her tent."

"Good. Hope she feels better when she gets back up."

Just then a shot sounded like rolling thunder from the distant woods.

"Two shots," I said. "That mean they've killed two deer?"

"Could be. Every shot doesn't necessarily mean a kill."

"How do you feel about it? The killing I mean?"

She gave a thoughtful frown and shook her head. "I got no problem with it. It's just something humans do. Those steaks we ate last night were living cows not long ago."

"Yeah. I know. It just seems a little different to go out in the woods with the intent to kill. Some wild thing that has no sense of what's coming … you know?" I could tell she was thinking I was just responding in an immature way. "Sorry. It's just my first time on a hunting trip. I have nothing against it either, really. I just never even thought about it before."

"So, your family never did any hunting, eh? How about fishing? You are a Texas girl, aren't you?"

Her question made me smile. "Yes, I'm a Texas girl. I really don't know about the hunting and fishing though. My father died when I was tiny."

"You poor thing. I had no idea."

I was sitting there wondering what I would say next when a shot rang out. We both looked in the direction it had come from. Then another shot. And then it was like all hell broke loose. Shots were ringing like fireworks on the fourth of July.

"Good lord," I said, laughing, "did they find a whole herd of deer?"

But Kathleen wasn't smiling. Her eyes were big and she looked terrified.

"Kathleen, what's wrong?"

"Something's not right." There was a catch in her voice.

"Not right?"

"That was too many shots. There's no good reason why they'd be firing so many shots."

"Really?"

"Yeah." She stared at me, her breath coming in gulps. A tear rolled down her face.

"What should we do?" My heart was starting to beat faster.

"I don't know. This has never happened before. I just can't imagine …"

"Should we go to town and get help?" My mind was racing. If something was wrong, I wanted to do something about it right away.

"No … not yet. We'll wait a little bit and see if they come back. It's getting close to mid-morning anyway."

I had the sense she was maybe kidding herself, like trying to hide what she was really thinking from both of us. "I'll wait a bit," I said, "but if they don't come back soon, I'm walking over that way to take a look."

Kathleen just stared at me with terrified eyes.

"Okay? Kathleen?" I didn't want her drifting off to fear land.

She nodded vigorously.

Waiting that next thirty minutes was one of the hardest things I've ever done.

I stood up. "I'm going. If something bad has happened, it won't be good to wait any longer." I started to walk north.

"Wait." I thought she was going to try to talk me out of going, but that wasn't it at all. "Here," she said, digging through a box beside Joe's truck. She pulled out a handgun. "You may need this."

I took the gun from her.

"Ever shot a gun?"

I shook my head. She quickly went through how to take the safety off. "It's a revolver, so you just point and shoot."

"Okay. Say a prayer that this is all a misunderstanding," I told her.

"I will."

As I walked away, she told me a few landmarks to watch for; a big red oak alongside a fence, then a break in the fence where I could walk through. The path would lead down to a creek bed that was usually dry. If I walked left along the creek I'd come to the spot where the deer blind was after a few minutes. She warned me to keep quiet and have that gun ready to use if I needed it.

So, I walked fast across that land I didn't know. All the way I wondered what I'd find. I suspected whatever it was it would not be good, but I couldn't form a clear picture of what might have caused all the shooting. I tried to be quiet, but I hurried on just the same. The gun felt heavy and hot in my hand. What would I find that would make me have to use it? I called on Grannie and she responded, but from a great distance. This frustrated me all the more. She was paying attention to what was happening here, but she couldn't come in close like she normally would. Something was holding her back. A barrier had been erected between us.

Everything played out just like Kathleen had said they would. Her instructions were good. After I'd walked along the creek bed a good while I came to a place where I could tell the men had been. There was a jacket on the ground. It was Joe's. A little further on I found a thermos. I crept quiet like, looking this way and that, holding the gun out in front of me the way I'd seen folks do it in the movies. I found the deer blind. It was shot full of holes and I saw blood on it. There were brass shells from spent bullets scattered all around.

I heard a groan. Real slow like I crept toward it. When I rounded a big oak tree, I saw Rusty slumped over against it. I rushed over and knelt beside him, which wasn't a good thing to do because it scared him and he let out a grunt. I think it was only a grunt because he didn't have the strength to scream.

"Rusty, it's okay. It's me, Sadie."

"Sadie?" His voice was weak, dry, whispery.

"Yeah."

"Sadie, can you get me a swaller of water? I'm so dry." The words came out of him real slow and the sound of his voice reminded me of dead autumn leaves stirring in a breeze.

"Where's the water?"

He raised a hand and pointed. I remembered the thermos I'd seen and I hoped it was water, not coffee. I ran back to it and picked it up, unscrewing the lid. It was water, thank God. I went back and helped him pour some into his mouth. It looked like a jolt of pain went through him when he swallowed. He coughed. "That's better," he said. "Give me more."

I tilted the open thermos up and filled his mouth with water. He sputtered but got most of it down. Again, he winced with pain.

"Can you tell me what happened?" I asked him.

"Over there ..." He pointed. "We found the girl." It was hard for him to talk. I looked down and saw that the shirt under his jacket was drenched in blood. That made me gasp, but I put a hand over my mouth to shush myself. I didn't want to make matters worse by carrying on. "I guess they came back here when they heard us shooting. I don't know why they did that to her." Rusty coughed hard and blood came out of his mouth. I wiped it away with my sleeve.

"Rusty, what happened to Joe and Thompson?"

"Thompson? I don't know ... they were still standing when I went down." He laughed. Of all things to do when he was bleeding to death, he laughed! "I'm all shot up, Sadie," he said real soft.

"I see that. Rusty, listen. I'm going for help. I want you to hang on, okay?"

"Help? What kind of help?"

"I'm going back to town to get the police."

He coughed hard and big drops of blood hit my jacket.

"Sorry," he said, noticing the blood he'd spit on me. "Can't do that. No police."

"No police?"

"No. Some of them were police."

"Police?"

"The ones who shot me. They were cops."

"Oh, Rusty, what's happening? I don't understand."

He forced a smile. "I don't get it, either. Why'd they have to do that to the girl?" He raised his finger again and pointed in the same direction he'd done before.

"There's a girl over there?"

"They killed her." He started coughing again and I thought he would never stop. When he did, I wiped the blood from his mouth.

"More water?" He nodded, so I poured a little bit in his mouth. "Rusty will you please try to hang on? I'm going to see if I can get one of the trucks down here to you."

"Remember?" It was a real struggle for him to talk. "Remember my bad dreams?"

"Yeah."

"Thanks for praying for me. It was a warning. Should've listened."

"Oh, Rusty …" My voice caught in my throat and I struggled not to bust out bawling.

His eyes got a faraway look and then he sort of whispered like he was trying to sing, "Welcome to the party. We're all just papers in the wind … run …"

Then he was gone. His whole body went limp and I knew his soul had left.

"Damn it!" I didn't want Rusty to be dead. Where were Joe and Thompson? Were they dead, too? I felt sick and helpless.

I heard Grannie calling from far away, "Get up on your feet, girl."

I stood up, wiped tears away from my eyes and walked toward the direction Rusty had pointed. I didn't have to go far. There was a big oak tree with stones laid around it in a pattern. A naked woman about my age was posed on her knees, with her hands nailed to a big board that had been attached to the tree with rope. Small deer antlers had been tied to her head with bands of leather, something like a crown or a head dress you'd see a native American wearing in a western movie. Her throat was cut and her eyes were gone. Blood ran from her eye sockets, like tears down her cheeks. A wide stream of caking blood reddened her chest and stained her pubic hair. The sickest thing was that she looked like she was smiling.

I threw up. I couldn't help it.

What kind of insane people would do this? Cops! Rusty had said at least some of them were cops. If the police were in on this, what was I going to do? I took the safety off on the pistol. I didn't care now if I accidentally discharged the weapon or not. After what I'd seen I was ready to shoot at anything or anybody I didn't know.

Cops!

I walked back as quickly as I could to the campsite. I didn't worry about making noise. When I came out of the trees, I saw Kathleen still sitting where I'd seen her last. I started to call out to her, but then thought better of it. I rushed toward her trying to formulate exactly what I'd say, how I'd explain what had happened. I realized even I didn't really know what had happened. I had no idea where Joe and Thompson were. Only that Rusty was dead and policemen had killed him. And the poor girl with the deer antlers. I guess it was cops that had done that to her. I was angry and sick. Sick and angry!

Kathleen's back was still toward me when I rushed into the camp.

"Something really bad's happened," I said. She didn't turn toward me. For an instant I thought she was dead, but I could see her shoulders quivering like she was crying. Maybe, I thought, she was too shook up to respond. I'd better be gentle with her. I walked around to the front of her. She raised her head and that's when I saw the tape over her mouth. Her eyes were wide with terror.

"Oh, my god …" The words just jumped out of me. Then I saw Trish all bloodied and lifeless on the ground in front of her tent.

Someone grabbed me from behind and put a big wad of cotton batting over my face. I knew it was drenched in some kind of chemical that would leave me unconscious. I struggled and tried not to breath, but it was no use. Whoever it was behind me had me trapped. I inhaled the stuff on the cotton, cursing myself for not being able to fight harder and hold my breath longer. The last thing I saw before I lost consciousness was a cop shooting Kathleen in the back of the head. She went limp and he grinned at me. I knew that grin. It was the same officer who'd asked for Thompson's driver's license at the side of the highway in Draper.

Chapter 20

When I woke up my skull was pounding with a hellacious headache. It was dark, but I could hear people moving around me and a few words spoken kind of quiet. Right away I remembered that cop bastard shooting Kathleen in the head. I realized they'd taken me somewhere and I was a captive. Maybe, I hoped, Thompson and Joe were in the same place and I'd find them. Feeling around, I realized my hands weren't tied. It seems I'd been rolled up tight in a blanket and just dropped off in a corner somewhere. Ever so slowly I loosened the blanket around me, gradually got my hands up around my face so I could pull it down and have a look at my surroundings.

I'd never been in a basement that I could recall, but that's what I imagined this place to be. It was a big square room with a stairway leading up along one wall to a floor above. The ceiling wasn't finished out; you could see the studs that supported the floor above. The walls around me were half brick and the other half concrete. All around me were bodies, just heaped willy-nilly on the floor, mostly women, but some young boys, too. They all seemed to be drugged, not moving, but not dead.

There were maybe six men moving around among the unconscious captives. Two of them had guns slung over their shoulders. The kind of guns you'd see in one of Jerry's action DVDs. They had big clips and looked like they could spit bullets faster than you could say Jack Robinson. You know, fully automatic guns. The four men without guns were moving around through the bodies, talking to one another and making notes on a clipboard. All six of the men were brown-skinned and I guessed they were Mexican. They spoke Spanish part of the time and English a bit, too.

One of them nudged a girl with his foot and said, "Trumbull gets this one. She's the kind he likes."

The guy with the clipboard made a note and hollered out something in Spanish. A couple of young women entered the room from behind a curtain. I hadn't noticed the curtain before. As they swept in, it seemed like that was a hallway leading off to God knows where. The two women were frightened, intimidated by the men and I could tell those guys were enjoying it. They barked some more Spanish at the women and laughed at the fear they saw in the women's eyes. The two women picked up the girl from the floor. It sickened me to see that the little girl was probably only ten or eleven. She was small and skinny and her head sort of lolled around on her neck. She tried to say something in Spanish, but one of the women shushed her. They held her up on her feet and walked her out of the room, through the curtained doorway.

Those men went through the room making an appraisal of every poor soul lying on that floor.

Sometimes one of them would say, "Get rid of that one." Then someone would come in and drag the rejected one out through the curtain. They weren't careful with them at all. I figured if they'd been rejected that meant they were worthless, damaged goods, soon to be dead.

As they worked their way through the room, I couldn't think of anything to do except pretend I was still unconscious. I watched through squinted eyes as they worked their way closer and closer. When they were right on top of me, I closed my eyes and did my best to look like I was out of it. One of them kicked at me through the blanket and rattled off a question I couldn't understand. Another one answered in Spanish, but I caught the word 'gringo.' I knew this was a sort of slang term for white guys among the Mexicans. They both laughed real hard. Then they stopped laughing right quick. I couldn't see with my eyes being closed tight, but I soon understood why they'd shut up.

"Where is she?" It was that cop. The one who'd shot Kathleen. I recognized his voice.

"She's here," one of the men answered. Then I felt another kick at me.

"Well, get her up and out of here. Take her over to the make-ready."

He didn't have to tell them twice. Right away I felt one at my shoulders and one at my feet, grabbing the blanket and lifting me off the floor. They carried me out through that curtain. I heard their boots clacking on what I imagined to be a tile floor for a good long while. Turning sharply right they carried me into a brightly lit room and then just dropped me hard on the floor.

"Hey, pendejo!" It was that same damn cop. "You damage the goods and I'm going to take it out of your hide! Comprende?"

"Sorry, boss man." One of them answered quietly.

"Get out of here," the lawman barked and I heard their boots clicking off into the distance.

"What's this?" It was the sound of a mature Mexican woman. She spoke English with a heavy accent.

"Just a little, white trash gal who ended up in the wrong place at the wrong time."

"Is this right?"

"Yeah. She ain't worth nothing. She's got more graffiti on her than a bathroom wall. None of them hot shots upstairs are going to want her. Thought I might bid on her myself."

"Oh, really?" The Mexican woman laughed. "You got a thing for illustrated women?"

"Not really. She'd be my first. She seems healthy enough, though. I imagine I could make good use of her. For a while anyway."

"Okay. If you're buying."

"I figured you'd see it that way. My money's as green as anybody's, eh?"

"True. We like your money as much as anyone's."

"I'm afraid my money ain't going to amount to much this time. Like I say, nobody else is going to buy her. I can bid low and get her all the same."

"How do you want her prepared?"

"What do you mean?"

"If we have an idea who will buy, we always try to make them more appealing. Trumbull likes them very young and submissive. No matter what he does to them he wants to believe they love it. A large dose of MDMA. See? Or if you talk about Mr. Massey. He, too, likes them young, but he wants them to be terrified when he has his way with them. Those we give a small dose of strychnine. And if we know other specific likes and dislikes, we try to oblige. A particular shade of lipstick? A certain style of clothing?"

"Oh, yeah, I get you. Well, I definitely don't want her fighting back. She's a little spitfire from what I've seen so far. Give her something that'll take the fight out of her. Clothes don't matter. She won't be wearing any while I'm making use of her."

"As you wish. Let me take a look at this girl."

Next thing I knew someone had grabbed hold of the blanket and tumbled me right out of it, spinning off onto the floor. I ventured a little peek through barely opened eyelids. It was that asshole cop. After he'd bitched at the two Mexicans for dumping me on the floor, he'd treated me no better.

He was grinning real big, looking down at me. "She's a fine-looking filly, ain't she? Why she'd want to cover her skin with all that, I couldn't say. Why would a girl want to do that?"

I caught my first glimpse of the woman. She walked with an extreme limp as she came closer to get a look at me. My first impression was that she looked a lot like Rita. She leaned down over me and at first, I thought she looked shocked. Surprise filled her eyes along with a sort of awe, then her face twisted into a very ugly expression of humor. She laughed. Loud. It was a taunting, attacking kind of laughter. Her laughter was mocking the cop. But, why?

He didn't like the sound of her laughter any more than I did. "What are you laughing about, you old bitch?"

"So, this is the one you want to own, eh? You want to fuck her? Hurt her maybe? What do you think Gooch will say about that?"

"Why the hell should I give a shit what Gooch thinks?"

The woman's expression turned very serious, very quick. "First, pendejo, Gooch is king here. Second, you try to steal his daughter."

"You stupid old hen! This ain't Gooch's daughter!"

"For anyone who has eyes to see, she is his blood. You are too stupid to notice."

The cop pulled back his fist as if he intended to smack the woman.

"Watch your mouth, old woman."

"I speak truth. If you know what you are talking about, bring Gooch in here. Let him see the one you think you wish to own. Go ahead. Hit me. Gooch will be doing much worse to you, my friend."

The cop got a scared look on his face. How could the old woman know? I only knew because my mother had told me. As far as I knew, mother had never told another soul. The woman physically resembled Rita, could've been her sister. I formulated the idea that she had a way of seeing things something like Rita's way, but darker. The cop kicked around on the floor.

"We bring Gooch to take a look at her. He'll decide what is to be done," said the woman.

"Well, I'll be damned."

"Yes, you will. Go get him."

The cop hesitated.

"Go."

Like a kid being sent to his room, that police man tromped out of the room.

The woman knelt beside me. She touched my face. "He's gone, little one. You don't have to pretend to be asleep."

I opened my eyes. For an instant I thought I might ask her how she knew I was awake, but that would've just been a waste of words and she would've thought me a fool. So, I just looked at her.

She laughed. "A strange, twisted path has brought you here. Fate cannot be denied." An idea crossed her mind and she laughed out loud. "Oh, Lucinda's going to want your blood. You know that don't you?"

"I was hoping Lucinda had nothing to do with all this," I said.

She shrugged. "Ah, hope. What good is hope? It makes us want what we know cannot be." She stood up. "Can you stand, child?"

"I think so." I got up on my feet, but I was kind of shaky.

"They will be back here soon. I think I can help you, but you are going to have to trust me."

I'm sure my expression told her I did not trust her.

"For a little time only. If I am going to get you out of here, you must appear to be under my control." She stared at me waiting for a response. When I didn't say anything right away, she said, "Or you can just let them do what they will with you. I have seen many young women come and go from this room. Maybe twenty years now? Maybe more. I was young like you when I came here. Pretty. Like you. I was luckier than some. Well, I suppose that depends how you look at it, eh? Maybe the dead are luckier?"

"Okay," I said, "what do you want me to do?"

"Let's get you into this." She pointed at a wheelchair. "You must convince them you are drugged. Do you want a ... sedative?"

"Fuck no!" My head hurt enough already. I wanted my wits about me as much as possible. I realized already that if my chance for escape came, I'd have to move fast. No hesitation.

She laughed slightly. "As you wish. But, understand. These men may try to test you to see if you are drugged. They may hurt you to make sure for themselves."

"I understand," I said, settling into the wheelchair.

"They will be back soon. You must not give yourself away. If they decide to hurt ... or to kill you ... I will not be able to stop them."

I nodded. "Why are you helping me?"

She looked at me long and hard. Not the kind of look you'd say was friendly, not the sort of look you'd expect from an ally. Finally, she said, "Simple. I hate Lucinda. You have come here to kill her. You are the light side of her darkness. How much does she know about you?"

"She's seen me. I think she tried to get a homeless man to kill me in Austin."

The woman got a faraway look in her eyes. I felt she was seeing with her other vision. "Yes. And she spilled her blood on your account."

"My account?"

"Si. That was exactly one year ago to this very day. You remember, no?"

"Has it been exactly a year?"

"She called you here. She will want nothing more than to see you suffer."

"Well, I feel the same way about her right now," I said.

She laughed. "Good. Keep that fire. But you must seem drugged when they come. Comprende?"

"I understand. What's your name?"

She seemed to consider whether or not she should tell me. "I am Consuela."

"Consuela, my partner, Thompson, may have been taken. Those men killed my friend, Rusty. If Thompson's alive, where will he be?"

"Yes. He is most certainly alive."

"Really?"

"Of course. Lucinda wants him, if only to keep him from being with you."

Then we heard a ruckus coming down the hallway. It sounded like several men all talking and having a good time, like a bunch of friends at a party or a football game.

"I think each of you will find exactly what you're looking for in one of these rooms," a man said, over the hubbub of the others.

"You're a hell of a host, you know that?" someone answered.

"We aim to please."

"This is the best time I've had since I can't remember when."

"Fun's not over. We have plenty of festivities planned for tomorrow as well."

"Is Dick coming?"

"No, he sent his regrets."

"Now, that's a real shame."

"Yeah, I like the way he hunts."

"Me, too, as long as I'm standing behind him."

They all laughed, sounding like they were just outside our room. Consuela leaned close to my ear. "Shhh," she whispered, then moved away from me and pretended to busy herself with something on a counter top.

"Gentlemen, continue on down the hall. Check every option. We want you to get exactly what you have in mind. If you don't see it, ask. I trust we can fulfill any desires. Now, excuse me. I need to duck in here for a moment and take care of business." There was a murmur of pleasant responses and the group passed on down the corridor. A moment later, I heard footsteps entering our room. My heart was pounding, but I forced my breathing into a slow rhythm, trying my best to appear out of it. I didn't dare open my eyes even the smallest crack. "Consuela, what's the problem?"

I had no doubt the voice I heard belonged to Archibald Gooch. Brother Archie.

"Your blood shines from her. Not that these fools would notice," Consuela answered him.

"Ah …" There was a long pause. I heard his steps draw nearer. I could smell his overpowering cologne. "So, this is the daughter of that little tramp that married Dan McWhorter?"

His words caused my blood to boil.

"Born the same year as your own Lucinda," Consuela said, softly.

"So, this really is your daughter?" I knew that bastard's voice. It was the cop.

"I thought she was locked up. I thought she was in Terrell."

"She's a nutcase, too?"

"Shut up, Harvey," Gooch snapped. "I know you're disappointed about not getting your bargain play-toy, but there are larger concerns to be addressed here."

"Yes, sir," the cop answered, all hang dog.

"Does she know she's my blood?" Gooch asked Consuela.

"I think not," the woman answered tentatively.

"Is she good and doped?"

"Oh, yes."

I guess Brother Archie didn't want to take her word for it. The next thing I knew, he smacked my face with his open palm. Hard. I grunted. Couldn't avoid it. But I stayed all limp and didn't open my eyes. I let my head move loosely on my neck. "Yes. I'd say she's pretty well under."

"You have to hit here so hard?" the cop asked. I knew damn well his concern was all about him having to look at my bruised face, if I ended up in his hands.

"Harvey, do I need to remind you to shut your stupid mouth?"

No answer from old Harve.

"Does Lucinda know she's here?" Gooch asked.

"I have not told her," Consuela told him.

"Let's keep a lid on it for the time being. Not that it's easy to keep secrets from Lucinda, but I don't want to deal with all her demands while our guests are here. Can you keep her drugged up until I decide what to do?"

"Of course. Patron, I sense she has the gifts. Like Lucinda."

"Interesting. I suppose that's to be expected. Keep her quiet and out of the way until the boys have finished having their fun. Is it possible we could make use of her? In the circle?"

"It is possible. If Lucinda allows it."

"Leave that to me. Put her in the wine cellar. That's one place no one will accidentally stumble onto her." Then he added, with more than a hint of a threat in his voice. "Don't let the little bitch wake up, Consuela."

"No, Patron."

"Right. And Harvey, you stay the fuck away from her. Understand?"

"Yes, sir."

"Now, let's try to get through the remainder of our festival without any further disruptions."

I heard the footsteps of the two men exiting the room. I waited a good long while before risking the slightest glimpse beneath my eyelids. Consuela was glaring at me. "Good job, little one. You fooled them. But you won't fool Lucinda if she finds you. Let's get you into the wine cellar. Just play dead until we are there."

Making my body as limp as possible, I let her wheel me out of the room and on a twisting, turning journey to the wine cellar.

Chapter 21

"Where are we?" I asked Consuela once we were safely in the darkest corner of the wine cellar.

"Under the church."

"How can I get out of here? Where is Thompson?"

She raised a finger to her lips. "Shhh. This thing will not be easy. When the time comes, I will help you find your man. Tonight, after dinner they will all be in the ritual room. They will be drunk. That will be the best time."

"What will they do in the ritual room?" I remembered what Lucinda had done beside the firepit. The big ritual tonight was probably a bigger, grander version. It was certain to include calling on dark forces and some form of blood-letting. I remembered the naked corpse I'd seen in the woods, that poor eyeless woman nailed to a tree. Clearly these men would not hesitate to conduct even grander ritual sacrifices if this evening was a special night to them.

"The less you know about their rituals, the better," Consuela answered. "Do not see what you do not have to see. The dark forces they worship slip into people through the eyes. The things you see, the thoughts you have about such things, these are the paths demons walk."

Through the eyes. Is this the reason the dead woman's eyes had been removed? The memory of that ghastly smile on her dead face sent a shiver up my spine.

"How did they put a place this size under the church without everyone knowing?"

"Many do know. Those who they do not wish to know are dead."

Many know. How many? It was a terrifying thought to consider that many, perhaps even most of the people in Draper were part of this bloodthirsty cult. "This is incredible," I said, "How long has this been going on?"

"Very long. The floor of the ritual room is from a place in Iran. They say it is thousands of years old. A remnant of Babylon. This place was built by the oil men who came here in the 1920s."

"The oil men? Why?"

"They serve an ancient mistress. She gives them wealth from the black blood of the earth. They give her power and satisfy her hunger with the pain and blood of the children of men."

I thought about this. These men were a part of a conspiracy reaching back into ancient times. If this was taking place in a Podunk town like Draper, where else might there be branches of the cult? Were they everywhere? Did ancient relics, impregnated with dark energy, line the basements of buildings in Washington, D.C.? How could I fight an organized effort as potentially huge as this one? If I escaped, how could I evade others of their group? Were they controlling everything? Was my hope of freedom just a cruel joke? "Consuela, what will I do once I'm out of here? Who can I go to for help?"

She laughed a harsh laugh. It was the kind of laugh that people use to mock one another. "*If* you get out of here. *If!* You will have to rely on your inner sight. If that fails you, you will die."

I stared at her, feeling confused more than anything else. Could I trust her? Why was she helping me? Was this all just a snare they'd set to torment me? I knew anything was possible if we were dealing with dark ancient forces. I remembered my dream from the night before. Then, I wished more than anything that Grannie was there beside me. But she'd been blocked by someone or something. I already knew that. And my other ally, Rita, was seemingly blocked as well.

Finally, Consuela broke the silence. When she spoke, there was an element of compassion to her voice. The harsh edge was gone from her words. "You have been here a day. I have been here more than twenty years. I have not seen the sun since that first day I was brought here."

"I'm sorry, Consuela. If I get out of here, I'll bring help. I'll get you out, too."

"No," her expression told me she considered herself defeated. "I will never leave here. It is my destiny to die in this grave where I have lived for so long. This I have known for years. There is no escape from this pit for me. I will escape only from my body when the time comes."

I started to contradict her, but then I remembered what she'd said earlier about hope. I figured she knew more about seeing the future than I did. "I will do whatever I can for you," I said.

"Yes. I know. And I will do the same for you."

"Why are you helping me? It has to be more than your hatred of Lucinda."

"It is more. You are the light echo of your dark sister. I am the dark echo of my light sister."

"I don't understand," I said without considering her words.

"Don't be a child!" The hard edge returned to her voice. "There is no time for childish games. Now! Use your insight."

I drew a breath and tried to imagine what she meant. A vivid picture of Rita came to my mind, but a younger Rita than the woman I knew and called my friend. I wished more than anything that I could consult with Rita, feel the comfort of her words.

"Speak!" Consuela barked.

"Rita," I said, still not fully wrapping my head around what was happening.

"Yes. Rita is to me what you are to Lucinda."

I couldn't believe what she seemed to be saying. My mouth dropped open for a moment, then I said, "Rita is your sister?"

Consuela nodded. I couldn't be sure in the darkness of that wine cellar, but I thought I saw a glimmer of light reflected on tears welling in her eyes.

"Consuela! Does she know you're here?"

"I am sure she understands I am in a dark place. She may not know that I am still alive."

"I know Rita would help you if she could."

"But she cannot help me. I am here because of my choices. I chose darkness. Rita cannot change that. She cannot help me anymore than you can help Lucinda. We are playing out the echoes of many lives."

I hugged her. She let me, but only for a moment, then she pushed me away. "I am going to get some things for you."

"Things?"

"Water. Food. Light. A weapon. You will need these. I will not bring them myself. Too much I am needed to make ready the festival. I will send someone I trust."

She started away from me and I noticed the odd rhythm of her limping walk. I knew she limped because they had fractured her leg when, long ago, she'd tried to escape. I saw it clearly in my mind. "Thank you, Consuela," I called to her before she left the room. She said nothing, just paused a second, before stepping through the doorway that led to the corridor outside the wine cellar. Far down the hallway I heard a young woman cry out in pain.

I sat back down on the wheelchair. I knew that if someone just barged in suddenly, I'd need to pretend I was drugged out of my mind. Plus, my head was still throbbing from the ether or chloroform or whatever it was they'd put me out with back at our campsite. I could feel my heart beating in my chest, a sharp, stabbing beat that told me each breath could be my last. I was tempted to feel sorry for myself, but only for a moment. Self-pity wasn't going to gain my freedom. A better option was anger. Better yet would be a cool-headed position of strategic thinking, if only I could manage it.

I knew Consuela was right about one thing; I needed to use my intuition. Without it I was done. I reminded myself to step back from everything and gain a broader perspective. I needed to look at the bigger picture. I knew that I had lived before. Many times. I knew that I had died before. No doubt many of those deaths had been painful, frightening. Yet, here I was, alive again. What I needed more than anything was to trust that this lifetime had a meaning, that it served a purpose. My belief in the creator, whoever or whatever had stirred all these realities into being, would give me the strength to face whatever challenges lay ahead. I could fight. I would fight. If only to become an inconvenience to the darkness that ruled this cult.

So, I leaned back in the seat and did a few neck rotations and tried to relax my body as much as possible to open up access to my higher mind. This was just the sort of thing I did every time Thompson and I meditated together in the solarium. Solarium. That word reminded me of Consuela's claim that she had not seen the sun for over twenty years. How terrible to be deprived of the sun's healing rays for such a long time. What would that deprivation do to a body, a mind, a soul?

The familiarity of the relaxation techniques did a lot to put me in the proper frame of mind.

"Grannie," I said softly, "I know you can't get close right now, but I also know that wherever you are, you're sending me light and wanting the best for me. I trust that no matter what happens here today, I am just playing my part in a bigger drama. I'll do my part willingly. And I'll fight these evil men with my last breath, if it comes down to that."

I decided to start with my immediate surroundings. I'd assess this wine cellar, see what impressions rose into my awareness. Breathing deeply, I turned inward to the blank slate of my third eye. Images flooded in on me suddenly. I saw bricklayers building the walls. They were men of another era, dressed in shabby clothing like something from an old silent movie. In a flash I knew that three men had been killed on this very site and buried in the wall to my right. Their spirits still struggled, restlessly resisting their fate even after all these years.

There was a jump to another time. My gut told me it was just after World War II. A red-faced man in a tuxedo struck a pretty young woman in a white dress.

He knocked her down and raped her right here on the floor. I saw the events unfolding at my feet. When he was done with her a sort of panic swept through him as he considered the consequences of his actions. This was no slave brought in from a poor village. This woman was a debutante, daughter of a wealthy oil man and politician. Her name was Colleen. The man strangled her. Later he concealed her corpse in an empty keg and buried her somewhere on the grounds, out among the trees. The man was never tried for his crime, but some of Colleen's family members suspected him and had shot him down a year later when he was hunting.

There was another sudden jump forward and I saw three men, huddled close together in the cellar, discussing a new drug they were going to test on the party-goers upstairs. They were excited at the prospect of what this potent concoction would do to the minds of their guests.

"What is it?" one of the men asked, grinning like a demon.

"It's called LSD-25," a man with the hint of a foreign accent answered. I knew instantly that this man was a member of one of the government intelligence agencies. He was tasked with finding mind-control methods to use on American citizens, with the object of manipulating and enslaving their minds. He clearly loved using humans as guinea pigs; he reveled in the godlike power he exercised over others. "Put this in the punchbowl, then stand back and watch. I assure you; it will be unlike anything you've ever seen." The man had gone by many names during his life but at that moment he was known by the name Forcht. Then, I was surprised to see that he was still alive and living in an assisted-living facility in Arizona. This old man had committed many crimes and now he waited like so many other fading humans for his days to run out. He would not be punished for his acts of evil. Not in this lifetime.

My mind wandered away from Forcht and I saw a scene that I knew was happening in the here and now. Trumbull, the red-headed politician from the billboards, was out in the woods with a couple of others. They were armed and dressed like hunters, but they weren't hunting deer. Crouched in a deer blind, they drank and shot the shit until someone below sent a young boy or girl running across the field in front of them. These runners had been given drugs to make them frantic.

When one of them entered the field of view Trumbull would say, "There goes one."

They'd confer over whose turn it was, then one of them would take aim and fire.

The captives had been told if they made it across the clearing into the woods beyond, they could go free. This was a lie and a pointless one. None of them made it across the field without being shot down.

The men in the deer blind carried on conversation like they were at the skeet range or the golf course instead of killing innocent kidnapped children.

"Gooch puts on a pretty nice spread," one said.

"Yep. This is a fine resort. One of the best."

"Looking forward to picking out a plaything tonight. Something shapely and young."

"Me too. I've had it with women out in the real world. It's good to be in a place where a man can get what he wants."

"Yep. Just grab 'em by the pussy, eh?"

They all laughed.

"Hell yeah!"

"If it's good enough for the POTUS, I won't argue with it."

"There goes one. Ted, it's your turn."

My stomach knotted.

The door opened.

It's difficult to describe what happens when the mind is required to switch quickly from the intuitive to the normal state of awareness. It's like you have two different minds with an ocean of space between them. Coming back into regular consciousness is a little like struggling to wake up from a dream. When I heard that door open, my heart jumped. That expanded consciousness I was using collapsed in on itself and tumbled down with a jolt into a space somewhere deep inside me. The image that comes to mind is one of those sea anemones that live deep in the ocean. They put out all these tentacle-feeler-things into the water around them, but at the first sign of a threat, all those writhing filaments disappear back into its crusty shell. Instead of a shell, my expansive consciousness sucked back into my skull. It's not a pleasant experience.

I tried to appear unconscious and prayed I would not give myself away.

Someone crept forward and stood in front of me. "Don't be afraid. Consuela sent me."

I opened my eyes and in the dim light I saw a young woman. She was terribly thin.

"I am Lupe," she said. "Here." She opened a bag and started handing me things: a bottle of water, a sandwich, a knife and a pistol. "Eat, drink," she said. "Put the gun behind your back in your pants. Keep the knife in your boot. Careful, it is very sharp."

"Thank you," I said, taking these things onto my lap, following her instructions.

Without another word, she turned and started out of the room.

"Wait," I whispered.

"I cannot. They will kill me." She slid out the door and was gone.

I opened the cylinder on the pistol and made sure it was loaded. Wondering how they got their hands on a loaded gun, I slipped the weapon into the waistband of my pants at the small of my back. The hunting knife she had handed me was in a flimsy leather sheath. That was a good thing, because when I slipped it out and touched the blade with my thumb, I found it was razor sharp. Without that sheath It would not have been possible to hide the knife in my boot for long without cutting myself.

Twisting the plastic lid off the bottle of water I tasted it. My mouth was incredibly dry and the water seemed a gift from heaven. I was tempted to gulp it down at once, but two thoughts prevented me; I didn't know when I'd get more and I didn't fancy my options when the inevitable need to empty my bladder occurred.

I sat in my wheelchair and waited. I did not cast my consciousness to gather more information about my surroundings. I was sick enough with the knowledge I'd just gathered. My normal state of mind, alertness, was what I needed if I wanted to stay alive. I felt much better about my chances now that I was armed. Still, I was deep underground, with no idea how to make my way to the world above. If a woman like Consuela had been stuck here for decades, I knew I wasn't just going to skip right out. Suppressing any fearful thoughts, I reminded myself that my intuitive mind could be relied on to provide me with any information I required on an as-needed basis.

The waiting. That was the hardest thing.

Chapter 22

Hours passed. Finally, I did have to squat in a corner. I just couldn't hold it any longer. After I relieved myself, I sat back down in the wheelchair and waited.

The door opened and the scrawny young woman who called herself Lupe, slipped in.

"The time is now," she said.

I stood up to follow her out, but she gestured for me to stay in the chair.

"The wheelchair. It is best if someone sees us."

I sat back down. Then I went back to my unconscious act, letting my head hang back loosely.

Lupe rolled me down one corridor and then another, twisting and turning in this secret underground maze. I was in awe of the size of the place. Then she stopped suddenly in front of a set of double doors.

"In there. Your man is there." She pointed with her chin.

I stood up. "Thank you," I said, pushing through the doors and hoping it was not a trap.

The room looked like a shipping department. There were scales and packing supplies and boxes. Directly in front of me, I saw a large bay door. Was this a way out? I walked toward it, then I saw Thompson.

There were metal poles in the room, supporting the ceiling. The psychos had taken a roll of clear plastic, the kind you use to wrap pallets of goods, and they'd wrapped Thompson tightly up in a clear plastic cocoon attached to one of the poles. Bundled up that way he reminded me of a fly trapped in a spider's web. He looked unconscious. His face was bruised and I could see a fair amount of blood smeared on the inside of the plastic wrap.

"Thompson!" I whispered, stepping up to him and rubbing his face. He responded to my touch by trying to jerk away. He managed to open one eye, but the other was swollen tightly shut.

"Say…" He was trying to say Sadie, but his mouth was too dry.

"Shhh!" I touched his lips and then opened my bottle of water and raised it to his mouth. I poured very slowly. He gulped the water but sputtered and let out a groan like it hurt him to drink.

"Sadie. Glad you're here," he whispered. He looked half dead and sounded like it took his last ounce of energy to talk.

"Don't talk," I told him, "just nod or shake your head. Can you stand if I cut you free?"

"I'll try," he whispered, ignoring my instruction.

I pulled the knife out of my boot and began slicing away at the thick wrapping of plastic. When the binding started to give way, I positioned myself to help support his weight. Even so, he fell to the floor, taking me with him.

"Sorry," he groaned.

"Thompson," I said, scrambling out from under him, "do you have any broken bones?"

"Don't think so," he said. "More water."

I poured water into his mouth. As he swallowed it, I tried to assess the damage his body had sustained. In his upper torso on the left side, there was a hole. He'd been shot. I looked at his back side. The bullet had passed through, but the exit wound was not a pretty sight. There were no bone fragments and not as much blood as there might have been. I figured no major blood vessels had been hit and I prayed that his left lung was okay. Regardless, it did not seem that he'd be doing much travelling under his own steam.

"You've been shot," I said. "How bad do you think you are?"

"Hard to say," he answered, softly. "Drugs." As if to illustrate the fact that he'd been tranquilized, a stream of drool fell out of his mouth and puddled under his face on the floor.

"What about Joe? Do you know where he is?"

"Dead. Lucinda killed him ... bitch."

"That means there's just you and me," I told him. "Rusty's dead. I was with him when he passed. Kathleen and Trish, too."

He let out a growl. I wasn't sure if it was anger or pain. Probably both, actually.

"Thompson, listen to me. I'm going to hide you over there in the corner, behind those boxes. I'm going to make it look like you took off down the hallway. You follow me?"

"Smart girl," he whispered, trying to smile.

"They have every kind of drug known to man here," I said. "Maybe they have some first aid stuff. At the very least, I'm going to get you some more water. I'm guessing we can get out through the bay door?"

"Truck's outside … just like the real deal."

I put my hands under his arms and dragged him behind some large cartons and propped him up against a wall. "Here," I said, handing him the pistol.

"Where'd you get …"

I touched his lips. "Don't talk. Just rest until I get back. You'll need your energy to help me find the way out. Now, listen. I'm going to try to get Consuela out. And some of those girls they kidnapped."

"Who?"

"Consuela. She's Rita's sister. I want to help her escape."

"Sadie … "

"Thompson, please just trust me. I've got to do this."

He looked at me with his one good eye and nodded. "Just remember …"

"Remember what?" I thought he was going to tell me he loved me.

Instead, he said, "The devil's a liar."

I kissed his forehead and stacked some boxes up near his feet, so he'd be harder to spot. As I moved the boxes into place a flap shifted and I caught sight of the contents. The box was filled with human bones, all clean and bleached white. My gag reflex kicked in, but I didn't have time to be sick and not enough food in me to really throw up.

I took the blood on the plastic wrap and smudged an intermittent trail out into the hallway. Hopefully, if anyone came into this part of the compound, they'd think he went back the way I'd come. I went back to the corner and peered over the boxes down at Thompson in his little hidey hole.

"I'm leaving now," I said, "but I'll be back soon. Hold on. Get your wits back and we're going to get out of here. Okay?"

"Okay." He flinched with pain I suppose, then said, "Sadie, mark your trail."

That was a good idea. If he hadn't brought it up, I don't know if I would've thought of it on my own. I had no idea how big this damn place was. It would probably be pretty easy to get lost. Over on one of the counter tops I spotted a black marker. That would do the trick.

I said a silent prayer for Thompson's safety and I went back through the double doors into the corridor. I made my first mark on the wall beside the door frame. A small arrow pointing at the doors. Big enough that I wouldn't miss it, but small enough that others who weren't already aware of the mark might overlook it. Every time I came to a corner, I listened carefully for any sounds of activity before advancing. At each turn I left an arrow mark pointing the way back to the shipping area where Thompson was hiding. The knife was in my right hand and I carried the marker in my left.

Before long I heard voices. I paused at a corner to listen.

"This sucks," a man's voice said.

"Stop your whining," another man answered.

"They're having all the fun upstairs and we're stuck here. For what? What are we guarding? No one's ever gotten out of here."

"Hang in there. You'll get to join the party soon enough."

"Right."

Then my blood started pounding in my chest and my temples. One of them was walking toward me. I backed off a bit and leaned against the wall like I was having trouble keeping my eyes open. I stashed the marker in my hip pocket and kept the knife out of sight at my side. In seconds, the man rounded the corner, a uniformed policeman. He stopped in his tracks, his eyes big as saucers.

"Please," I said weakly, squinting at him and trying to sound completely pathetic, "please help me."

He took me for a drugged-up victim. A big grin appeared on his face. "Sure, little lady," he said. "I'll help you."

From around the corner, his companion called out, "You say something, Luke?"

I waited for him to step right in close. Then with every ounce of energy and the most single-pointed intention I'd ever mustered, I drove that blade straight into his heart all the way up to the hilt. He looked surprised. His expression would've seemed comical under other circumstances. I caught most of his weight as he collapsed and pulled the blade out of him as he went down. That was a mistake. His heart squeezed out a geyser of blood all over the front of me. No more being inconspicuous tonight. Hopefully, anyone else I encountered would think it was my own blood and not consider me much of a threat. I was trying to make his fall as quiet as possible, but he made enough of a sound that I knew his buddy would come to investigate.

"Luke?" I heard the guy's footsteps. Not really hurried, but still only seconds away.

I pulled Luke's revolver from its holster and switched off the safety. I aimed where I thought his buddy's torso would appear as he rounded the corner. In the split second it took for him to register the blood-drenched bitch with a gun pointed in his direction, I squeezed off a shot. It was a hit, but not a kill. I saw a hole open up near his shoulder. The impact spun him around and back out of sight behind the corner. I didn't have time to think. I raced to the corner just as he was trying to raise himself off the floor. I fired a second shot into his back and stepped in for a definite kill shot to his head.

"Shit," I muttered. That had been noisy. I needed to move. I put an arrow on the wall above his body as if two corpses wouldn't be marker enough. *Just in case.* That's what I told myself as I imagined a team of janitors tidying up the area before I returned. *Move it, Sadie!*

Muffled, distant-sounding, I heard little snatches of some kind of weird music. I moved toward it, marking every turn I took with an arrow pointing the way back to Thompson. I hoped by the time I made it back to him, he'd be more clear-headed and up to travelling.

When I peeked around the next corner, my heart jumped and my temples pounded. Not four feet away, right in front of me, someone stood. Automatically, I raised the gun and was about to squeeze the trigger, when I realized it was Consuela. She grabbed my arm and dragged me down the hallway.

At first, she said nothing, but when we came to a turn I whispered, "Wait." I broke free of her grasp and marked an arrow on the wall. Up to that point she wore an expression of anger or maybe concern. For a split second she allowed herself a smile.

"Smart girl," she hissed, before grabbing my wrist and pulling me forward again. We came to a door, which she unlocked with a key. She shoved me through the door and closed it behind us. Now that we were in a relatively safe position, she glared at me. There was no mistaking it now. She was angry. Angry at me? I was puzzled. "Maybe not so smart, eh?"

"What?"

"You fired three shots."

"So?"

"To kill how many?"

I saw where she was going. "One," I admitted. I'd spent three bullets and drawn attention with a great deal of noise. Who knew how many more enemies I'd encounter before I escaped this place?

"You've used half your bullets, girl! Here." She placed a handful of bullets in my palm.

I removed the empty shells from the pistol and reloaded. I shoved the remaining bullets in my pocket. She was still staring at me like an angry bull. "Sorry. I'm new at this," was all I could think to say in my own defense.

"You have the inner vision. Use it. Do not fire three bullets when you can kill with one. In your heart you already know this. Focus."

"Okay." She was right. It was true, I already knew this. I'd already demonstrated that I could access information at will when I was waiting in the wine cellar. There was no reason to doubt the same aspect of consciousness would guide my hand when I needed to fire the gun. That same 'knowing' would direct the bullet to its intended target.

"Your man is well?"

"He's drugged up, but not too bad. Just weak. He has a bullet hole near his shoulder, but he hasn't lost a terrible amount of blood. It's not as bad as it might have been."

"Lucinda. She wants him. She keeps him safe."

I felt like we were wasting time talking. I wanted to do what needed to be done and get out of there. "What now, Consuela? Where are we? What do I do?"

She gestured with her chin. There was a staircase ahead of us and I noticed the music was louder, though still muffled.

"The ritual is happening now. Their minds are drunk, with alcohol and the lust for power. They are in a dream, which keeps them from knowing what you've done. This will not last, little one. When you get close to her, she will know you."

I understood what she was saying. The stream of consciousness I'd used to see the visions of the past and present in the wine cellar had temporarily taken my focus away from the here and now. It was a bit like the fog of a dream. I could see that it would be difficult, if not impossible, to remain focused in both realities.

"No offense, Consuela," I said, "but, aren't we wasting time?"

She slapped me. Now, that I was not expecting, but it damn sure got my attention.

"No one knows this time better than I. I have dreamed it for twenty years. I can only help you if you allow me to."

I heard the truth in her words, but I also saw the shadow in her eyes. This was a woman who had not only witnessed great evil but had taken an active part in it. Perhaps not willingly, at least not always willingly, but there was blood on her hands. When I looked in her eyes, I saw a darkness emanating from her heart that I could not penetrate. I could not understand it, nor would I want to. If I came to understand it, I would become a part of it. Her expression softened a little.

"Here." She took something out of her pocket and offered it to me. I opened my hand and she dropped a gold cross on a chain. This was the last thing I expected to see. Why would she have a Christian symbol like this in her possession?

"What is this?"

"You will return it to Rita."

"Rita?" I certainly didn't think of Rita as a Christian either.

"I stole it from her to sell for money. To get out of that village where we were born."

"Yet, you still have it."

"I was younger. I have learned much since then. I was drawn to the shadows and my desire led me here. I had no need for money to bring me to my destiny."

"Rita was Catholic?"

"We were raised as Catholics as were all the children in our village. That was long ago. As you know, the soul cuts its own path through life."

I nodded and put the cross in my pocket. I wondered what Rita was doing at that very moment. Was she thinking of me? Thinking of the sister she had not seen for many years?

"Now we go into the ritual chamber."

"What are we going to do?" I felt myself tensing, resisting the unknown.

"I cannot tell you what will happen."

"You don't know?"

"I know what will happen. I cannot tell you because you would not believe. Not yet."

Strange. A momentary wave of peace swept through my entire being. For a split second I trusted that everything would be all right. Then it passed and I was as confused, tense and fearful as I had been.

Consuela started for the stairs and I followed. As we climbed, the music became louder, though it was never blaring. It was dreamy, like something you'd hear in a movie where the main character was drugged or hypnotized. The air became thicker as we neared the top of the stairs. Their desire for power was tangible. The people in that room above were all focused on acquiring power and using that power to glorify themselves at the expense of others. I braced myself, but I was unprepared to see what I did when Consuela stepped aside and gave me a glimpse into the chamber.

The first thing I saw was Lucinda plunging a knife into a naked young girl on an altar in the center of the room. My mind rebelled, not wanting this image to be true. I felt sick and my heart pounded. Then something else I would never have expected happened. My mind shifted gears into a space I'd never known before. At least not that I could recall. There was a great big sound like rushing wind and the scene in the ritual chamber slowed down and appeared to become even darker. At the same time a light opened up above us.

I looked up and saw a bright tunnel leading off into another reality. I could see my Grannie and my mother was right there beside her. They were both watching what was going on with me and sending me their most positive thoughts, but were unable to come any closer. They seemed incredibly distant, but even so I was comforted by the thought that they were witnessing this part of my life, no matter how far away they were from this dark place.

Above Grannie and Mom, I caught a glimpse of Rita. She was smiling, but I could see she was as frustrated as I was by her inability to help me directly.

"Do you see that?" I asked Consuela, returning my gaze to her. Consuela was trembling and tears streamed down her cheeks. Her eyes were directed at her feet, though I knew she sensed the bright light above. It was too bright for her, too painful to look at.

"I'm sorry you had to witness the killing," Consuela whispered. "It was the only time you could pass beyond Lucinda's power … while her soul was drunk with power."

"It's okay." I touched her cheek. Then I looked into the chamber where things seemed to be happening in slow motion. I took in every detail. I could stare as long as I wished, still I understood that I would not reengage with that time-stream until I was ready. The scenes I witnessed in that chamber were hellish, but I'd been given a safe distance of detachment, so I could take in every detail, see it clearly for what it was, without being sucked into a crippling emotional response.

Lucinda was naked except for some jewels and a long strip of translucent cloth hanging from her crotch. The knife in her hand was buried deep in the heart of the girl on an altar carved from stone. Images on the altar seemed to come alive, gnashing their teeth in the flickering light cast from candles all around the chamber, hungrily lapping up the hateful energy of the place. To the dark forces of evil in attendance there, the perversions being acted out by these people were as tasty as a fresh piece of toast dripping with honey. The jewels hanging from Lucinda's neck and wrists had been chosen for their ability to magnify these energies. She believed, as long as she wore these stones, no harm could come to her. Her nakedness was more than just a lurid show for the guests; she wanted to bathe in the blood of her sacrifice, absorbing the lifeforce energy. I knew that the girl on the altar was an innocent, that their victims all these many years had been chosen because of their innocence. In that same instant I realized this was why Consuela had been kept alive and made a servant in this hellish pit. She'd lost her innocence, willingly given it up, long before she'd been brought to this place.

Surrounding the altar on all sides were men in dark robes, each satisfying an unholy appetite. Some were eating human flesh or drinking blood from brass goblets. Others were raping naked children on small tables that ringed the altar in concentric circles. In the outer ring of the circular chamber were the newcomers to the cult. These consisted of policemen and other workers whose services were needed to support the secret organization. Most of these were men, but there were a few women present as well. All of them seemed in awe, enthralled by the otherworldly spectacle playing out before them. Every one of them without exception, both male and female, were masturbating. Brother Archie himself was seated at a table to the right of the altar. In his hand was a sort of demonic parody of a rosary, made of human vertebrae strung together. Slowly, he slid each vertebra over the palm of his hand while silently mouthing the words of a dark invocation in a long-forgotten language. It seemed odd to me that he took a subordinate position to his daughter. Then I realized that the power this group worshipped was identified as feminine, a black goddess from the abyss, openly worshipped in the dawn of human history, but long since relegated to the hidden places of modern civilization.

The scene continued to play out as slow as molasses from the jar in my grannie's kitchen. I saw Lucinda begin to withdraw the knife from her victim. The light above me grew brighter and I heard a sound like a distant trumpet. Consuela looked at me and using her mind instead of her mouth she said, "Now!"

Like a puppet controlled by an unknown mechanism, I stepped into the outer ring of the room. Without thought, I went straight to the guard on my left, firing a single shot into his head as I took the weapon from his holster with my other hand. Moving in a separate time from that experienced by the reveling cult members, I encompassed the outer ring of the room, firing a single shot into the brains of each of the servants. There were thirteen of them in all and all were armed, so as I expended my bullets, I simply grabbed another weapon.

"Keep moving!" Consuela shouted with her mind.

I glanced at the altar. Lucinda was still just beginning to withdraw the knife from the bloody girl's heart. An inkling of my disruption was making its way toward her consciousness slowly but surely. Of this I was certain.

I stepped into the second ring of the evil sanctuary. The atmosphere was denser there. On the table immediately before me, a fat old man was butchering a small body that was barely recognizable as human. I put my gun to the butcher's temple and squeezed the trigger, snatching the machete he was holding as I moved forward. I made the circuit of the second ring, killing all seven of the adherents with swiping blows to their throats. Still the actions of all these dark sorcerers were barely perceptible. None of them knew yet that they were dead.

I risked another look at Lucinda. The knife was not yet out of the girl's chest, but it seemed that Lucinda's head had begun to tilt upward ever so slightly.

In my head I heard Consuela shouting, "Go!"

The air in the third circle of the chamber was thick, dense with the most malevolent intent. The third ring contained only three members; Brother Archie, the red-headed politician named Trumbull and another man whose name I do not know, but whom I recognized as an important politician in Washington, DC. I'd seen his face on television and in newspapers and magazines. He'd always seemed to me to have a sort of baby face and a childlike smile. I knew now that these were the masks he wore to deceive the sheep he preyed on. With all my might, I struck a blow to the baby-faced politician, disconnecting his head from his body. That disarming smile remained on his face. Next, I spun around, delivering a deep gash in the throat of Trumbull. It didn't take his head completely off but fell only slightly short of decapitating him. I stepped into position in front of Brother Archie—my own father—and raised the machete over my head, preparing to bring it down on top of his skull. His eyes were on the bones in his hand.

Then he shocked me by looking up. He spoke to me with his mind, just as Consuela had done. "Oh," he said, "It's you."

I understood that he did not mean, "Oh, it's you, Liza McWhorter." His actual meaning was, "Oh, it's you, Amos." His dark soul recognized me from that lifetime. And I recognized him. "What are you doing here?" he asked. "Aren't you afraid of getting dirty?"

Without thinking, I responded, "Do two walk together unless they have agreed to do so?"

His expression did not change, but from deep within the pit of his soul, I heard him laugh.

"Do not let him trick you!" Consuela shrieked.

I stole a glimpse of Lucinda. Her eyes were rising, but not in my direction. I realized that Consuela was using magic of her own to cloud Lucinda's perception. She was distracting the witch so I'd have the opportunity to succeed. This was the dream she'd held all those years, intending that someday it would manifest and sweep over the dark reality of this evil underground world. The tip of the knife blade was not yet withdrawn from the sacrificial child.

I glared at Archie, the sorcerer and shepherd of two flocks; those who would commit any evil act in exchange for temporal power and those blind sheep above ground who allowed him to baptize them.

Archie's voice took on a plaintive tone. "I have done much good in this world," his mind claimed to mine.

Words flowed out of me without my conscious intention. "All the evil-doers among my people will die by the sword, all those who say, 'Disaster will not overtake or meet us.'"

"I am your father," he said.

"I will destroy her ruler and kill all her officials with him." Came the words from deep within me.

"Amos," he said, "you don't know when to quit."

"You brought me here for this. From your own deepest desire, you conjured me forth to put an end to your evil."

A sort of impotent cry came from within him. Then I buried the machete so deep in his skull I was unable to pull it out.

"Move!" Consuela screamed.

Time popped back into a familiar gear and I was moving in the same flow with Lucinda. The knife in her hand rose quickly from the corpse before her. She stared at the chamber, seeing the blood flowing from the bodies of all of her followers. I felt her sense of dread, it flowed out of her like the billowing heat from a vast furnace, heavy with smoke and oppressive. She could not believe what she was seeing, much less that she had been powerless to foretell this attack.

Consuela was gloating and her savage lustfulness for this moment of revenge was palpable. It swept over all in this sanctuary and rocked Lucinda on her feet. She shook it off and only now was she aware of my presence. When her eyes fell on my face, I saw fear, a soul-deep sense of dread that reached all the way into the darkest pit of hell. This lasted just an instant.

I wheeled away from Brother Archie and pulled a pistol from my belt, raising it toward Lucinda's head.

Her fear transformed to desperate anger. With her free hand she struck out at the gun, forcing it away from her. I turned with the power of her blow and as my finger squeezed the trigger, the bullet intended for Lucinda bore through the dark atmosphere of the bloody chamber and collided with Consuela's forehead. Her head exploded in a crimson blossom of gore.

"Yes!" I heard Consuela's soul shout before her body collapsed. She was glad. Glad to be out of the prison of this lifetime, even if it meant another dark trial for her soul.

I turned back to Lucinda, but it was too late. Just as my eyes met hers, I felt the knife glancing off my ribs and penetrating my heart. I was done for.

Then, just like before, the light above us grew brighter and time slowed down. Lucinda glanced up but was unable to bear the light. Her face filled with terror and she screamed, "No!"

A sound like a trumpet swept through the chamber on a mighty wind, tossing Lucinda's hair. Somewhere high above us, I heard a voice saying, "It is done."

An avalanche of information flooded into my consciousness. So much so, that I'd say for a while, I became a different sort of creature. I was no longer human. But what I was, I can't really say.

I knew that Lucinda had made a terrible mistake by using the sacrificial blade on me. In her fear and anger, she'd forgotten that it was only to be used on innocents. For thousands of years since those ancient days when this blade was forged, only the blood of innocents had been spilled with it. With that occult iron blade buried deep within me I rode through time, experiencing the death of each and every human sacrifice it had claimed back to the moment its metal had been consecrated to that shadowy goddess of the abyss. Those ancient sorcerers had made a pact with darkness in order to conquer the hardships of life on this primitive planet. But the bargain had doomed their souls to hardships they could never imagine in the murky nightmare realm where that goddess dwelled. I was brought into this life as her half-sister by the willful lust of our father precisely so that this moment could occur. I was not an innocent. I had relinquished my innocence willingly, early in life so I could become the instrument that would bring an end to this evil.

The horror in Lucinda's eyes was unlike anything I'd ever witnessed. She looked at the knife in my chest and a moan echoed out of her into the room.

I saw the blood flowing out of my wound. I saw her hand on the handle of the knife. Firmly, I removed her hand, then I pulled the blade out of my body. It slid out of me easily. Under normal circumstances I would've viewed the wound in my chest with dread, expecting to pass out and die in short order. Instead, I felt an inexplicable peace.

Completely without any intention on my part, an energy began to flow out of me. It was something like when your nose just starts to run and you don't really have any control over it. Or when your period starts to flow unexpectedly. Or when you're aroused and the wetness pours out between your legs. It was just automatic, like it was just a fact of life, something of a relief. The energy swept out of me and in its release, I felt relief, I might even say pleasure. When I looked down, to see what form this energy might take, I saw that it was a stream of fire. The fire swept up Lucinda's legs and quickly engulfed her. She screamed, but her cries sounded more like rage than pain. The anger roared out of her and a stream of fire flew across the room to where Consuela's body lay. Consuela burst into flame.

Turning away from Lucinda, I saw that the energy and the fire it manifested flowed out of my body in every direction. A river of fire poured from my body, sending tributaries to each of the sorcerers in the room. They exploded like cans of gasoline. Each of their victims including the girl on the altar, dematerialized and flowed together into a single cloud of golden light. This light moved upward and merged with the light from above. When I looked up, I could see nothing in the incredibly bright expanse above.

I am at the fig tree. I reach for a piece of fruit, but the tree turns to light. I am in a vast expanse of desert. Nothing grows here. Only the light. I am not troubled by the lack of life because I know the light is the source of all life. All things are purified here.

Behind me the sanctuary was in flames. I descended the stairs. Far away I could hear voices. Looking down at my blood-drenched clothes I felt curious. Automatically, my hand reached for the hole in my chest, but it was gone. Healed. Feeling detached, but uninjured, I followed the arrows I had left on the walls to guide me back. On my way I passed the bodies of the two guards I had killed earlier. No janitors had cleaned up my mess. The thought crossed my mind that these two had not perished in the fire because they were not yet too far gone. They still had a shot at becoming something better than what they had been in this life.

Coming near the loading dock, the sound of voices grew louder and when I rounded the last corner, I saw Lupe approaching me.

"You are all right?" she asked.

"Yeah, I'm okay. How is Thompson?"

"He is better. He worries about you." She smiled at me and led the way into the dock.

The room was filled with young people. Most of them seemed to be Hispanic. Lupe called out something in Spanish and they all turned to stare at me, falling silent. She gestured to a boy at the dock door and began raising the metal door by tugging at a chain. Outside the dock was a big, boxy truck. It looked just like an official delivery truck you'd see every day. I realized this was how the cult had delivered slaves to the place without attracting attention. Lupe and the boy began shuffling the others into the back of the truck.

I went to Thompson's hidey hole.

"You okay?" I asked him.

He grinned. "Fine now. I've never been so happy to see someone in all my life."

"I feel exactly the same way. Can you walk?"

"I think so. Still a little foggy headed. Can you help me get up on my feet?"

I took his good arm and helped him up. He groaned. I knew that the bullet hole was hurting like hell. When we got into the back of the truck, I said, "You want to lie down?"

"No. Take me up front with you."

"Up front with me?"

"Yeah, so I can tell you how to drive this thing. I'd do it, but I don't want to take the chance of passing out at the wheel."

"I'm driving?"

"Who else? You've done tougher things today haven't you?"

"Yeah. That's true for damn sure."

He laughed, then groaned as he leaned down to kiss me.

"You need this," Lupe said. When I turned, I saw she was pushing a folded set of gray overalls at me; the kind mechanics wear. She was right, I realized, when I saw the amount of blood on my clothes. I shucked my shirt and stepped into the coveralls.

"Thanks," I told her. She just nodded.

Thompson and I climbed into the cab while Lupe and the boy settled everyone in the back. Thompson told me what to do and with a few jolts and the sound of grinding gears, we started up the ramp. The entrance to the loading dock had been concealed quite well. The ramp took a gradual climb up to surface level where it came out in a grove of oak trees. Even if it had been daylight, unless you were looking for the ramp's entrance, you'd probably never notice it. I drove along a dirt track that led to a concrete driveway and gradually out to an actual street. As I pulled onto the street, I saw a huge column of smoke over a blaze of firelight coming from the Zion Hill Church of the Redeemer.

"Drive nice and slow," Thompson said. "Don't do anything that'll attract attention."

"I'll do my best, but I'm not making any promises," I told him. "I'm not used to steering a dinosaur like this."

"You're doing fine. Just take it slow."

We were headed out of Draper when I heard the first sound of sirens. I wasn't too concerned about anyone stopping us. I felt pretty certain that most of Draper's police force were already incinerated.

"What about your truck?" I knew how much Thompson loved that truck and the thought of losing it was a sad one even if we had bigger problems on our plate at the moment.

"They didn't expect any of us to make it out of there," he answered. "I'm sure they swept our campsite clean as soon as they captured you."

"I suppose you're right."

"If they've been running an operation like this one, they know better than to leave any loose ends lying around. They'd destroy any evidence that we were ever there."

"Where we headed? To Jerry's mom's place?"

"No. Head south. Lupe's from Piedras Negras. We'll go there. She says there will be safe places for these kids down there."

"I sure hope so." I couldn't help but think that these kids had already been abducted from places like Piedras Negras.

"It's our best shot. We can't try to hand them over to the police in Albany. Too close. Who knows if some of them were in cahoots with these bastards?"

"You're right." I told him about the politician Trumbull and the guy I recognized as being a bigwig in Washington.

He made a disgusted sound. "Shit."

"It's okay," I said. "I got a feeling things are going to be okay for us. For a while anyway."

"Excellent. I'll trust your gut." He groaned and shifted in his seat.

"What should we do about your wound?" I asked.

"Nothing yet. In Mexico, antibiotics are sold over the counter. You can get me some in Piedras Negras. In the meantime, when we stop for gas, we'll pick up some ibuprofen. That'll take the edge off the pain without making me loopy."

"Sounds like a plan. It's a long way to Piedras Negras, isn't it?"

"Yeah, three or four hundred miles. But you said you had a good feeling about things. Right?"

"Yes, sir."

"Once we get these kids to safety, you can get me to Rita. I know I'll be fine if she works on me."

"Yeah, Rita!" I told him about Consuela and the gold cross in my pocket. I explained everything that had happened in Gooch's compound to the best of my ability. The shifts in reality were hard to put into words. I told him flat out about every one of the people I'd killed and how I'd done it. When I got to the part about the fire, I was at a loss to explain the source of the flames, so I didn't try. I just told him like it was, making no effort to give my story a more plausible spin. What I'd experienced was like a nightmare. I'm sure that's the way it must have seemed to him when he heard it. He listened carefully, letting me spill my guts without interruption. When I finished, he just sat there, staring at the road ahead of us.

"What are you thinking?" I asked him after a good while.

"I don't know what to think," he admitted.

"Are you okay?" For a moment I felt vulnerable. I needed some reassurance that we were still in this thing together. What I'd just told Thompson was the sort of story that got people locked up in Terrell.

"Yeah. It's pretty mind-blowing, you know? When you wandered into Skin Dreams that day, I never would've imagined any of this ever could've happened."

I was hoping he wasn't beginning to blame me for this whole mess. "It all started when Lucinda wandered into your life," I reminded him. "Imagine where you'd be right now if I hadn't come along."

"God, I don't want to imagine," he said, heaving a sigh. "You say Rita's sister was there for over twenty years?"

"That's what she told me. She said she hadn't seen sunlight since she entered that place."

"Thanks for saving me from a similar fate, Sadie."

"My pleasure," I told him, grinning from ear to ear. I knew he thought I was a keeper for sure.

"There's a gas station," Thompson said, pointing to the road ahead. "Pull in there. We'll top off the tank and you can get me some pain killers. We'll get some food and water for everyone, too."

I pulled in close to the gas pumps. He handed me his wallet.

"Pay for everything inside. Take Lupe with you. I'd help out, but I don't want anyone noticing this hole in me."

"Gotcha." I climbed in the back and told Lupe the plan, asking her to tell everyone to be quiet until we were back on the road.

Inside the store we bought all sorts of chips and cookies, some lunch meat, some bread and a couple of flats of bottled water. I told the young woman behind the counter to open up the pump next to the truck so I could fill up.

"Is it hard to get hired on there?" she asked me, pointing at the truck.

At first, I didn't understand what she meant. When it clicked, I said, "Oh, heck no. If they'll hire me, they'll hire anybody."

She smiled real big. I'd given her hope. Clearly, she wanted a better job than operating a cash register at an out of the way gas station. "Maybe I'll put in an application," she said cheerfully, swiping the credit card.

"Might as well," I answered. "Couldn't hurt."

"Pump ten's on for you," she said.

I carried water and food out to the truck, gave Thompson the bottle of pain killers and pumped gas. When I went back inside to retrieve his card, the girl thanked me. "I appreciate you telling me to apply," she said. "You encouraged me. That made my day."

"You are so welcome ..." I looked at her nametag, "... Wendy. Encouragement's the least we can offer one another. Right?"

"Right." She was beaming. "Come back, soon," she called as I was walking out the door.

"I'll try," I answered, in the sincerest voice I could muster. What I was thinking was I'd just as soon never see that part of Texas again.

Chapter 23

Lupe had people in Piedras Negras who were glad to have her back. We really couldn't risk crossing the border in that truck. It would've attracted too much attention. We waited in Eagle Pass and her people came across the border to get her and all the other kidnap victims we had with us. They brought antibiotics for Thompson, which he started taking right away. Lupe's relatives seemed uncertain about us. They were glad to have her back, but under the circumstances I guess it was normal for them to think poorly of white folks. She clearly stood up for us and they saw that Thompson had taken a bullet. All of them thanked us in the end for helping Lupe and the others escape.

I inspected Thompson's wound and it didn't look any worse than it had when I'd first laid eyes on it. I figured Lucinda's spell of protection was still in force. I couldn't wait to get him to Rita, so she could sweep away any influence the witch had over him and replace it with positive healing energy.

"What are we going to do now?" I asked him once Lupe and the others had left us to ourselves.

"I think we need to abandon this truck and rent a car to drive home."

"All right. What about Jerry?"

"He's a big boy. We'll call him and tell him to catch a bus home. If he asks why, we need to say we can't explain until he gets home. I think it's important not to discuss any of this on a phone or by email. Ever."

"Gotcha."

I went to a Walmart and bought some bandages and a fresh shirt for Thompson. Once we'd cleaned him up and got him presentable enough to rent a car without raising any suspicions, we had breakfast and waited for the rental car place to open.

Everything went without a hitch. The car people bought his story about having his truck stolen and needing a ride home. It was mostly true. The only lie he told really was where the truck disappeared. His bruised face and swollen eye caused a few double-takes. I suppose they assumed he'd been beaten when our truck was stolen.

It was a little over 200 miles back to Austin. By the time we made it home I'd driven over 600 miles in a single day. Probably seems like no big deal, but I took a little pride in that accomplishment. It was a first for me. Up until then, I doubt I'd driven even fifty miles total. The fact that more than half of that 600 miles was behind the wheel of that delivery truck entitled me to a gold star by my name. That's the way I looked at it anyway.

It felt so good to be home. Right away Thompson got a shower. I changed the dressing on his wound and he went to bed for some well-deserved sleep. I was too keyed up to sleep just yet, so I told him I'd call Jerry and Rita. I had to use a burner phone he kept for emergencies, the same phone he'd used earlier to contact the folks who supplied my fake ID. The bastards in Draper had taken our phones when they took us captive. We were just damn lucky that Lucinda had let him keep his wallet.

Why would she do that? I allowed myself to speculate for a while. I imagined that Lucinda believed she could turn Thompson to her side. Make him one of the cult members. I suppose she thought he could take daddy's place once the old man was gone. Maybe even take over as the shepherd of the flock at Zion Hill Church of the Redeemer. I was glad we were away from that place and equally glad the cult members and their sanctuary had been destroyed. But the thing was too big to be swept away with a single act. A dark enterprise as well-organized as that one would have tentacles reaching into all sorts of unexpected corners. Thompson and I would have to watch our backs from now on. There would be no cut and dried end to it. No happily ever after.

I called Jerry knowing full well he wouldn't answer. He never does when the call is from a number he doesn't recognize. When the call rolled over into his voice mail, I left a message.

"Jerry, it's Sadie. There's been a change of plans. Call me as soon as you get this."

I disconnected thinking he'd probably call back right away. Tempted to make some coffee, I decided against it, realizing it would just make it harder for me to sleep. I was exhausted, but my nerves were still on edge. I decided on food, hoping my system would relax a bit if I fed it. Just as I took the first bite of a tuna sandwich I'd thrown together, the phone rang. I jumped. No two ways about it, I was nervous as hell.

"Hello," I said, trying hard to make it sound like my mouth wasn't full of food.

"Hey, Sadie, I got your message." Jerry was his usual upbeat self. He was glad to hear from me. Hearing his childlike enthusiasm, I realized I missed him, too. "How was the hunting? You guys bag a deer?"

"No. We didn't get anything. Jerry, we can't pick you up. You're going to have to catch a bus back home."

Now, he sounded less than enthusiastic. "Really? Why? I don't get it. What's wrong."

"I don't want you to worry, but I can't discuss it over the phone. We'll explain everything once you're home."

"What the fuck, Sadie? What's going on?" It sounded like anger was creeping into his voice. I should have expected it. He wasn't used to being denied information. The three of us were completely honest with one another.

"Thompson's truck was stolen." I figured that would take the edge off his anger, without revealing anything about what had really happened in Draper.

"No shit?"

"No shit."

"Well, how'd you guys get home? You are home, aren't you? And why are you calling me from this strange number?"

Curious Jerry, the most curious guy I know.

"Jerry, I know this is real hard for you. I wish I could tell you more, but I can't. Not yet. Will you please just trust me on that? I really need you to just trust me. Can you do that?"

When he spoke again, I knew he'd do as I asked even if he didn't like it.

"Okay," he said. "Well, shit, I don't suppose there's any point in continuing this conversation since you're operating under a veil of secrecy."

"Sorry. When will you head back?"

"Tomorrow, I guess. I'll have to check out the bus situation. I have no idea how often they run."

"It'll be good to have you home, Jerry. Do you need us to send you money for the bus?"

"No, I don't think so. If I don't have enough to cover it I'll let you know. Should I call you on this number?"

"Yes."

"Just tell me this; you two are all right, aren't you?"

"Yeah, we're okay." That was mostly true. It didn't feel like a lie to say it.

"That's good. I'll call you when I know my travel plans."

"Okay."

"Bye for now." He hung up.

I finished my tuna sandwich, then called Rita. She answered right away.

"I'm so glad you called."

"Rita, we need your help."

"I knew that. I sensed it. I've been calling your numbers but got no answer. I know what happened to you is not good. Are you okay?"

"I'm fine, but Thompson needs your help."

"He's hurt. Is it bad?"

"Let's not talk about it over the phone. Can you just come to our place as soon as possible?"

"I don't sense that it's an emergency. Not life and death. Is it okay if I keep my last appointment of the day before I come your way?"

"That's probably best. Thompson's asleep right now, anyway."

"Good. I'll see you soon, Sadie."

"Bye."

The food must've helped my metabolism calm down a bit. The next thing I knew I was waking up on the sofa to the sound of Rita knocking. Rubbing my eyes, I got up and let her in.

"I'm so glad to see you!" She gave me a big bear hug. It felt great to be in her energy field. I just hugged her back for a long time. Then, we let go of one another and I closed the front door.

"Want some tea?" I asked her.

"No." She shook her head. "Is Thompson still asleep? Should we wake him?"

"I'm sure he'd want me to wake him up, now that you're here."

"Okay. Wake him up. If he doesn't feel like getting out of bed, I'll come to him."

It took me a couple of nudges to wake him up. I told him Rita was in the house and asked if he wanted to join us in the living room. He groaned when he sat up, but said he'd be there in a minute. He wanted to go to the restroom. After peeing and washing his face, he came into the room.

"Hey, Rita."

"How are you, son?" I liked the way Rita sometimes called him son. I knew she felt sort of maternal toward him.

"I'm going to live."

"Come over here and make yourself comfortable."

"Where do you want me?"

"I want you in whatever position feels best to you."

He took a seat on the sofa with his legs stretched out onto the coffee table. "This is good," he said, settling in.

"All right." Rita began doing her passes over his body with the palms of her hands. She spoke very quietly, so we couldn't make out the words, but I knew she was speaking a prayer of protection and healing. "You've been shot," she said, just matter-of-factly.

Thompson was going to reply, but she shushed him.

"Tell me later."

I sat and watched quietly while she scanned his whole body, swept away dark energies with her hands and directed lifeforce energy wherever his body needed it. This thing she was doing she called Reiki. I don't know how it works, exactly, but it does work. Rita'd told me a few times she'd like to teach me Reiki. And I wanted to learn, just hadn't made the time for it yet. She worked on him for about an hour, then she closed a circle around him and shook her hands vigorously in the air.

"I'll take that cup of tea now," she said, sitting down.

I got up and went to the kitchen. "You want anything, Thompson?"

Before he could say anything, Rita called, "Nothing for him but good clean water. Lots of it. No beer or coffee for at least a day."

I started water heating for Rita's tea and brought Thompson a cool bottle of water.

"Now it's story time," Rita said. "Fill me in."

Thompson and I took turns telling her everything we knew. I brought her a cup of hot water and, as usual, she took a tea bag out of her purse and made her own herbal concoction. When I got to the part about Consuela, she began to tremble. I fished the gold cross necklace out of my pocket and gave it to her. As she stared at the thing, I could see she was reliving memories from long ago. I got her a box of tissues for her tears and runny nose.

"Thank you, dear," she said, drying her face, blowing her nose. "You know, there are times in life when no matter how much you want it, there is no peace to be made. I didn't want the conflict with Consuela. I never did. But it was always there. No matter what I did I couldn't release that aggression. I always wondered if she was still alive. I hoped she was. Now, I think she might've been better off dead."

I knew exactly what she was talking about. Lucinda wanted me dead as soon as she knew I existed. Maybe she'd known for a long time about me. I didn't know about her and even if I had I wouldn't have hated her. In the end, when I did want her dead, she ended up killing herself. Her blind hatred killed her.

For a long time, the three of us said nothing.

"What do we do now?" Rita asked, slapping her hands down on her knees. It wasn't a question so much as a way of letting us know she was moving on to other thoughts.

"That's the question," Thompson said.

"Well, I say you get your truck back." Rita was thinking, the gears were turning and she nodded as her plan started coming together in her head.

"How?" Thompson snorted like he thought that was nigh impossible.

"First, you file a report that it was stolen. Do you have full coverage?"

"Yes." His expression started to turn hopeful.

"They did steal your truck. I doubt they destroyed a perfectly good truck like yours. And they haven't had much time to unload it. It's probably still in Draper. You have to file a police report to be eligible for an insurance claim. Once you report it stolen and where, the Draper police may get in touch with you."

"The last thing we want is to go back to that town," I said.

"I know, dear, I know," Rita said. "But I also know Thompson loves that truck. If they call him and tell him to come get the truck, we'll arrange a little surprise for them."

"Surprise?"

"There's strength in numbers," Rita said.

We filed the report and waited. Sure enough, a few days later we got a call from a law officer in Draper. He was real friendly. Claimed they'd found the truck parked in front of a convenience store in perfect condition, keys in the ignition.

"Well, isn't that convenient," Thompson told the officer.

"Yes, sir," the man answered. "Looks like today's your lucky day."

Thompson made arrangements to pick the truck up. Then, we called Rita. By the next day she'd arranged for a convoy of ten cars full of people to travel to Draper with us. One of our travelling companions was Ray Rodriguez, a cousin of Rita's who just happened to be a well-known journalist for the paper in Houston. By this time Jerry was back home with us. We'd told him the whole story. He had more than a little trouble swallowing what I told him happened in the underground sanctuary. He asked me lots of questions, but finally gave up with a shrug on trying to make it fit with his conception of reality. Jerry insisted on coming along with us to retrieve the truck.

When we pulled up in front of the police department, a little brick building adjacent to the fire station, we'd just gotten out of the car when two men in uniforms came out to meet us. One was middle-aged and balding, the other looked not much older than me.

"What's all this?" asked the bald one. The other just chewed on a toothpick.

"I'm Thompson. I called you about picking up my truck."

"Did you feel like you had to bring your whole family with you?" The man asked. There was an edge in his voice. Seemed like maybe he was boiling inside, but trying hard to hide it.

"Hello, officer," Raymond Rodriguez said, stepping forward. "I'm Ray Rodriguez. I write for the Houston Chronicle. You fellows did such a great job of finding Thompson's truck, I thought I might do a little story about it. You know, back the blue, that sort of thing."

The cop was speechless. He managed to spit out a few words, despite his angry surprise at having ten carloads of witnesses on hand for the exchange. Thompson signed some papers and they led him to a fenced area behind the station where some cars were parked, including his truck. Joe's vehicle and Rusty's were back there, too. It made my stomach do flips to see them. The cop got a cocky look on his face and said, "I understand you were hunting out on a lease with Joe Farrell."

Of course, they knew that. They'd known it since we were first approached by that other bastard on our way into town. I've got to hand it to Thompson. He was cool as a cucumber when he answered.

"We were supposed to meet Joe and some others, but they never showed up."

"That right?" The cop's smile faded as he tried to figure out what to say next without tipping his hand. I guess nothing came to him. He kept his mouth shut.

"Thanks," Thompson said.

Then me and Thompson and Jerry climbed into his truck and drove away. Thompson gave the cops a sarcastic little friendly wave and a big smile. They just stared. The ten cars full of Rita's friends and family fell in behind us and escorted us safely back to the Austin city limits.

On the drive back home, we talked.

"I'd say that went well," Jerry commented.

"Yep," Thompson agreed. "We're out of the woods for the time being."

"You expect more trouble?"

"Hard to say. One thing we do know; this organization, cult … whatever you want to call it, has got some powerful members. We may have knocked out the local chapter, but what about the others? Will they care enough to come after us? Will they be afraid of drawing more attention? There's so much we don't know."

"Maybe we can find out anything we need to know," I suggested.

"How?" Thompson asked.

I told him and Jerry about the 'casting' I'd done while I was in the wine cellar. How I'd been able to see things that had happened long before and elsewhere on the property.

"Pardon my saying so," Jerry said, "but couldn't all that be just your imagination? It's not like you had any independent verification of any of that. Right?"

"I can't really explain it to you, Jerry," I said. "At least not in a way that you'll really get it. There's a difference between an idle daydream and grabbing hold of an actual event with your mind. Telepathically. That's the word I was looking for. When I get something I can trust, I just know it, down deep in my soul."

"I want to believe you, Sadie," he answered. "Truly I do."

"You think you can 'cast' for information about other members of the cult?" Thompson asked.

"Yeah. I think I can."

"I hope you do," Jerry said. "I, for one, would love to get some info we could independently verify. I want to believe in your ability. I want to know I can trust it."

"One thing you can believe and trust," Thompson said, "is that Sadie pretty much single-handedly took out that whole group. I was useless, just hidden away behind some boxes, waiting for her to come get me."

I smiled at Thompson and put my hand on his knee. He winked at me.

"I'm not saying she's not a bad ass. It's just …"

"What?" I asked him. "We're all friends here, Jerry. Speak your mind."

"Okay." He cleared his throat. "You have a history of violence. Nobody's doubting that."

"Self-defense," Thompson added. "It's important to remember anything she's done was done in self-defense."

"Granted. I get that. It's just that nothing I've experienced has prepared me to accept your account at face value. I'm not calling you a liar. But, the talk of time slowing down while you hacked people to death? You say Lucinda stabbed you in the heart? Not that I'd put it past that bitch to try, mind you. It's just so much to wrap my head around, okay? I may be the slow learner in the group. I guess you'll just have to be patient with me until my level of understanding catches up to you guys."

He'd put it out there, clear as day. I couldn't fault him for any part of what he'd said. Suddenly, it just struck me as funny. I couldn't help it. A cosmic joke? You could call it that. I laughed out loud and Jerry just shook his head, unsure how he should respond.

"You're absolutely right, Jerry. It's just insane at first glance."

"And second glance," he added.

"Yes. Who's that guy you're always watching on YouTube? The one who wrote the books about magic mushrooms and DMT?"

"McKenna. Terence McKenna."

"Right. Isn't he always saying, 'not only is the universe stranger than we imagine, but it's stranger than we can imagine'?"

He nodded. "Yes. He does say that."

"And doesn't he say, 'everything you know is wrong'?"

"He does."

"And aren't some of his experiences, the things he talks about in his lectures, as far out there as anything I've told you?"

"None of his experiences involve killing people, but yes, he's been through some weird shit."

"And you believe him?"

"I suppose I do."

"Then, I'd say your mind underwent an adjustment to accommodate his alternate version of reality."

"Way to go, Sadie!" Thompson said, busting out laughing.

"Your point is well-taken," Jerry admitted. He chewed on his lower lip, mulling over this new frame I'd placed around the subject.

I went on. "You seem to believe I killed all those people. It doesn't challenge your view of reality that I single-handedly slaughtered, what …" I counted them up in my head, "twenty-six people and burned the church down?"

"It's possible you had help," Jerry said, weakly.

"Possible, yes. But, I didn't. This universe is stranger than anyone knows. I don't understand it, but I know what I've told you is true. Think this over. A huge portion of the population believe in a god they've never seen and a devil, too. I imagine they believe in the devil mostly just to have someone to blame the bad stuff on. Is that widely held belief system any stranger than what I've told you?"

"Do you believe in a god?" he asked me, looking real serious.

"I do think there's something or someone behind all of this. Yes, I do. I don't know if it has a personality or if it's just a force, like gravity. But something is making all this happen for reasons of its own. You can call it god or devil or whatever. To my way of thinking, there's no difference between the god of the old testament and what I'd think of as a devil."

"Agreed," Jerry said. "You've given me a lot to consider, Sadie. I want you to know that I am willing, eager even, to become a believer in your extraordinary abilities."

"Thanks, Jerry."

"Don't mention it." He gave me a timid smile.

"Well, now," Thompson said real loud, "If we're finished probing the depths of the cosmos, let's talk about what we're going to eat when we get home. I'm feeling hungry."

"Yeah. That's a topic I can relate to," Jerry answered.

"For some reason, a big greasy chili burger is striking my fancy. What do you think?" Thompson nudged me.

"Chili burger sounds okay," I admitted.

"Jerry?"

"Why the hell not?"

"Chili burgers it is! We can all agree on that."

The next day we reopened Skin Dreams for the first time. There were a lot of voice messages on the landline at the shop. Mostly regular customers wanting to know why we weren't open. I called all the regular's back and told them we were up and running again and encouraged them to come in as soon as possible. By the end of the day we'd done four tats and it was good to have some cash flowing in again.

That night when I was in the shower, I felt Grannie. Real close like old times. She told me she was proud of me; said I was a real woman now and I'd stepped into my own. She didn't explain what stepping into 'my own' meant exactly, but I understood. I had come through the shit storm and I was still standing. I knew I could cast into the world around me and gather information if I needed to. Grannie wrapped me up in a warm feeling and told me it was time for her to move on. Now that made me cry. I couldn't help it. She was telling me she couldn't come and visit anymore. Other tasks in other realities were calling to her and she needed to attend to them. She'd put them off for as long as she could. Now it was time for her to let go of any attachments to this world. I was the only reason she'd stuck around. She'd looked after me as long as she could. There was no more forestalling the inevitable.

Then she was gone.

I didn't know what the future held for me and Thompson and Jerry. But I'd been led to a home and a life that suited me just fine. It was a life worth fighting for and I vowed I would fight for it whenever I had to. Whatever fighting I had to do couldn't be any worse than what I'd already gone through. That's how it seemed to me. I thanked Grannie for watching over me all those years and I let her go. When I was done crying, I dried off and joined Thompson in our bed.

ABOUT YOUR AUTHOR

Bret McCormick is a native Texan, writer, artist and filmmaker. His 1986 feature film, The Abomination has a small, but fierce international cult following.

Bret has edited or co-edited five anthologies of horror fiction.

He lives with his partner, four dogs and four birds in Bedford, Texas.

Learn more about Bret and his films at: www.collectorsreleases.com.

Bret McCormick

Other HellBound Books Titles
Available at:
www.hellboundbookspublishing.com

The Toilet Zone
RESTROOM READING AT ITS MOST FRIGHTENING!

Compiled and edited by the grand master of 80's schlock horror, Bret McCormick, each one of this collection of 32 terrifying tales is just the perfect length for a visit to the smallest room....

At the very boundaries of human imagination dwells one single, solitary place of solitude, of peace and quiet, a place in which your regular human being spends, on average, 10 to 15 minutes - at least once every single day of their lives.

Now, consider a typical, everyday reading speed of 200 to 250 words per minute - that means your average visitor has the time to read between 2,500 to 4,000 words, which makes each and every one of these 32 tales of terror - from some of the best contemporary independent authors - within this anthology of horror the perfect, meticulously calculated length. Dare you take a walk to the small room from where inky shadows creep out to smother the light and solitude's siren call beckons you?

Dare you take a quiet, lonely walk into... The Toilet Zone

ROAD KILL: TEXAS HORROR BY TEXAS WRITERS - VOL 3

Everything is bigger in Texas - including the horror!

A Piney woods meth dealer clones Adolph Hitler. A nightmare exorcist meets an inexorable fined. An eyeball collector gets collected. The apparition of a lynching victim tracks down his executioners. A Texas lawman is undone by shades of his past. A Baphomet recruits converts as a local summer camp. The tales of the baker's dozen who appear in this anthology demonstrate why everything is scarier in Texas…

Including tales of terror from
Jeremy Hepler
Madison Estes
Bret McCormick
James H Longmore
ER Bills
Shawna Borman

And many more...

Follow Him

True love doesn't die - it devours. Just outside the sleepy town of Dreury, a mysterious cult known as The Shared Heart has planted its stakes. Its followers are numerous. More join every day. Those who are lost and suffering seem to be drawn to it; a home for the broken. When Jacob finds himself in need of such a home, he abandons his dead name and gives himself over to the will of The Great Collector. However, love refuses to let Jacob go so easily; his ex-fiancé, Nina, kidnaps him in the hopes that he can be deprogrammed. As she attempts to return Jacob to the life they once had, a terrible fear creeps in: what if there isn't enough of her Jacob left? When The Great Collector learns of his missing follower, the true nature of The Shared Heart is unleashed. Nina discovers what Jacob already knows: that hidden behind the warm songs and soaring bonfires is a terrifying and ancient secret; one that lives and breathes and hungers. And it's coming for them.

Satanic Panic

An incredible homage to 1980's horror!

Satanic Panic, a mass hysteria created in the nineteen eighties, has returned to a small college town in the Midwest.

Ritualistic murders and the presence of the occult have bled below the surface of the town in the form of icy accidents and other coincidences.

And when three lifelong friends find themselves on the radar of a killer—and leader of a satanic cult—they must fight for what's good without being seduced by the evil that possesses their campus.

Invasive Species

A monster has come to Maldus, Arkansas, and the residents of the small mountain town are too busy to notice. With the monster comes something even more terrifying and threatening than gnashing teeth or razor-sharp claws.

The monster has brought change.

The residents of the small mountain town are too busy to notice at first. Busy with things such as addiction, racism, work, or land deals. Unnoticed, the change the monster brings in its insidious wake spreads like wildfire.

Unnoticed, the town of Maldus falls prey to an Invasive Species.

An Unholy Trinity

3 TERRIFYING NOVELLAS, 3 SUPERLATIVE AUTHORS, 1 BIG, FAT, JUICY BOOK!

ENÛMA ELIŠ (When on High) – Terry Grimwood.
The Babylonian Creation story is a tale of monsters and cataclysmic wars. An epic saga dominated by the gods Tiamat and Mardak, bitter rivals who battle for supremacy over the unformed universe. It is a story replete with Minotaurs and scorpion men, dragons and monstrous blood-sucking demons.
A myth, a fantasy...
But when a traumatized ex-soldier rescues a young woman, washed up and barely alive on the shore of a sleepy English seaside town, the fragile borders between myth and reality begin to crumble and gods and their legions wake from their long-slumber.

THE REMNANT - C. Bailey-Bacchus
When fifteen-year-old Bianca Baker is blinded by rage and hatred, her inner demons take control and turn an ordinary school trip into a horrific tragedy. Witnesses

to her violent act, succumb to Bianca's aggression and agree to say events were a terrible accident. Sixteen years later, those involved find the past clawing its way from the shadows to haunt them, and this time there is no way it will stay buried.

ALICE IN HORRORLAND - Vanessa Hawkins
Alice is an 11 year old orphan living within the veins of industrial England. When she meets a mysterious gentleman with the power to turn into a white rabbit, she finds herself tumbling down a manhole into Horrorland.
Here the creatures are strange and uncanny, lost in a revolution of madness. Drug addicted Caterpillars, grinning cats and homicidal Mad Hatters gambol around Alice like blood-drunk mosquitoes. However, at the center of it all is the Queen of Hearts: said to have given up her own a long time ago…
Horrorland used to be so wonderful… Can Alice make it so again?

**A HellBound Books LLC
Publication**

http://www.hellboundbookspublishing.com

Printed in the United States of America

www.ingramcontent.com/pod-product-compliance
Lightning Source LLC
Chambersburg PA
CBHW032113180726
48284CB00002B/555